A Garden in Paris

Books by Stephanie Grace Whitson

CONTEMPORARY FICTION
  A Garden in Paris

HISTORICAL FICTION
  PINE RIDGE PORTRAITS
  Secrets on the Wind
  Watchers on the Hill
  Footsteps on the Horizon

  DAKOTA MOONS
  Valley of the Shadow
  Edge of the Wilderness
  Heart of the Sandhills

  KEEPSAKE LEGACIES
  Sarah's Patchwork
  Karyn's Memory Box
  Nora's Ribbon of Memories

  PRAIRIE WINDS
  Walks the Fire
  Soaring Eagle
  Red Bird

NONFICTION
  How to Help a Grieving Friend: A Candid Guide
  for Those Who Care

STEPHANIE GRACE WHITSON

A Garden

in Paris

BETHANY HOUSE PUBLISHERS
Minneapolis, Minnesota

A Garden in Paris
Copyright © 2005
Stephanie Grace Whitson

Cover design by Paul Higdon
Cover photo: © Willy Ronis/RAPHO – Les amoureux de la Bastille – 1957

Published by Bethany House Publishers
11400 Hampshire Avenue South
Bloomington, Minnesota 55438

Bethany House Publishers is a division of
Baker Publishing Group, Grand Rapids, Michigan.

Printed in the United States of America

Library of Congress Cataloging-in-Publication Data

Whitson, Stephanie Grace.
  A garden in Paris / by Stephanie Grace Whitson.
    p. cm.
  Summary: "The motto, 'It is never too late to be what you might have been,' haunts Mary Davis. Newly widowed, she has the notion that if she can return to Paris with her increasingly distant daughter, perhaps she'll be able to reconcile with the past and find a new future"—Provided by publisher.
  ISBN 0-7642-2935-4 (pbk.)
  1. Americans—France—Fiction. 2. Mothers and daughters—Fiction. 3. Paris (France)—Fiction. 4. Widows—Fiction. I. Title.
  PS3573.H555G37   2005
  813'.54—dc22   2004024192

DEDICATION

To Lois Gladys Leppard
who believed in this story
and my ability to tell it.

ABOUT STEPHANIE

A native of southern Illinois, Stephanie Grace Whitson Higgins has resided in Nebraska since 1975. She began what she likes to call "playing with imaginary friends" (writing fiction) when, as a result of teaching her four homeschooled children Nebraska history, she was personally encouraged and challenged by the lives of pioneer women in the West. Since her first book, *Walks the Fire,* was published in 1995, Stephanie's fiction titles have appeared on the ECPA bestseller list and been finalists for the Christy Award and the Inspirational Reader's Choice Award. Her first nonfiction work, *How to Help a Grieving Friend,* was released in 2005. In addition to serving her local church and keeping up with two married children and three teenagers, Stephanie enjoys volunteering for the International Quilt Study Center and riding motorcycles with her blended family and church friends. Widowed in 2001, Stephanie remarried in 2003 and now pursues full-time writing and a speaking ministry from her studio in Lincoln, Nebraska. Visit her at *www.stephaniegracewhitson.com* or write 3800 Old Cheney Road, #101–178, Lincoln, Nebraska 68516.

A Garden in Paris

PROLOGUE

November 2003

Omaha, Nebraska

THE ONLY PROBLEM WITH HER life, Mary thought, was that she didn't have one. Sam had been gone for two years, but she was still playing by his rules. The weight of the charade was too much. She would take the pills.

The nurse and the sheriff had accounted for every prescription medication the day Sam died. They'd taken the Oxycontin and hundreds of dollars worth of other pharmaceuticals off to be destroyed. Except for the sleeping pills. The hospice nurse had trusted Mary with those. Had even urged her to make use of them until she could see her own doctor. Had she looked in the bottle, the nurse would have had second thoughts. Mary had been collecting pills for a long time. She knew enough about computers to Ask Jeeves and follow a few links until she was convinced, even taking into account reduced potency, that she had enough to do the trick painlessly.

She hadn't expected her hand to tremble so when she opened the bottle. She hadn't expected to spill the water from the glass on her bedside table. As the water trickled across the tabletop and dripped onto the sculptured carpet below, Mary pondered the realization that, while she wanted to think she was the kind of person St. Peter would be glad to see in line at the pearly gates, when it came right down to it, she had no real assurance as to what might be on the other side of what Sam had irreverently called "the dirt nap." She put the lid back on the bottle of pills, tucked it under the bank of pillows propped up against the headboard, and leaned back. Staring up at the ceiling she scolded herself. *Mary Elisabeth McKibbin Davis, you're fifty years old. You have no life of your own, no future plans, and no guts to do anything about it. No wonder Sam spelled Elizabeth with a z instead of an s. No wonder he named your daughter after his mother. Elizabeth Davis had a spine. Mary Elisabeth McKibbin has none. Elizabeth Davis went to market. . . . Mary Elisabeth McKibbin stayed home.* She fell asleep repeating her bittersweet version of the old nursery rhyme.

By the next evening, Mary was grateful she had put the pills away. Earlier that afternoon, she had wandered into a store and found a cheap little piece of junk with a motto that offered hope. She couldn't get it out of her mind. And then there was that magazine cover, featuring the *Sea Cloud* slicing through the water, her sails unfurled against a brilliant blue sky. Reading the article, Mary had learned that the ship's home port was a small town in Southern France called Arcachon. Her heart pounded as she reread the article, searching for the captain's name.

Instead of taking the pills . . . she wrote a letter.

ONE

November 30, 2003
Dear Jean-Marc,

If this letter reaches you, it will be a miracle of the God whose existence you denied all those years ago. It's been a long time since that evening when Sam took the microphone away from the band-leader and surprised everyone by announcing our engagement. You were standing by the door, looking at our table across the crowded dining room. I'll never forget the look you gave me just before you turned to go.

It was nearly thirty years ago. It was yesterday.

I went to your hotel the next day. But you were gone.

I have a grown daughter. My hair is short now, and I have given up both trying to tame the curls and cover the gray. If we were to pass on the street, you might walk right by and never know it was me.

Do you still play Chopin? Did you spend that summer sailing around the Mediterranean? I thought of you often, even though I did not keep my promise to come with you.

Do you remember the first day you took me sailing? When we anchored for lunch, you tore off a chunk of the baguette your mother had packed in that old basket and spread brie on it. You insisted eating something would make me feel better. And you were right. The seasickness receded. I still love brie.

It will be Christmas soon and I have decided to return to Paris. My daughter might be with me. Sam will not. He always said he would die first, and unlike me, Sam always kept his promises.

I suppose this ridiculous letter is a sign that I'm growing old. They say old people are prone to try to relive the past. And they forget things. The other day I couldn't remember my own phone number. But after all this time, I still remember your address.

I used to try to imagine you aboard the Sea Cloud. *And now I have seen the article in* Seafaring *magazine and learned that your dream came true—she is yours. When I have thought about you over the years, I have also imagined you married to that lovely chanteuse who flirted with you so mercilessly when you and I were together. You seemed to find her annoying, but she was devoted to you, and I have hoped that perhaps you finally allowed her to see the man I knew. I've even let myself picture you with children and grandchildren. A man who can tell stories like you should definitely have grandchildren. But the article makes no mention of a family— just a humorous quote from you about the* Sea Cloud *being your best wife yet.*

I don't know all the reasons I feel compelled to put this in the mail. I suppose I am hoping that somehow you will let me know that you have forgiven me. My life has not been all broken promises.

I'll be thinking of you Christmas Eve in Paris. If you think of me, picture me . . . Well, you know where I'll be.

She had been writing furiously, but when it came to signing the note that had suddenly become a letter, Mary hesitated, leaning her head against the wing of the chair she used at her desk. The sun was beginning to nudge towards the horizon, streaking the sky with pink and orange, and backlighting the stand of trees beyond Sam's garden. Mary lay the pen down to watch the sunrise through the great bay window opposite her desk. As the sky brightened, she absentmindedly smoothed the frayed edge of the old silk robe she'd pulled on in the predawn dark. Sam had always hated the color, which approximated the muddy creek water flowing through the southern end of their property. The smoothness of the silk accented the fact that she had yet to dip into the jar of hand lotion this morning. Dry skin. Another harbinger of aging. Another regret.

She reread the letter, still not certain how to sign it. *Your friend*? Hardly an accurate description, of either their relationship or their parting. *Love*? Too cavalier. *Sincerely*? Too formal.

When she leaned forward, putting her elbows on the writing desk so she could rest her chin on her folded hands, the robe's wide sleeve fell back, its frayed edge tickling her arm. Sam had urged her to throw it away long ago.

"You look like one of those homeless women who goes picking through the piles at the Salvation Army," he had complained the first time she grabbed it out of a pile off the dressing room floor.

"It's *comfortable*," she had grumbled. "Why can't I be comfortable in my own house?"

Sam had come up behind her and put his arms around her, resting his chin on the top of her head and staring at her in the mirror. "The house staff will never respect you if you bumble about in that." He had her yellow silk dressing gown over his arm. He held it out. "*This* is what the lady of the manor should wear." With his free hand he traced her jawline and let his hand play down the lapel of the mud-colored robe. He nuzzled her ear. "Would madam care to change?"

Funny how memories like that came more often lately. That little incident had happened on their first morning back from their honeymoon, although Sam had always reminded her to call it their *wedding trip*. On that long-ago morning, the young bride Mary Elisabeth McKibbin Davis had pulled the old robe off and donned the new without any more argument. Looking down at it now, she fingered the worn silk, realizing just how symbolic of the rest of her life that incident would be. She had had to change garments a lot in the past thirty years.

Sighing, Mary reached out to pick up the framed motto sitting beside the lamp. Running her finger along its scratched metal frame she mouthed the words, *It is never too late to be what you might have been.* She'd picked it up the day before in a shop down in the Old Market district. It was the kind of place Sam despised and Mary was drawn to—a musty collection of high-ceilinged rooms boasting shelves crowded with bric-a-brac and racks of old curtains and clothing creatively tagged *Vintage.*

Mary turned the frame over, smiling when she realized the piece of masking tape pricing it at 50 cents was still affixed to the back. It was the only thing she'd bought in her ramblings yesterday—a day she was supposed to be at the stationers ordering invitations for Elizabeth and Jeffrey's wedding breakfast. She would have to do that today. Even if the wedding wasn't until next May, Liz was already fretting. If Mary thought about it, her daughter's apprehension hurt her feelings. Liz seemed convinced that with her father gone everything would fall apart, including her wedding plans. As if it had been Sam who kept track of things all these years.

The red rim of the sun peeked over the distant hills, and crimson light flooded the room. Mary placed the motto back beside her Tiffany desk lamp, remembering how Sam had complained when she insisted the desk be placed opposite the great bay window.

"It will distract you from your work," he had said. "No one puts their desk in front of a window like that."

"I do," Mary had insisted. "I want to see outside." Sam had relented about the placement of her desk. He had stood his ground, though, when it came to the subject of work. His definition of the word was as far removed from Mary's as the English estate in his family history was from the Irish shanty in hers.

Mary soon realized that what Samuel Davis called her *work* would have made her father shake his head in disgust. But then, Michael McKibbin had only the money in his pockets and no experience with managing funds earned by the previous generation. Sitting at a desk answering invitations to charity functions would never qualify as work to a McKibbin. And although Mary had done it for over a quarter of a century, she'd never really considered it *work,* either. Thank God Elizabeth did all that now. At last, Mary was free to do what she wanted. If only she could find what it was she wanted to do. She looked down at the letter, running her finger over his name. *M. Jean-Marc David.* Three first names. She'd teased him about that.

As the light turned golden in the room, Mary snatched up the old ball-point pen she had dug out of her desk drawer and signed the letter. *Fondly, Mary.* She could still hear Jean-Marc's voice whispering her name with that gorgeous bass voice of his. It had taken her three years of practice, but she thought she knew how to pronounce a proper French *r*. But when Jean-Marc said her name, she realized she had it all wrong. It wasn't trilled, and it wasn't pulled to the back of the throat the way the Germans did it. It was . . . Well, when Jean-Marc said it as part of her name, it was beautiful.

Her hand trembled as she addressed the envelope. *This will end up in the bottom of some mailbag in Arcachon. The neighborhood is probably a parking lot by now. That's what they do in resort towns. They build up and take out the old neighborhoods. With their view of the bay, the Davids probably sold out long ago. Even if they didn't, if Jean-Marc went out to sea as planned, he would have sold the house as soon as his parents died. And surely they are dead by now.*

Mary stood up. Walking around the desk she went to the wall of leaded windows and climbed onto the upholstered cushion in the bay. She grabbed a pillow and hugged it to herself. Down past a low hedge, the sun was illuminating the tops of the hundred-year-old pine trees that served as a boundary between the groomed lawn and the prairie beyond. Several of the pines hosted decades-old bittersweet vines that wound up their trunks and provided garlands laden with orange berries for the five mantels in the house every fall. In the morning light the berries shone bright, and Mary realized the first frost had come and gone, and no one had harvested the bittersweet. Just as well. Had anyone mentioned it, Cecil Baxter would have forced his arthritic knees to climb one more year, and Cecil was far too old to be climbing trees. She was going to have to hire help before next spring and would need to think long and hard about how to bring *that* up without hurting Cecil's feelings.

Stretching again, Mary stood up and went to the opposite side of the room and into the half-empty dressing room. She had never managed to care enough about clothing to fill all the hanging space, much less the shelves and drawers.

"You all right, ma'am?" A soft knock on the bedroom's double doors accompanied the low voice.

"Just moving a little slow this morning, Irene. Come on in."

She opened the lingerie drawer, but then hastily retreated to her desk to get the envelope and tuck it into her robe pocket while Irene set a breakfast tray on the bench at the foot of the bed.

The older woman's eyebrows drew together. "You're not coming down with anything, I hope. Holidays coming and all."

Mary nodded toward the broad expanse of windows. "Gorgeous morning." She turned away and headed back toward the dressing room, calling over her shoulder. "I'm driving into town this morning. I'll likely pick up something for lunch at Val's." After pulling on faded jeans, she slipped her bare feet into a pair of beaded moccasins before yanking a sweater out of her drawer.

Irene's voice at the door behind her made her jump. "How much weight have you lost?"

"Thirty-eight pounds," Mary answered as she pulled the sweater over her head. "And ten more to go." She turned around and patted her stomach. "Not bad for an old gal, huh?" She reached for an ivory linen blazer. "Can I get you anything in town?"

Irene shook her head. "Have Val make you one of her malts. Put some meat back on those bones."

Mary chuckled. "Don't worry, old friend. I'm not exactly wasting away." Once again turning her back, she grabbed a leather clutch off a shelf and quickly transferred the envelope out of the robe pocket and into her purse. She squinted and peered into the full-length mirror. Lifting her glasses she pursed her lips, frowning slightly. Those two lines at the corners of her mouth were getting more pronounced by the day. Maybe some wrinkle cream. Maybe Botox. Meredith at the club went for regular injections and swore by her doctor. And she *did* look a little younger.

Irene cleared her throat. "You going to the post office?"

Mary straightened up. "Why?"

"Saw you tuck a letter into your purse." Irene nodded toward the leather pouch. "If you're going to the post office, I'd appreciate it if you could get a roll of stamps."

"Of course." Mary brushed by her. "Don't forget. I won't be home for lunch." She hurried into the bedroom and stopped by the breakfast tray long enough to take a gulp of coffee. "Bye." Mary paused. "And thanks again for the help with the dinner party last night." She rested her hand on the doorknob. "I don't think I've ever told you, Irene, how much you've meant to me. You've saved me from many a social nose dive over the years. Last night was no exception."

Irene snorted and shook her head. "No such thing. They would have understood."

"That's what you think. They would have *pretended* to understand. But I would have been the talk of the club today if you hadn't called and reminded me to get home. How could I have forgotten about dinner with the Goldenhirsches?" Mary paused. "I *like* Maude. Really."

"Well, it's likely she's forgotten a dinner or two in her day," Irene offered as she bent over to arrange the pillows on Mary's bed. "And Elizabeth was here. It wouldn't have been a complete disaster."

"Well, maybe Maude would have let it go. But Elizabeth would have been mortified. I know she's counting on the Goldenhirsches' support for help with the new oncology wing."

Irene straightened up. "Elizabeth would have lived. It's not like she's never forgotten anything. And her own mother's birthday is a darned site more important than dinner with rich friends!"

"Now, Irene," Mary said, "That was last year. She was under

a lot of stress trying to run the business without Sam. And I did tell her I didn't want a fuss made over it."

"Well, then," Irene said. "I guess you got your wish."

Mary smiled. "You know, you saved the day at my first dinner party, and you saved the day at the last. I owe you big time. I love you for all you've done. Now g'bye. I can't handle standing here watching you make my bed."

"It's my *job* to make your bed, Mrs. Davis," Irene said.

Mary paused at the door and looked back. "If you sense an earthquake later this morning, it's my fault. I'm dropping in on the foundation board meeting."

Irene's eyebrows shot up. "Really."

Mary nodded. "Something—well, several somethings, actually—that Elizabeth said at dinner last night make me think it might be a good idea."

"That George Kincaid business," Irene said.

Mary sighed. "Sam wouldn't like it. I really don't want to get involved, but after arguing with myself half the morning, I've decided I owe it to him to fix it."

"Good luck," Irene said, plumping a pillow.

"Thanks. I'll need it." Mary flashed a smile and headed down the hall toward the back stairs. *Back stairs.* Sam had never wanted her to use them. *"That's the servants' entrance,"* he'd always said. The stairs were narrow and steep, and the walls had always been painted white. As she descended them this morning, Mary paused, looking down the flight of stairs toward the hardwood landing. *Yellow. We'll paint the walls yellow. And hang some of those black-and-white photographs of Paris I saw at Target.* She could almost hear Sam snorting his displeasure. *All right, then. I'll buy a digital camera and take my own photographs.*

IRENE LUMBERED toward the unmade bed, worrying over the George Kincaid business and grumbling about the untouched breakfast on Mary's tray. She smoothed the sheets and tucked the quilts in place, taking special care not to stress the fragile fabric on the top one. Mrs. Davis had hauled it home from an antique shop a month ago, exclaiming over the age of the chintz and the border fabric she called a "pillar print"— whatever that meant. She'd folded it at the bottom of her bed and said it was too fragile to really use but she just wanted to enjoy it for a while before deciding where to display it.

Finishing with the bed, Irene paused and looked out the windows just in time to see the silver Austin Healey make its way down the winding drive and out onto the road. That was a good sign. Mrs. Davis hadn't driven that car much since the mister passed on. And she was going to a meeting down at the office. Taking an interest. That was good, too. Maybe she'd turned a corner.

Humming while she worked, Irene moved around the room, drawing the sheer blinds down on each set of windows in the bay, straightening the desk top, plucking a piece of thread off the carpet. When she grabbed the coffee cup Mary had set on her bedside table on her way out the door, her toe hit something and sent it rolling under the bed. With a grunt, Irene bent down to retrieve it. A bottle of pills lay on its side, barely hidden by the damask bed skirt. Irene reached for it, lifting her glasses and squinting at the label. *Take one to two capsules by mouth at bedtime as needed for sleep. May cause drowsiness. Alcohol may intensify this effect. Use care when operating a car or dangerous machinery.* Irene opened the bottle. It held a collection of pills. Different sizes. Different colors. Lots and lots of pills. *Enough to kill a horse,* she thought. She slumped down onto the window seat and closed her eyes.

Oh, Lord. No, Lord. Irene sat for a few minutes looking out the window. Her husband came into view, perched on the riding lawn mower, his spindly legs sticking out either side. He guided the mower along the edge of the perennial bed, then stopped beside the reflecting pool and got off. He looked toward the house. Looking for her, Irene knew. They were supposed to harvest the late elderberries growing along the back of those beds today. The ones Mrs. Davis had asked Cecil to try to save from frost.

Irene looked down at the pills again. She stood up and dropped them into her apron pocket. *Just when I thought she was coming back to life.*

Something she'd heard on *Oprah* came to mind. People did that, sometimes. Set things in order. Just before they—*Now stop that, Irene Baxter. That's nonsense.* But was it? Was it really? Mrs. Davis and Elizabeth hadn't been getting along. Truth be told, Liz hardly ever came around these days. And what was that Mrs. Davis had said about last night? Something about it being her *last* dinner party? And why'd she suddenly decided to go to that stuffy foundation meeting, anyway? *George Kincaid.* She wanted to set things straight about that. What, Irene wondered, would happen once that got straightened out? And what was in that letter Mrs. Davis was hiding in her purse, anyway?

Irene picked up the breakfast tray and headed for the hallway. At the bedroom door, she turned back around to survey the room, scolding herself for being so dramatic. Mrs. Davis was slowly taking back her life. Wasn't that quilt on the end of the bed a sure sign of that? She was learning about something new. And what about the lost weight? She was looking ten years younger. And was driving the Austin Healey again.

Still arguing with herself, Irene headed to the back stairs. At the top of the stairs, she looked back toward the master suite. Morning light was streaming out into the hallway through the open doors.

Too big for one lonely woman. Too big, Lord. The pill bottle in her apron pocket bumped against the handrail. At the sound of all those pills rattling around, Irene sighed. *Help me know what to do.*

TWO

HAD ANYONE WARNED HER ABOUT what would happen once she stepped through the massive Davis Enterprises boardroom doors, Mary Davis would likely have turned left instead of right when she got off the elevator, descended the stairs to the first floor, slipped out the back door into the narrow alley behind the old brick building, revved up the Austin Healey, and escaped. Never mind that she had spent nearly a quarter of a century perfecting the art of being someone she didn't know. Never mind she had learned to spend a great deal of her life in places she didn't like. Given a warning as to what would happen between her and Elizabeth, Mary would have avoided the meeting and raised the subject of an architect for the Samuel F. Davis Oncology Wing of Creighton University Hospital over dinner at Vivace—with Jeffrey Scott at the table to smooth his fiancée's ruffled feathers.

But she had no warning. So Mary arrived early enough to schmooze and pretended she didn't notice how surprised the board members were at her presence. She asked Derrick Miller how his son was doing at Creighton, inquired after Harvey

Fagan's aging Basset hound, and soothed Millie Patton's concerns over what to serve at the next foundation fund-raiser.

And then, Elizabeth arrived.

"Look who's here!" Harvey Fagan put his arm around Mary's shoulders and squeezed before pulling out the leather chair at the head of the boardroom table for her.

Grateful that Harvey's back was turned so he did not see Liz's silent appraisal of her mother's blue jeans and moccasin-clad feet, Mary slid into the upholstered armchair next to the chairman's. "I'm just listening in," she said.

There was an edge to Liz's voice from the minute she called things to order. Mary wondered if Elizabeth and Jeff had had a spat. That was happening all too frequently these days. A broken engagement at this point would not only be a nightmare logistically but also a mistake. Jeffrey James Scott was the best thing to happen to Elizabeth Davis in a very long time, and Mary hoped Liz knew it.

"The string quartet has confirmed," Millie Patton was saying, "but their fee has gone up considerably since last year."

Elizabeth frowned. "Gone up? How much?"

"Well," Millie looked around the table. "Several hundred dollars, actually. But you said you wanted them. So I went ahead." She paused. "I suppose I should have called you."

"No," Elizabeth said, shaking her head. "It's fine. A call would have been nice, but I meant for you to be in charge." She looked down at the meeting agenda and checked off one item.

Watching her, Mary wondered at Liz's uncanny ability to be completely polite and yet make it apparent that what she was feeling was exactly the opposite of what she was saying. In the boardroom, Elizabeth Davis was nearly a carbon copy of her father. Which was, Mary thought, not necessarily a good thing, either for the volunteer foundation members seated around the table this morning or for Liz.

Mary forced her attention back to the agenda. The group discussed several more items, and the longer the meeting went on, the more disgruntled Mary became at her daughter's systematic bullying of the committee. She did what she could to mediate and to soften the blows Elizabeth was landing.

"Well," Elizabeth said, laying aside the agenda, "those items are taken care of." She picked up a slim file folder. "But there's still the matter of an architect." She opened the file and pulled out a piece of paper.

"We reached a consensus." Harvey Fagan spoke up, looking around the table. Everyone smiled and nodded their agreement.

"I read that in the file," Elizabeth said. "But I can't agree to it."

The tension level in the room rose palpably. Mary sat up straighter. She looked around the table at the other committee members. Millie Patton's mouth was drawn down into a thin line that emphasized the fine wrinkles descending from the corners of her mouth to her chin. Derrick Miller was fiddling with his pen trying to avoid eye contact with anyone. He looked up only when Mary spoke.

"You and I both agreed to abide by the committee's findings," she said.

Elizabeth shook her head. "George Kincaid should never have been on the list. He's made himself the laughingstock of Omaha more than once and choosing him for this project is—"

"Compassionate," Mary said. "The publicity will do him good."

"The Samuel Davis Foundation is not a rehab organization," Liz said.

"No one here said it should be," Mary replied. "It is, however, named for a man who was one of George's best friends." She leaned toward the table and put her hands palms down on either side of the file before her. "Your father would agree with the committee. And heaven knows George could use the good press doing this project will give him."

Liz's left eyebrow arched slightly. Her nostrils flared. She stood up. "Could I talk to you in my office, Mother?"

Mary laughed. "I don't think there's a need for that, dear."

"Please." Liz left the room without a backward glance.

Mary looked around the table. Millie was studying the meeting agenda, pretending to jot something down. Neither Derrick nor Harvey met her gaze, either. She took a deep breath. "Listen, folks, we've finished everything else. Millie, you've done fine work." When Millie looked up, Mary smiled warmly, adding, "You did the right thing with the reception music. Thank you." She turned to the men. "Derrick, Harvey," she said, "you two have a good round of golf later this afternoon. And greet your wives for me." She stood up. "And thank you again for your selflessness on behalf of the foundation. You've all spent a lot of hours working on this project when you could have been doing a thousand other things. Someday I'll find a way to thank you." Mary patted Derrick Miller's shoulder. "You tell that boy of yours to come and talk to Liz next week about a summer internship." She headed for the door.

The minute Mary closed Liz's office door behind her, Liz held up her hand. "It's my last one. Promise." She put the cigarette out before turning to look out the expansive windows behind her desk. Folding her arms across her torso, she waited. Tension showed in every line of her elegantly clad body, from her two feet planted about a foot apart on the imported carpet to her ramrod straight back and squared shoulders. "Would you mind telling me what is going on?"

Mary slid into one of the leather club chairs in the seating area in the corner. "Well," she said, tracing the grain of the leather with her index finger as she spoke, "we are finalizing plans for a reception after the groundbreaking ceremony for the Samuel F. Davis wing at Creighton. And discussing the details."

Liz wheeled around and faced her mother. "That's not what I meant. And you know it."

"George?" Mary asked, looking up at her.

"George Kincaid is a drunk," Liz blurted out, "and I will not have his name associated with this project. And I'd appreciate it if you would refrain from embarrassing me in front of the foundation committee that way. You haven't been to a meeting in ages and to have you show up unannounced like that and then treat me like a child was—" Liz drew in a breath. "It was inappropriate."

Mary frowned. "It is never inappropriate to raise a voice of reason and kindness where none has been heard," she said. "And if you were embarrassed, I'm sorry, but I didn't do that to you. You did it to yourself when you held George's name up to ridicule."

"I said nothing in that boardroom that isn't common knowledge," Liz snapped. "I was just the only one gutsy enough to say it."

"Just because something is common knowledge doesn't mean it has to be aired publicly. The last thing George needs is another group of people ignoring the quality of his work and refusing to come alongside him when he needs it."

"The quality of his work?" Liz snorted. "What work? What

work has he done in the last two years? He's been locked up in detox."

Mary leaned forward to rest her chin on her folded hands. She sighed before motioning to the other club chair. "Take a cleansing breath and sit down, Elizabeth. We're having a discussion, not a joust."

Liz blinked a few times. She went to the chair Mary had pointed out, but instead of sitting down, she stood behind it, bracing her hands on the back.

"As to your comment about my not coming to meetings, I don't think that's quite accurate," Mary said. "I've been at nearly every meeting I was told about." She paused, letting what she had not said—which was that Liz had had a number of meetings without Mary being informed—have its full effect before going on. "I've been charming and offered my opinions—most of which have been ignored. But I'm not mad. And I don't really know why you are. Have you and Jeffrey had an argument? You came into that meeting with a gi-normous chip on your shoulder." Mary pronounced the word *gi-normous* slowly, hoping the use of Jeff's favorite descriptive term would make Liz smile.

Liz did not smile. Instead, she flung the word back at Mary, "If I have a gi-normous chip on my shoulder it's because I'm under a gi-normous amount of pressure, and I don't see anyone coming alongside *me* to help. And now my own mother is siding with the committee and helping them make a huge mistake."

"Well," Mary said, standing up, "if it turns out to be a mistake, I'll take full responsibility."

Liz snorted.

"Is that funny?"

Liz shook her head. "Come on, Mother. You've never taken responsibility for anything in your life—except the flavor of the coffee and the freshness of the canapés at Daddy's soirees.".

Mary sat back down. Hard. Her heart thumped. She inhaled sharply, as if recovering from being hit. She swallowed and fought back the tears that sprang to her eyes.

"I'm sorry, Mother. That was . . ." Liz reached out to put her hand on her mother's shoulder.

Mary waved her away, shaking her head. "I think," she finally managed to say, "I'll be going." She pushed herself out of the chair and headed for the door.

"Mother. Please," Liz said.

Mary looked at her daughter, painfully aware of the anger in Liz's Nordic blue eyes. Her father's eyes. She looked away, swallowed, and then looked back into those eyes. "I don't fault you for thinking you can ignore my opinions, dear. I've been walking around in a fog since your father died." She smiled. "But I'm waking up. And I'm going to have more to say about things in the coming days." She put her hand on the doorknob. "Now I'm going to grab my purse and my folder from the boardroom and scoot home. And you, Elizabeth, are going to call George Kincaid and congratulate him on winning the bid for the new wing. It's the right thing to do." Mary's next words were said slowly and with special emphasis. "And what's even more important, *it's what your father would have wanted.*" When Liz opened her mouth to protest, Mary interrupted her. "That's the way it's going to be, Elizabeth. You can bully the committee, but you cannot bully me. Not anymore."

As she walked down the hallway toward the boardroom, Mary passed by the lighted oil painting of Samuel Frederick Davis that hung just opposite the elevator doors. She paused to look into the deep blue eyes. *It's taken a long time, Sam. But I'm finally going to fight back. I hope it isn't too late.*

On her way home, Mary mailed the letter.

THREE

Liz

IT TOOK ME UNTIL I WAS eighteen years old to finally give myself permission not to love my mother. Don't get me wrong. I love my mother. But I don't *love* her. There's a difference the English language can't quite express. I don't know if there's a language anywhere that does, but I'd like to think that somewhere there's a family structure that allows for a daughter to respect and cherish her mother in the ideal sense without loving her in the emotional sense.

Maybe it's wrong to say I don't love her. Certainly I appreciate her giving me life and changing diapers and making my life easy. It's just that she and I have never connected. I've always been more like my father. He and I could share unspoken jokes across the dinner table that went right over my mother's head. When we watched a movie as a family, it was Daddy and I who laughed at the same scenes. Mother would politely join in, but more often than not it was just that—she was only being polite. She really didn't think the campfire scene in *Blazing Saddles* was funny. Daddy and I practically rolled on the floor every time we watched it.

I struggled all through high school to make a connection with Mother. She did everything all my friends' mothers did. She worked on committees and gave her share of parties. She was nice to my girlfriends and compassionate to the boys I dragged home and then summarily dumped one by one. She applauded my good grades and gave one of the most memorable graduation parties in our class. She even cried at the baccalaureate.

But for all those happy memories, there isn't one moment of time when I can say she and I really connected. We have always been like two dancers just slightly out of step with each other. It's as if somewhere in our heads we hear music, but the melody isn't the same. Or maybe it's that we both want to lead. Or follow.

I felt guilty about this all through my high school years. Like there was something lacking in me that made Mother disapprove of me. Finally, the year I graduated and went off to college, I gave up trying to understand her. I stopped asking her opinion of things and accepted the fact that we just didn't have anything in common. She was the quintessential homemaker. Not to denigrate her chosen field, mind you, but I could never see myself doing the June Cleaver thing. I grew up telling Daddy I was going to come to work with him someday, and I didn't change my mind. After high school graduation I headed for business school. Business school led to graduate school, which landed me my MBA and the right to work beside my father.

The happiest moment of my life was the moment I walked toward my new office at Davis Enterprises and saw my name on the door. Mother sent flowers. Daddy took me to lunch.

Working for Davis Enterprises was everything I'd imagined. Except for one thing. Two years after I received my MBA, Daddy was diagnosed with pancreatic cancer. He did his best to teach me everything he knew in a few weeks and then went home to die. I'm still not very happy with him for giving up so quickly. I spent hours on the Internet investigating alternative therapies and treatments, but Daddy said no, he wanted to be at home with Mother. He didn't want to travel, he said. I've always suspected that what was really going on was Mother didn't want to travel. She's never been one to stray far from home. It seems like she could have gotten past that for Daddy's sake. Maybe he could have lived a little longer.

I don't know what would have happened to us during those hellish days when Daddy was dying if it hadn't been for Jeff. We met at a business conference I didn't want to go to and almost skipped out of. I'm glad I didn't. We were already engaged when Daddy was diagnosed, and it means a lot to me to know that my father approved of Jeff.

Jeff fills in all the gaps in my breach with my mother. His own mom died of cancer, so Jeff understands what it's like to lose a parent that way. And he reminds me to appreciate having Mother around, whether I understand her or not.

I thought Daddy's dying would bring Mother and me closer together. It hasn't. The things about her I don't understand just keep multiplying. I hurt just as much as she does, but a person can't just come to a grinding halt when they lose someone they love. Daddy told us both he expected us to keep living. I never thought my mother and dad had any great deep love affair going. But maybe I was wrong, because since Daddy has been gone Mother seems to be losing her grip on life. She doesn't get out unless you count going out to lunch at Val's. She never invites people in unless it's something I've planned for the foundation. When I suggest she needs a social life, she just gives me the look that says I don't understand. Which, truth be told, I don't. I *know* that as a widow she's the "odd number" at a dinner party, but if she'd give half the energy to becoming an interesting person that she gives to wandering aimlessly around the Old Market or poking through antique shops, it wouldn't matter if she was part of a couple or not. If it weren't for me insisting that she do things for the foundation from time to time, I don't know if she'd even bother to get dressed some mornings.

Even Irene is worried. People think she's just the housekeeper, but she's a lot more than that. Irene and Cecil Baxter have lived in the cottage just behind the main house for as long as I can remember. Cecil takes care of the grounds and the cars. Irene takes care of the meals and the house.

Most of the time they treat all of us more like their surrogate children than their employers. It used to irritate Daddy to the point that he once threatened to replace them. I didn't think Irene knew about that, but the next day she baked two pies. Rhubarb and gooseberry. And three dozen kolaches. Daddy never again objected to Irene treating us all like family. And Irene went out of her way to address Daddy as "sir" and Mother as "ma'am" in the presence of outsiders. She even acquiesced to Daddy's request that she wear a uniform. For company.

Irene says Mother just needs time. But after this morning's display at the foundation meeting, I'm beginning to think she needs therapy. She isn't herself, that's for sure. I want her to take an interest in things, and that would naturally include the foundation, but it just isn't like her to pick a fight in front of the committee like that. Of course I regret hurting her feelings. But I'm grieving, too. The oncology wing for the hospital is important to me, and I don't want it ruined. George Kincaid was a great architect. Once. But his best days are long gone. Daddy would have realized that. I don't know what Mother was talking about, saying that he would have championed George's come-back. The Samuel Davis I knew wasn't a man to risk important ventures on weaklings.

And for Mother to contradict me in front of the committee . . . well, that was just bad form. Again, Daddy never would have done that. And no one would ever have attempted it with him, either. I'm beginning to think I made a mistake when I tried to get Mother more involved. Clearly, she's misunderstood what I had in mind. It's a good thing she's invited Jeff and me to dinner tonight. I don't know what's going on with her, but I'm going to find out. And we're going to clear the air about this George Kincaid business, too.

FOUR

"MOTHER, YOU ARE KIDDING. RIGHT?" Liz stifled a laugh and looked across the dining table at Jeffrey, her blue eyes sending an unspoken message. Jeff looked down at his plate, inspecting his steak like a biologist examining a Petri dish.

Mary was reminded of the way Liz and Sam used to relay unspoken messages to one another across the dinner table. She spoke to Jeff. "That's a new sauce I asked Irene to try out." She looked at Liz and smiled. "And no, I'm not kidding. My passport came yesterday, and I'm ready to book the flight."

Apparently Jeff's radar was on a different setting than Sam's had been. After taking a bite of steak and sounding his approval, he winked at Mary and said, "You go, girl!"

"I thought you said you were going to get more involved in the foundation," Liz said frowning. "Running off to Paris and missing the holiday gala doesn't sound like getting more involved to me."

"Were we at the same meeting today?" Mary asked. "Because if I recall correctly, Millie has the entertainment and the food in hand, and both Derrick Miller and Harvey Fagan will be there to welcome guests." She paused. "Nothing earth shattering is going to happen. All we were going to do was smile and thank people for coming, anyway."

"Maybe that's all *you* were going to do," Liz snapped. "But there's a *lot* of PR to be done before we can even think about breaking ground. And Samuel Davis's wife being absent would make a negative impression."

Mary shrugged. "I think we should just let people have fun at the dinner. We're already expecting them to bid outrageous prices for things they don't need at the auction. That's enough begging for one evening. I think hosting more intimate luncheons would give us a better idea of who we can really count on. I'd be happy to set up a half dozen or so for after the first of the year. After I come back." *If I come back.*

"When did you come up with this idea?" Liz demanded.

"I didn't," Mary said. "It's Millie's. But after thinking about it, I like the idea. In the long run, building relationships with benefactors is going to be much more effective than one-shot events like the gala."

"Maybe *you* have time for a string of intimate little luncheons," Liz said. "But I don't. I have a business to run, a wedding to plan, and a life to live." She grabbed her steak knife in one hand, her fork in the other, and began to cut the thick filet on her plate.

Mary took a drink of water before continuing. "There's something I don't understand, Elizabeth." As usual, the use of her daughter's given name caught the young woman's attention. "You've been harping at me for months to take a more active part in the foundation. I did that today. I'm offering to do it after the first of the year. But you don't seem to be very happy about either of these things."

"I didn't realize that your idea of taking an interest would mean embarrassing me in front of the committee," Liz said. "And I also didn't realize your idea of taking an interest would mean leaving the country instead of coming to our main fund-raiser— and then doing an end around with the benefactors at a string of private events I've already told you I can't attend."

"You can't possibly sit there and tell me that your luncheon schedule for six weeks from now is filled," Mary said. "I appreciate that you're a busy young woman, but no one is that busy."

"She's got you there, Bitsy," Jeff said.

Mary silently blessed him for trying to cool things down.

Liz cast an angry frown in his direction. "All right," she said. "Maybe I could make time for one or two." She sat back and sighed. "I don't suppose it's a completely bad idea."

"Thank you," Mary nodded her head.

"But George Kincaid is off the project. I won't compromise on that."

Mary took another sip of water. She closed her eyes for a moment, then opened them and glanced at the oil portrait of herself and Sam hanging above the fireplace on the far wall. Inhaling deeply, she spoke with what she hoped was an authoritative tone. "This isn't an appropriate topic for the dinner table, sweetheart. As your father used to say, disagreements over dinner cause indigestion, and that's not good for anyone."

"Right." Jeff nodded. He gestured at Liz with his fork. "So let's stop talking fund-raising and go back to the subject of Paris. Which, I predict, you will love, Mary."

"What, exactly, makes you think she'll love it?" Liz challenged.

"You would too, *ma chérie,*" Jeff said, mimicking a thick French accent.

"Really? What makes you think that?"

"Well," Mary agreed, "you have a Monet print hanging in your office. The spot where Monet painted the original is only a day trip from Paris. Then there's the Musée d'Orsay—dedicated to the impressionists. And the Rodin museum. Not to mention the Louvre."

Liz smirked. "You sound like a guidebook, Mother," she said. "And you have to admit that's a little strange, considering the fact that you've never traveled."

When Mary didn't say anything, Jeff spoke up, "If you're thinking you want to see what you've been missing, I repeat, 'You go, girl'." He raised his glass. "Here's to trying new things."

Liz got the message, and Mary recognized her forced smile. "Jeff's right, of course. It's wonderful that you're trying something new, Mother. But . . . can't you wait until after the gala?"

"I want to be there for Christmas," Mary said. "In fact, I've already made reservations at a small hotel near the Sorbonne."

"You're going to be gone for Christmas?"

"Now don't be angry. You can't tell me you two won't enjoy having a romantic holiday to yourselves." Mary grinned. "Irene won't know what to do. She hasn't cooked a Christmas dinner for two in decades. She might actually have to *relax* on Christmas Day!"

Liz had been fiddling with her earring while she listened. Now it fell out, bounced off her lap, and disappeared somewhere under the massive cherrywood table. She swore softly.

"I'll get it," Jeff said, and slid out of his chair.

"Can I help you, Mr. Scott?" It was Cecil Baxter, coming in from the kitchen, impeccable in a dark suit and tie, looking nothing like the gardener he was at heart.

Liz waved him away. "Jeff's getting it."

Jeff reappeared, Liz's earring in hand. Cecil retreated to the kitchen with instructions to bring in dessert, and the subject returned to Christmas in Paris.

"I've been wanting to do this for a while," Mary said.

"I'm amazed," Liz said. "Daddy hated to travel. I thought you did, too."

Mary shook her head. "I used to love it."

"Did Daddy know that?"

Mary chose not to answer.

"Why didn't you just tell him?"

There it was again. That tone. The one that made her feel like things were her fault. Mary sighed. She looked out the window. Cecil came back in carrying a footed cake stand crowned with an unusually tall chocolate cake. "As a matter of fact, honey, I did tell him."

Liz frowned. "Really? And he just . . . ignored it?"

"It's a little more complicated than that," Mary said. She waved Cecil to her side. He set the cake before her and went to the sideboard to retrieve dessert plates.

"I suppose it is," Liz said. She shook her head. "Of all the things I might have imagined you saying to me, 'I'm spending Christmas alone in Paris' wasn't on the list."

Mary smiled as she took her knife from the side of her plate and sliced into the cake.

"*Mother,*" Liz scolded. Standing up, she went to the sideboard, opened a drawer, and produced a silver cake knife.

"I'll have some," Jeff said, and held up his plate.

Mary started to slide a piece of cake onto the small dessert plate, but it ended up frosting side down on the tablecloth.

"Be sure you let Irene serve the guests at those intimate little luncheons you're planning," Liz chided. "You'll find it's a little awkward to ask for a hundred thousand dollars while you're scraping chocolate off the damask."

For the second time in as many days, Mary felt her daughter's words land in her midsection.

"Oh, Liz," Jeff said, his voice gently scolding as he set his dessert plate down.

"Well," Liz said stubbornly. "It's the truth. Those events require tact and style."

"Neither of which I have, apparently," Mary said, dipping the tip of her finger into the dollop of chocolate frosting on the table and licking it off with a flourish.

When Liz responded, it was to take up the one subject Mary had banished from their dinner table discussion only moments ago. "Now that you mention it, Mother, it *wasn't* very tactful of you to contradict me in front of everyone at that meeting today. Daddy always made certain he and I presented a united front at board meetings. You and I should be careful to do the same."

"Are we back on the subject of George Kincaid?" Mary asked.

Liz took a deep breath. "Listen to me, Mother. No one is telling you not to participate in the foundation. Your presence is welcome. I had grown tired of making excuses for you. People were beginning to think Samuel Davis's widow had gone over the edge."

"Liz . . ." Jeff reached over to take her hand.

She shook him off. "No, Jeff, she needs to know the truth."

"The truth?" Mary asked.

Liz nodded. "You don't know because I've protected you. Made excuses for you. Given reasons why you don't go to the club anymore. Why you've lost so much weight. Why you never go to church." She seemed to gain steam the longer she spoke.

She listed meetings Mary had failed to attend, ways she had disappointed Liz, failing upon failing upon failing piled higher and higher. Liz ventured back in time, to embarrassments Mary had never known about. She mentioned her senior prom. "Honestly, Mother, you came to the door *barefoot*. You didn't even bring the *camera*. It was like it meant nothing to you. And now, after all these years, suddenly you want a voice in the company? You think you can give me orders?" Liz's voice rose as she landed the final blow. "Daddy left *me* in charge of the company, Mother. That should tell you something."

Mary stood up. For a moment, she stared into her daughter's stormy blue eyes. When she looked past Liz to the portrait looming on the far wall of the dining room, her heart began to pound. Tearing her gaze away from Sam's blue eyes, she took a deep breath before saying quietly yet deliberately, "I have a majority interest in the foundation's organization and function, Elizabeth. So whether we agree on the subject or not, George Kincaid is the architect for the Samuel F. Davis Memorial Oncology Wing at Creighton University Hospital." She rested her fingertips on the damask tablecloth as she continued, "Millie Patton is in charge of the gala. Derrick Miller and Harvey Fagan are the greeters. Harvey is going to be the master of ceremonies. And I," she said, pushing her chair back and heading for the door, "am going to Paris."

She managed what she hoped was a dignified exit. Jeff tried to stop her, but she waved him away. Once outside in the hallway, she sank momentarily against the wall, stifling a sob, trying to catch her breath. The sound of approaching footsteps forced her to hurry away. She scuttled down the hallway and hurried up the grand, sweeping front staircase and across the balcony. Once in her own quarters, she went to the bedside table. There would be no sleeping tonight unless . . .

Swiping the tears off her cheeks with the back of her hand, she reached to search beneath the bank of pillows at the head of her bed. *Nothing.* Holding her breath, she knelt beside the bed and reached beneath it. When her hand met empty space, she peered under the dust ruffle. The pills were gone. Sitting down on the carpet, Mary raked her fingers through her hair, wondering what to do.

IRENE HESITATED in the dark hall, leaning toward the door, almost pressing her ear against it, listening. She raised a lightly clenched fist to knock, then thought better of it and reached for the knob, relieved when it turned. *At least she didn't lock me out.*

The door opened soundlessly into the darkened room. Her toe caught the corner of the hooked rug Mary had just positioned at the foot of the bed a few days ago, and she stumbled. When she placed a hand on the bed to steady herself, a spring creaked.

"Go away. Please. Whoever it is, just go away." A dark shape rose from the desk chair across the room and turned toward Irene. "Oh," Mary said softly. "It's you." She paused again before saying, in a voice strained with false cheer, "I'm all right, Irene. Go on to bed. It's late."

"You're not all right," Irene said. "No mother on earth would be all right after a child said things like that. Cecil and I heard every word—all the way in the kitchen, for goodness' sake." When Mary turned away to look out the window, Irene followed her gaze. Moonlight illuminated the garden sculptures, peopling the garden with ghostly figures.

Mary went to the window seat and sat down. "It wasn't really a surprise." She drew in a long, ragged breath. "Although the intensity of her feelings did take the wind out of my sails."

"She was cruel," Irene insisted. "She'll likely be around to apologize tomorrow."

"Maybe," Mary said, her voice quivering. She glanced over her shoulder to where Irene waited, still standing. "Well, if you're not going to go to bed, at least come and sit down." She patted the cushions beside her.

Irene complied, sitting primly, her hands in her lap, her back straight.

"You get along so *well* with your children," Mary said. "Where did I go wrong? What is it I do? Don't do? Say? Don't say?" She swept her hair back off her face.

"It's not you," Irene said. "It's her. She doesn't see."

"Doesn't see what?" Mary muttered.

"Anything," Irene blurted out. "What it's been like for you. She doesn't know any of it."

"Well, she's not to blame for that," Mary said. "I promised Sam not to talk about Paris." She paused. "Whatever else can be said about Mary McKibbin, at least she kept *that* promise." She shook her head. "Elizabeth doesn't think there's anything to me but what she's been shown. I'm just 'the little woman' who plans parties . . . and occasionally drops chocolate cake on the white tablecloth."

"*I* know there's more to you than that," Irene said. "And I'm the *maid*. Seems like your own daughter might get her eyes off herself just long enough to see the way things really are with her mother."

"Don't be so hard on Elizabeth. She's had it rough. All the responsibility dumped on her shoulders—"

"She loves it, and you know it," Irene said. "Loves all the decision-making. Loves bossing people around. Always did, even when she was little. She was probably the inspiration for that Mary Engelbreit's 'Queen of Everything' saying."

Mary chuckled. "Well, at least 'The Princess of Quite a Lot.' She did have Sam under her thumb from the minute she opened those blue eyes." She murmured, "Not having him here is awful for her."

"Of course it is," Irene agreed. "But she should look around her and count her blessings. And after she counts her blessings, she should think about *you* for a change. She's been whining for over a year about you not taking enough interest in the foundation. And now you do, and she gets all high and mighty."

"It wasn't quite that bad."

Irene raised both eyebrows.

"All right," Mary acquiesced. "It was." She sighed and stretched her arms above her head. "Well, what's done is done." She stood up. "I'll call her tomorrow and apologize. It'll be all right."

Irene slapped her open palms against her knees. "You'll do no such thing! It's Elizabeth who should be apologizing. She should be in here right now, begging you to forgive her for the things she said."

"Maybe some things just can't be fixed, Irene. Maybe it *is* too late. I lost her little by little to Sam from the day she was born. I saw it happening and I let it be. I told myself I was lucky Sam was so devoted, so completely accepting. I was so glad he made time for her—"

"That," Irene said. "is an understatement. If you ask me—and I realize you didn't—but if you ask me, that man, God rest his soul, cared too much for Elizabeth and too little for you."

Mary sighed. "You can't love a child too much. You don't believe that for a minute."

"It wasn't a matter of too much loving," Irene agreed. "But his priorities were wrong. He—" She stopped in midsentence.

"It's all right," Mary said. "I know I took a backseat to Liz in Sam's life. In his heart, too, if I'm completely honest. I came to accept it." She shook her head, "And then, when her father died and the center of Liz's universe collapsed, I folded in on myself." She sighed. "She may have kept her distance from me, but I did nothing to fight it. Until this week, I've made no attempt to get seriously involved in the things that interest her. You know that."

"You've had your own sorrows to handle," Irene interjected. "And precious little help handling them, either, if you don't mind my saying so." She caught Mary's hand and pulled her back down beside her on the window seat. "Remember, honey, I wasn't much younger than you when my first husband passed on. And when he died, I wanted to climb into that grave right beside him. I know what it's like to go through days when all you can do is remind yourself to breathe. And I know what it's like, watching a man die by inches, helping him to the commode, preserving his dignity in the face of things that make you cringe. You could have hired nurses for all that, but you stuck by him."

"I *wanted* to do those things," Mary protested. "No one made me."

"That makes it even more wonderful. And all the more tragic

that Miss Know-it-all Elizabeth can't see what a wonderful woman you are."

Mary shook her head. "I'm not a wonderful woman. I'm a fraud. A backwoods country girl who's been pretending to be an heiress. Sam created the charade and then insisted I continue it." She got up and walked to the wall opposite the bay window.

It was dark, but Irene didn't need a light to know what Mary was looking at. The only photo from Mary's past was the one with the Rolls Royce in it. Even Elizabeth assumed it was a photo of a young Mary McKibbin showing off her father's Silver Cloud. Only Irene knew the truth. It was a photo of a poor American student in France, earning some extra money by modeling a designer gown in a car show and riding in a limousine owned by a friend of Samuel Frederick Davis—the man who would meet the model . . . and change her life.

Mary spoke up. "But Sam is gone, and I can't keep up the charade without him." She turned around to face Irene. "I don't *want* to."

"You should tell her," Irene said.

Mary shook her head. "It's too late. I should accept that. Maybe it's for the best."

Irene reached over to pick up the framed motto that she had noticed while dusting yesterday. *It is never too late to be what you might have been.* She hoped that even in the dark her employer would get the point. "She's turning into her father," Irene said. "How could that be for the best?"

"Sam had good qualities, too," Mary said quickly. "She has his drive. His memory for details. His . . ."

"Lust for power," Irene said. "And his ability to run over anyone standing in the way."

"She's single-minded," Mary said.

"She's self-centered and strong-willed," Irene retorted. "And she should listen to her mother."

"Well," Mary said. "She's obviously not inclined to do that." She turned back toward the window. "And to be honest, I don't think I have the will to force her to listen." She swept her hair back off her face. "I'm not even sure it matters."

The two women were quiet for several moments, Irene sitting on the window seat, Mary standing beside her, staring at the night sky. When Mary moved and Irene realized she was brushing a tear off her cheek, the older woman reached up and took her hand and squeezed it.

"I've lost her, Irene," Mary said, her voice breaking. "She's the only thing left in this world for me to love, and she doesn't want my love. And I don't have the strength to fight for her. The truth is, I don't even know if I want to. Sometimes I don't like her very much. How can a mother feel that way about her own child?" She suppressed a sob.

Irene pulled Mary down beside her and collected her into her arms. Even as she demonstrated what Cecil called her "mother-hen tendencies," anger seethed inside her. Anger against Elizabeth Davis for her inability to see her mother's need. Anger against whatever force it was that seemed to strengthen the wall keeping the two women apart. And anger against Sam Davis, who had brought an innocent girl into his world and systematically stomped every bit of enthusiasm for life out of her.

When Mary's tears subsided, Irene shuttled her toward the bed, took the old silk robe from her outstretched hand, and draped it across the back of her desk chair. She tucked her employer into bed, and as Mary settled back against her pillow, Irene put one open hand on her head and whispered a brief prayer.

When Irene opened one of the massive double doors to leave the room, Mary called her name.

"You sleep now," Irene said gently. "It's almost a brand new day. I'll be asking the Lord to give you something to rejoice in."

"Thank you." There was a pause and then Mary called out again. "Irene."

"Yes, ma'am."

"I wouldn't have taken them. I had plenty of chances."

"Yes, ma'am."

"You can throw them away."

"Already did. You sleep, now." Irene closed the door.

FIVE

Jeff

IF I'D KNOWN ALL THAT WAS going to happen when I met Liz Davis, maybe I would have run the other way. Maybe, but I doubt it. She's beautiful, capable, and intelligent. Just about everything a guy could want. Add to that the fact that she seems to be very excited about spending the rest of her life with me, and anyone can see I'm in this thing up to my eyeballs.

The problem is the invisible wall between Liz and her mother. Nobody in their right mind wants to be caught between two women who can't get along. Sometimes I think I'm not *in* my right mind or I'd have checked out long ago. Or told Liz to grow up and give her mother a break. Or maybe asked Mary to try a little harder. But I like Mary, and I love Liz . . . and so I mostly keep quiet and hope for the best. Mostly.

The majority of men, if put in my position, would just shrug and let things be—*if* they even noticed a problem. But I can't pretend it doesn't matter whether Liz and her mom get along or not. And I *do* notice. Anyone who tells you adult children no longer need their parents is an idiot. I know that because my mom died when I was twenty-five. To this day I find myself picking up the phone to call her about something—and realizing she isn't there. And I get choked up. Mom and I were close because it was just her and me against the world after my dad left. I was thirteen years old. I had a younger brother and a younger sister, and I remember putting my arms around my mom and telling her we'd make it. And we did. Luckily, I was bright enough to get a good scholarship to a local college. I also got a couple of offers for some pretty highbrow schools, but I wanted to be near my family. In fact, I lived at home for a couple of years. Mom finally kicked me out of the house when I was a junior. Said I needed to learn some lessons she didn't want to watch me learn. She was right.

My mom was an amazing lady who managed single parenting so well, I never guessed how much she missed being married. Until one night I came home late and found her watching the movie *Sabrina* and sobbing. "I always wanted a love like that," she said. She told me how she felt like she had failed us all by not making things work out with Dad. All those years had passed, and I didn't have a clue she was hurting like that. I gave her a big hug and told her she was terrific. And I decided I was never going to let her forget it.

Danny and Sarah were both in college when Mom died of a rare kind of lymphoma that kills quickly. She was gone before we even had a chance to come to terms with her cancer. Which, in some ways, was a blessing, I guess. I don't have the painful memories of an extended illness like Liz and Mary have of Sam. Mom just went into the hospital and never came out.

I had a good job, and for a while the three of us Scott kids all huddled together in my apartment. We got through it together, and we're still close, even though Danny lives in California now, and Sarah's in Denver with three kids under the age of four.

I don't have much patience with Liz and her complaints about her mom. Actually, she doesn't complain. Not like you'd think. She just doesn't seem to value her mother. And there are times when I think she's a little embarrassed by her. It makes me mad. In fact, the only really big fight Liz and I have ever had was about her and her mom.

Mary Davis is terrific. She's homey and down-to-earth, and where she got that in the middle of the life she's lived I'll never know. Liz doesn't seem to know much about her mother's past. That would bother me, but Liz says her mom said her life began when she met Sam Davis, and there's nothing more to say.

I think I liked Mary from the minute I saw her. Liz' was bringing me home to meet her parents. She'd warned me that the house she grew up in was big. That was the understatement of the year. The Davises don't live in a house. They live in a ten-thousand-square-foot mansion plopped in the middle of a forest. But you don't get to see the house unless the guy at the entrance opens the gate. When guests are expected, old Cecil Baxter puts on a uniform and waits in the little booth beside the gate.

Well, you can imagine how I felt. There I was, this guy who grew up in an Arts and Crafts house that was maybe eight hundred square feet. My room was at the top of a steep staircase that came down into my sister's closet. In other words, Danny and I got the attic.

There we were, driving up the driveway in my Volkswagen bus with a Grateful Dead decal on the rear window. We turned left and this mansion came into view. I wanted to turn around and run. But then the door opened, and it wasn't a butler. It was a woman in jeans and an oversized plaid shirt that made her look even smaller than she is. And she was barefoot. Come to think of it, I'm quite certain I liked Mary Davis from the first moment I saw her.

But Mary's outfit didn't please Liz. That was obvious right away. "Hello, Mother," she said. She didn't even hug her. She introduced me and then said, "I'm sorry we're early. I'll drag Jeff out to the pool. That'll give you a chance to change for dinner."

Even though I had just met Mary, I saw the hurt expression flit across her face. I opened my mouth to say something, but she was already walking away. I looked back at her as Liz dragged me through the entry hall and toward the back of the house. She was standing on the bottom stair looking at us. When she caught my eye, she smiled. But only with her mouth. I hadn't known her for more than a month before I realized that you never see Mary Davis's eyes smile. If I hadn't known her before Mr. Davis died, I'd just say it was grief. But if it's grief, Mary has something else she's grieving besides her husband's death.

Liz's dad wasn't as easily won over as her mom. Sometime during the year after he died, I learned he'd done a background check on me. Apparently he didn't find anything to object to. I've often wondered what would have happened if he had. Liz loves me, but I doubt our relationship would have survived the disapproval of her father. Thankfully, it was never an issue. Sam Davis was slow to warm up to me, but after about six months of dinners followed by chess games I deliberately lost, he must have decided I was all right. He started calling me Jeff instead of Jeffrey, and once or twice when I was saying good-bye he gave me a friendly slap on the back. When he let me drive his Austin Healey one night, I knew I was finally on his good side. I don't know what it was about that car, but Samuel Davis didn't let anyone near it. He didn't even let Liz drive it, and he gave Liz just about everything she wanted. I only drove it that one time, but it was about as big a thrill as I imagine I'll ever have. Not because of the car, mind you—but because it was Samuel Davis's car.

So, here we are on the other side of Sam's funeral, and I've been hoping something would happen to enable Mary and Liz to reach across whatever it is that's standing between them.

The funny thing is, most people who know Mary and Liz Davis see nothing but doting mother and devoted daughter. Although after that board meeting yesterday, it sounds like a few people might be getting an idea. Still, for the most part, I'd say you have to be around them in a more intimate setting, for long periods of time, to catch on to something not being quite right. They seem to have figured out how to dance around each other so things will go all right between them. And that, in my humble opinion, is the problem. They're content with just "all right." It drives me crazy. They have lunch with each other once in a while, and they get together on birthdays and holidays and take pictures. Liz has an 8-by-10 of herself with Mary on the credenza in her office. It was taken last Thanksgiving. Mary's arm is around Liz's waist, and if you didn't know Liz like I do, you'd think they look happy in that picture.

The fact is, neither of them has been happy since Sam died. He was the glue that held those two women together, and after he was gone, things started to unravel quickly. Liz let her irritation with what she calls her mother's "slumming" show. Mary stopped feigning interest in the Davis Foundation and quit going to meetings. I don't think she darkened the door of Davis Enterprises that first year. I think that was Mary's way of tossing down the glove. Sort of a challenge. But Liz didn't protest. Sam made sure she could carry on without him at the helm. She is, as everyone says, her father's daughter. She's doing a great job at the office. She didn't protest when Mary stepped back.

I've wondered before if Liz is enjoying the power and the control a little too much. If she was a little *too* willing to take over. What happened last night at the mansion makes me think I've glossed over a part of Liz that I need to stop and take a serious look at.

Mary, God bless her, is apparently taking a new interest in the foundation—largely because of George Kincaid. That guy's been the subject of a lot of gossip in those social circles. He was a friend of Sam's from the old days, and Mary's sticking by him even if nobody else does. So, Liz threw a fit about that. But the way she did it—well, I hate to say it, but it was almost mean. I know she's never had a sense of humor when it comes to her mother's more laid-back tendencies. But she made such a big deal out of that chocolate cake falling on the tablecloth that I was ashamed for her. And it killed me to see what it did to Mary. I probably should have done something. But it's tough to know how to run interference. When I think ahead to, say, five years from now, if I'm honest with myself, I have to admit that being in the middle of these two is going to get really old really fast.

SIX

Arcachon, France

CLOSING HIS EYES, HE STROKED the piano keys, his fingers tentative against the cool ivory. One, two, three chords, and then a pause as he repositioned himself on the scarred piano bench. His hands hovered over the keyboard. He flexed his left wrist, pursing his lips at the crackling sound of bone against bone, pulling his fingers in against his palm and making small circles in the air until the crackling stopped. Once again, he moved, as if the bench must yield its polished surface to his body and help him find the familiar place where he had once sat for hours practicing the exercises his tutor demanded.

Without opening his eyes he felt his way into position on the keyboard, his fingertips easily locating the first chord again. This time the melodies rang true, and his left wrist supported his hand well enough for him to glide through the first few pages of the music. He opened his eyes after the first measure, but not because he needed to see the music. He knew his place in the score. Indeed, it was burned into his memory just as permanently as the image of the young lady who once sat next to him admiring his prowess as his fingers flew into the scherzo, never faltering, never missing a note. But that was then. And now it was more than a quarter of a century later. He ignored the first missed note and kept playing. He winced at the second. With the dissonance of the third, he slammed his palms down on the keyboard abruptly, letting the jangle of sound play on his raw nerves while he sat motionless at the piano, thinking.

The sound had faded before he reached up to pat the breast pocket of his white silk shirt, running his finger over the outline of the envelope he'd been carrying around since yesterday. She'd sent it international overnight mail. He had wondered at the sense of urgency after all these years. Surprised by the emotions the sight of her handwriting had awakened, he'd ripped the large envelope open. At the sight of the smaller envelope inside, he'd hesitated, tossed the outer envelope away, and tucked the letter in his pocket. He took it out now, running his fingertips across the return address first, then his own name. He started to open it, then stuffed it back into the pocket and got up, crossing to the wall of windows that looked out over the hillside.

Pine trees had once obscured his view of the bay, but he'd cut them down years ago, ignoring the protests of his neighbors. He'd never regretted the days spent sawing up those trees. They had yielded fuel for the small stove that warmed this room on the few days when heat was required. But the labor had yielded a greater treasure than wood. It had opened up the entire rear of the house to an unhindered view of the bay. Long ago his parents had told him that he must have been born with seawater in his veins. Maybe they were right. Something happened to him when he went inland. Only one time had anyone been able to keep him away from the sea for more than a few days. But he'd shaken the dust of Paris off his feet back in 1974 and vowed never to return.

His cell phone jangled. *"Oui?"* He shook his head. *"Pas aujourd'hui.* Not today, Dominique. I have an appointment."

"You don't have anything on your calendar today," the voice whined. "I checked with Paul before calling your private line."

"I have errands to run before I close up the house. And I have to go over a few things with Paul."

"You treat that boat like a wife," the voice complained.

"Actually," he said, "there are at least two women in the world who would tell you I treat her better than a wife."

The woman on the other end of the line was impervious to his oblique warning about his history with women. She laughed. "I'm not worried. I skew the data in these matters. Now stop joking and tell me what you want for *le déjeuner.*"

He could feel the muscles in his jaw tense up. Why *had* he agreed to give Dominique Chevalier a ride to her parents' villa halfway across the country? He'd sensed there was a hidden agenda to her wheedling that ride, but then convinced himself he was being egotistical. She was young enough to be his daughter. Almost. But her car was in the shop, and it *was* ridiculous for her to ride a train when he would pass within a mile of her parents' front door on his way to see Celine and the boys. It would have been rude not to offer.

"Is there some problem with you getting away tomorrow?" He tried not to sound too hopeful.

"Of course not," the voice purred. "I just wanted to treat you to lunch before we leave. To thank you."

"You've already thanked me. It's no trouble, really. The villa is on my way to Celine's." He forced a positive tone. "I'm happy to have the company."

"There's no way to convince you to join me for lunch today?"

"None," Jean-Marc said. "I'll see you tomorrow morning. I should be there by nine." He hung up before she had a chance to say anything more, slipping the phone into his pants pocket and heading for the door. He brushed his graying hair off his forehead and pulled on a jacket and cap before going outside.

"Which car, sir?" Paul called out from where he stood polishing the green fender of the vintage Triumph parked in the first stall of the six-stall garage.

Jean-Marc's eyes glanced across the row of polished hoods and spotless hubcaps. "Actually," he said, grinning, "I was hoping I could borrow yours."

Paul laughed. Reaching in his pocket he tossed his boss the keys to the rusty Peugot parked beside the garage. "The rent's going to have to go up, if you keep putting miles on it."

Jean-Marc nodded and touched the bill of his cap in a mock salute. "Name your price. And take the Triumph out for a spin if you like."

"You're kidding—right?"

Jean-Marc shook his head. "Not kidding. Aren't you having lunch with your girlfriend today?"

"I have lunch with my girlfriend every day," Paul retorted.

"Well, take her someplace special, today," Jean-Marc said, heading for the Peugot. "I won't be back for a while. I'll meet you down at the docks later this afternoon. We can trade cars back then."

Twenty minutes later, Jean-Marc guided the Peugot into a parking place and headed off through the trees toward the backside of the Dune du Pilat. Dumped along the Atlantic Ocean by some ancient hurricane, the Dune du Pilat had swallowed part of a pine forest. As he climbed, Jean-Marc passed several dead trees jutting out of the sand. He paused halfway up to catch his breath, finally cresting the top of the dune and inhaling deeply. The sea was calm today, gray in color, gently lapping at the beach below. He hadn't been here in years and yet, except for a stairway erected to facilitate the climb, little had changed. Just to his right the German bunkers waited, silent sentinels from a long-ago conflict where an occupying army had erected defenses against an Allied landing that eventually took place in Normandy far to the northeast. As a child he had spent entire days playing in and around those bunkers, reading the graffiti left by German soldiers, climbing over the sand in mock battle with his friends.

Now he wondered about the men who'd carved their names in those walls. If they were alive they would be octogenarians by now. From this side of his own childhood and lost loves and marriages, he wondered about those men, how it had been for them when they returned home. Had their wives and lovers been waiting as promised? Or had they returned to bombed-out homes deserted by their families?

The wind swept up the dune and sent a shiver through him. He should have brought a blanket. *A bottle of wine,* he thought ruefully, as he touched his breast pocket again. He headed down the dune toward the beach. Hunkered up against a huge piece of driftwood, he watched the waves for a while, judging the height and strength of the wind, more from force of habit than any real interest in the conditions at sea today. The *Sea Cloud* was moored for the winter. Tomorrow he was heading overland for a holiday with his daughter and her twin sons. He'd secretly planned to take them all to Greece for Christmas.

Frowning, he took the letter out of his pocket. It was almost Christmas. What if . . . He sighed. Disappointing Xavier and Olivier wouldn't exactly strengthen his relationship with his daughter. As it was, they rarely spoke. He'd hoped this holiday might improve things.

He looked down the beach to where, in the distance, a couple walked hand in hand. Closing his eyes he thought back to the afternoon nearly thirty years ago when he'd brought a girl to this very spot. They'd picnicked and talked and watched the waves. He'd never been that close to a girl before. At least not one as lovely as she.

He smiled, remembering his youthful resolutions. He wasn't going to be like the other boys he knew. He was going to wait until it meant something. He was an anomaly and he knew it. French men had a reputation to uphold, and they usually went about upholding it as soon as possible with as many young women as possible. Jean-Marc David had no use for this conquering of women for no other reason than to add a story to the collection of half-truths and lies young men told one another about their romantic prowess. Such idiocy did not fit his philosophy of life at all.

But the American girl sitting next to him on the beach stirred him in ways he'd never allowed himself to feel before. When she flopped back on the sand and put her arms up over her head and stretched like a lazy cat, it was all he could do to stay on his own towel. He had pushed his sunglasses up on his nose and turned his head, pretending to watch the sea when he was really watching her sunbathe. His eyes took in every curve of her youthful body as she lay on the sand, her eyes closed, her chest rising and falling in a maddeningly slow rhythm.

"It's so beautiful here," she said. She smiled without opening her eyes. "I bet you bring all your girlfriends here."

"I like it here," he agreed. "But I've never brought a girl here before today."

Her blue eyes flew open and she turned her head and stared at him, doubting. "Oh, I believe *that*," she said.

He shrugged. "Believe it or not. As you please."

She turned toward him and raised up, supporting her head with one hand, her elbow cushioned in the sand. "So if you don't bring girls here to the dune, where do you go?" She shrugged slightly. "I mean, I'm just curious about how the French culture works. It's been hard to get to know anyone in town."

"We tend to be very private about our family life," Jean-Marc explained. "It's nothing against foreigners, really." He smiled. "Monsieur Bertrand had to . . . twist the arm, I think you say, to get any of us to come to that dinner at the lycée."

"So why did you come?"

"I am in his debt. He intervened on my behalf when my parents didn't want me to go to sea."

"Really? And what did your parents want you to do?"

"They are both teachers. They wanted me to teach."

The girl shook her head and lay back on the sand. "You'd hate being cooped up inside a classroom. Anyone can see that. All they have to do is watch you when you're sailing." She giggled softly. "Maybe you could teach sailing." She turned her head and opened one eye halfway. "Do you think your parents would agree to that compromise?"

"Maybe I could teach you."

Both blue eyes flew open again. "Really? Would you?" She sat up abruptly and brushed the sand off her elbows. "I'd never even been on a sailboat before you took me out. Oh, I'd *love* to learn!" There was fire in her blue eyes.

He grabbed her clumsily and managed an awkward kiss on her mouth, apologizing the minute he pulled away.

"Don't apologize," she said. "I was beginning to think there was something wrong with me." She snatched his hand up and held it, looking down. "I mean, you're French, right? And you haven't . . ." The blue eyes sought his. "I mean, you haven't even tried to kiss me until now."

"I haven't tried to kiss any girl," he said. "Ever."

"*Never?*"

He shook his head. "I wanted it to mean something. Even the first time." He blushed. "So I guess I am not the typical French boy you expected to meet."

"No, you aren't." She touched his cheek, traced his jaw. "But you're *exactly* the kind of French boy I *hoped* to meet."

Remembering those romantic moments on this same beach, the fifty-year-old Jean-Marc David sat watching the couple walking along the edge of the water until they were little more than two tiny dots in the distance. *"You're exactly the kind of French boy I hoped to meet."* He'd believed her with all of his untried heart. He had taught her to sail. Taught her how to avoid seasickness, took her home to meet his parents, played Chopin for her. . . . and walked out of her life on a day so long ago he was surprised it could still cause him pain.

He should have thrown the letter away. At least out here at the dune no one would know he was reading it. Even as he opened it and stared down at the handwriting, he envisioned how he would tear it into tiny bits and throw it into the sea and watch the waves carry it away.

> *Dear Jean-Marc,*
>
> *If this letter reaches you, it will be a miracle of the God whose existence you denied all those years ago. . . .*

He paused and looked past the print toward the horizon.

He'd lost a good friend once over the idea of God.

He kept reading. Rereading. Amazed at how, after all this time, the sight of her name and the knowledge that her own hand had written it could raise his blood pressure. Whether it was anger or resentment or some lingering affection, he wasn't sure. But he didn't tear the letter into tiny pieces and send them out to sea. Instead, he tucked the letter back into his pocket, climbed back up the dune, descended to Paul's old Peugot, and headed home.

SEVEN

"YOU AREN'T LISTENING TO ME, BITSY." They were seated just inside a broad expanse of windows at their favorite Italian restaurant. Jeff reached across the polished mahogany table and put his open palm across the back of her hand. "You need to go see your mother."

"Don't call me Bitsy!" Liz snatched her hand away.

"Whoa," Jeff said. The smile disappeared. "You really *are* upset. Over twenty-four hours later, and you not only haven't talked to your mom, you haven't cooled down one bit, either."

Liz hunkered down in her chair. "You know I don't like being called Bitsy," she said. "And you also know this isn't some little spat over nothing." She picked up her napkin, snapped it open, and spread it across her lap. "I just don't understand her."

"That," Jeff said, "is the understatement of the century."

"Well, then you explain it if you're so smart. She's never shown the least bit of sincere interest in anything to do with Davis Enterprises or the foundation. And suddenly she's got a bee in her bonnet about George Kincaid, and it's like she's going to take over or something."

"Voicing her opinion about the architect is hardly—"

"What she's done is a lot more than voicing her opinion. You heard her at dinner. She practically ordered me to use him. And that's exactly what she did at the meeting. And when I balked, she overruled me—*in front of the entire committee*."

"Aren't you the one who told me your father left her in charge of the foundation?"

"That was purely for the public. He knew it would look better that way. No one—including my father—ever expected Mother to think she could actually *run* the thing."

"Ouch." Jeff winced visibly. "That's really harsh." He hesitated before continuing. "If I didn't know better, I'd think you're showing signs of being threatened by your own mother. And that you don't really like her very much."

Liz shrugged. "We're just different people, that's all. It's nothing personal. I'll admit we haven't exactly come through these last two years shoulder to shoulder. But we've managed. I thought things were going along all right. But then all of a sudden she changes everything, strolls into a meeting, and takes over. And if that wasn't enough, suddenly she's leaving the country. What's *that* about, anyway?"

"Maybe you should ask her," Jeff prodded.

"What's she expecting? Some great awakening beneath the Eiffel Tower?" She shook her head. "I'm not kidding, Jeff. This is just too weird. Maybe she needs therapy."

Jeff leaned forward. "Listen to yourself, Elizabeth. It's *Paris*. I hardly think a woman needs therapy because she wants to go to one of the most beautiful cities in the world."

Liz reached over and patted Jeff's hand. "I think it's very attractive, you know."

"What?"

"That you care so much. About Mother and me and our troubles." When Jeff opened his mouth to talk, she interrupted him. "I know, sweetheart. I know. If you had a mother walking the earth. . . ." She sighed. "You're right, of course. I should try harder to get along with her."

"You make it sound like it's so hard," Jeff said. He leaned forward. "Let me see those baby blues, Elizabeth." When she looked up at him, he said, "Let it go. Whatever it is. Whether it's one thing or a hundred. Let it go. Stop harping about the meeting. Love her. Be thankful for her. Shall I provide a list of her good qualities?"

Liz tossed her head. "All right. You've made your point. I'll call her. But I need to let the smoke clear for a couple of days before we kiss and make up."

"MIZ DAVIS not down yet?" Cecil slid onto a barstool and waited for his wife to serve up the same breakfast he'd eaten for over twenty years—two eggs, over easy; two slices of bacon, crisp; and one piece of dark toast, dry. "It's time we cut back that hedge. But I don't want to do it without her okaying it."

Irene snatched the toast from the toaster while she talked. "Now, honey, you know she trusts you when it comes to the gardening. Just do what you think needs doing. Mrs. Davis won't think you're hinting that she can't manage . . . like some people we know would."

Cecil chuckled. "The fur did fly the other night, didn't it?" He clucked his tongue against the roof of his mouth, slurped coffee, and looked up at the clock. "Were you able to smooth things over for her?" he asked, raising his eyebrows and nodding toward the ceiling to indicate Mary's quarters. "I've not known her to sleep this late before."

Irene slid two eggs out of the frying pan and onto Cecil's plate. "You've not known her to cry herself to sleep two nights in a row, either. Even when Mr. Davis passed on." She poured two cups of coffee and sat down next to her husband, buttering her own piece of toast and slathering it with apple butter.

Wiping his plate with a crust of dry toast, Cecil stuffed the last bit of breakfast into his mouth and headed for the back door. He paused, his hand on the doorknob. "She's got you to watch over her. She'll be all right." He winked. "Take her some of your cocoa. And breakfast in bed. That'll cheer her up."

"Great minds run in the same channels, I guess," Irene said, nodding toward the counter where she had already put out a tray with plans to serve Mrs. Davis in her room. She reached for the cocoa just as Cecil closed the door behind him and headed for the garage.

The morning was perfect. Crisp fall air, and leaves from the maples overhead crunching as Cecil walked across the brick drive. He paused halfway there, taking in the beautiful sight of the lawn sweeping down the back hill away from the house, toward the creek. He turned to look up at the house, then toward the cottage he and Irene had occupied for decades. *You've had a good life, you old coot.* Opening the door that led into the garage, he fumbled with the switch that would raise the doors. He'd polish the old Healey, right after he rode the golf cart around the acreage checking on . . . well, he'd think of something that needed checking as soon as he got that hedge trimmed.

What in the world? He bit his lower lip. Where only yesterday there had been an Austin Healey, there was now an empty parking space. And a very small oil spot.

"Baxter!"

At the sound of his wife's call, Cecil ducked out of the garage and looked up at the main house where she stood at one of the windows in Mrs. Davis's private quarters. He didn't wait for her to speak before heading toward the back door. He knew what she was going to say, anyway. Mrs. Davis had flown the coop.

"GONE?!" LIZ exclaimed. "Where?"

"I was hoping you could answer that," Irene said.

"Well, I haven't heard from her."

"You haven't talked to her since the other night?"

Liz bristled. "You know it's best to let things settle a little before we make up. And I have a company to run, in case you've forgotten."

"Don't you take that tone with me, young lady," Irene snapped. "You may be able to bully half of Omaha with it, but I've changed your diapers, and I'm not impressed."

"Do you have a point? I have a board meeting in five minutes."

"Your mother has disappeared. The Austin Healey is gone, her bed is made, and there's a piece of luggage missing."

Liz sat down at her desk. "She mentioned Paris. Do you think she's actually gone and done it?"

Irene's voice lowered. "I found one of your father's bottles of sleeping pills under the bed the other day."

"I hardly think that's reason for concern," Liz said. "You told me yourself you don't clean like you used to."

"True," Irene answered, "but the thing about *this* bottle of pills was that it was full of all different kinds of pills. Like someone had been collecting them. For quite a while."

"What are you saying?" Liz closed her eyes. She knew exactly what Irene was saying. She leaned her head against the high back of her leather desk chair. "I'll be right there."

"Don't you think you should'a told her you know Miz' Davis doesn't have the pills with her?"

Cecil was leaning against the doorframe. It was the closest thing to a scolding Irene had ever heard from him. "I think," she said, "that Miss Elizabeth Davis needs someone to yank a knot in her high-and-mighty tail." Irene bustled across the kitchen and began to wipe down the counter with a vengeance.

EIGHT

THANKFUL THAT CECIL HAD LEFT the front gate open, Liz braked just enough to whip her Carrera into the lane leading to the Davis home, then accelerated again, squealing her tires as she followed the curving blacktop around the first of two ponds. Only when she saw that Jeff had already arrived, did she slow down just enough to keep from screeching her brakes as she stopped in the circular drive in front of the house. Jeff descended the stairs and opened his arms. Liz went to him, closing her eyes as she leaned into his embrace. "Thank you," she murmured.

"For what?" Jeff wanted to know.

"For coming."

"Thank you for asking. I like being needed." He held her a moment longer, then pulled away and led her up the front stairs.

"I thought Irene would be watching for us," Liz said as they made their way through the front hall, beneath the winding stairs, and toward the back of the house. "Irene? Cecil? We're here," she called.

"In the kitchen." Irene's voice, usually mellow and low, had a shrill tone Liz didn't like. She smiled weakly when Jeff squeezed her hand.

In the kitchen, Cecil welcomed them. He was using a towel to dry the few dishes perched in an old-fashioned rack beside the kitchen sink.

Irene removed her hands from the soapy dishwater, dried them on a second towel lying on the counter beside her, and reached into her apron pocket.

Liz recognized the stationery, a simple gray laid her mother always used. Taking the note from Irene's hand, she crossed the gleaming kitchen floor and slid onto the dining nook bench beside Jeff, positioning her mother's note so he could read along with her.

> *Dear Irene,*
>
> *I have lived in fear for too many years. Fear of not pleasing Sam became fear of not pleasing Liz. Both of those fears have gotten so far out of hand that, for a while, I have been afraid to live. I started collecting those pills you found. Don't worry. That's over. While I am not certain what it means to "really live," I am certain I want to find out. It feels like a new beginning. I really do want to believe that little motto on my desk—that it never is too late.*
>
> *Part of me wanted to tell Liz the "whys" of Paris and Christmas Eve. Part of me wanted to beg her to come along. But fear won out. After that scene at dinner the other night, I realized it is best that I go to Paris alone.*
>
> *Please don't worry. I suspect that after a little mucking around in the past, I'll be home—changed for the better, I hope. Tell Liz that once I have figured out how to use the Internet cafés, I will be in touch. I am not giving up on George Kincaid and neither should she.*

Have a wonderful holiday. Do you remember how to cook for only two?

Love,
Mary

Liz could feel tears gathering in her eyes. When she tried to blink them away, Jeff put his arm around her.

"I think you should go after her," Irene said. "She hasn't been herself, and in spite of what she says in that letter, I'm worried."

Liz inhaled deeply. She swiped at the tears threatening to spill down her cheeks.

Jeff patted her shoulder. "Relax, honey. She said she'll e-mail. And she told you not to worry."

"I'm *not* worried," Liz said, shrugging out of his embrace and jumping to her feet. She marched to the cupboard, grabbed a glass, and filled it with cold water before speaking again. "I'm mad."

"Mad?"

"What do *you* have to be mad about?" Irene asked.

Motioning toward the letter with her half-full glass, Liz answered. "All that . . . drama. She doesn't get her way on the foundation, and she throws a fit and runs off. Talk about making a mountain out of a molehill!" She rushed ahead. "I guess she made her point, though. Saddling me with the most important fund-raiser of the year. She couldn't have picked a worse time to leave. Or maybe a better one—if she wanted to make a point or get attention."

At the look on Irene and Jeff's faces, Liz got defensive. "Well, it's the truth. She's been building up to something like this for weeks. And now she runs off just when there's something really important for her to do. I wouldn't be at all surprised if those pills you found were planted for effect," she said. She chugged down the rest of the water and slammed the glass on the counter.

"What if they weren't?" Jeff said.

"I know they weren't," Irene snapped. She glared at Liz. "And I can't believe you'd suggest such a thing. If you'd get your eyes off yourself and on someone else for a change, you'd know it, too."

"Now, honey," Cecil interrupted for the first time, putting his hand on Irene's shoulders and shooting a look of appeal in Jeff's direction.

"Mary's not the type for dramatics," Jeff agreed. "This is completely out of character for her."

"She hasn't been herself," Irene said. "Have you noticed how much weight she's lost?"

"All right," Liz sighed. "I'll go up to her room and go through her desk. Maybe I can find something about her plans." She motioned for Jeff to follow her and headed up the back stairs.

In Mary's room, the couple stood looking out over the garden for a minute before Liz turned around and went to her mother's desk, looking through the drawers. "I don't see a thing out of order," she finally said.

"Would you know if there was?" Jeff asked.

Without answering him, Liz closed the last drawer and headed into the dressing room, wondering as she looked around what clothing had hung on the few empty hangers.

"Either she travels light," Jeff said, "or she doesn't mean to be gone for long."

"Maybe she's going shopping there—wherever *there* is," Liz said.

"Does she like to shop?" Jeff asked. "I never thought she was the type."

"The type like me?" Liz challenged.

"What?"

"You said you didn't think Mother was the type to shop. Exactly what type is that?"

"You know what I mean," Jeff said. "She doesn't care much for clothes. Seems to me every time I've seen her lately she's had on the same jeans with an oversized man's shirt. I used to think that was part of her grieving process—wearing your father's shirts. But then I remembered she was dressed that way the first time I had dinner with you. They probably aren't your father's shirts, after all."

"Oh, no," Liz said. "She bundled all of Daddy's things up the day he died and sent them off somewhere. The Salvation Army, I suppose."

"Why does that bother you?"

Liz whirled around. "The day he died? The very day?"

"She'd had plenty of time to think it through."

"Then why did she send them to a rummage store?" She rubbed her forearms briskly. "The idea of strangers pawing through my father's things . . ."

"Did you tell her how you felt?"

Liz shook her head. "I assumed she would feel the same way."

"Maybe," Jeff offered, "Maybe she couldn't stand to see them hanging there in the closet. Maybe it hurt too much."

Liz snorted and looked away. "I'm sure that was it." She headed for Mary's dressing table. With a small exclamation, she reached down and picked something up.

"What is it?" Jeff asked.

Liz wheeled around and held up the smooth gold ring. "Her

wedding ring," she said. She nodded at the china tray where she'd found the ring. "And those diamond earrings—my father gave her those on their twentieth anniversary. He joked about it. Said something about her finally having earned them." Liz slipped the wedding ring on her index finger, letting it rest between the first and second knuckles.

"She earned them?"

Liz shrugged. "I wondered what that meant, too, but Mother wouldn't tell me." She looked up at Jeff, frowning a little. "It didn't seem to be a good thing, now that I think about it."

Jeff nodded. He touched the gold ring. "Do you think this is a bad sign?"

Liz shrugged. "I haven't a clue."

"I agree with Irene. You should go after her."

"Go after her? Where, exactly? She didn't tell us which hotel."

"That would be easy enough to find out. I bet it would only take a few phone calls to travel agencies here in town. Or a little hacking of her computer if she made her own arrangements."

"What would I say to a travel agent? I've lost my mommy?" Liz turned around and put the ring back on the china tray next to the earrings. When Jeff was silent, she looked up, catching his expression of disapproval in the mirror. "All right. I'll have my assistant make the calls. I'll check her computer. And we'll go. *After* the gala."

Jeff shook his head. "I'll see you off. But I'm not going."

"But you always—"

"I always serve as a buffer between the two of you," Jeff said.

"I need you," Liz protested.

He shook his head. "No. You want to hide behind me. There's a difference." He headed for the door. "I'll be downstairs."

"BUT . . . what about lunch?" Liz's voice was shaking as she delivered the mild protest. She started to get up from her desk chair, but Jeff held up his hand and motioned for her to stay put. He stepped away from her and put his hand on her office door handle.

"I didn't get a lot of sleep last night," he said. Then he hesitated before dropping his hand to his side. He turned back to face her, averting his gaze for a moment before saying, "I didn't want to say it over the phone. I don't really want to say this at all." He moistened his lips and bit his lower lip.

Watching him, Liz had the faint impression of a soldier who repositions his body "at ease" but still maintains his bearing.

"I think we need to take a step back," he said. His eyes locked on hers. He waited.

"I don't understand," Liz said.

"I need time to think. You need to patch things up with your mom."

"But—"

"Just a step back, Bitsy. A little space." He reached for the door. "I'm serious, Liz. Put some energy into figuring out what's wrong between you and your mom. That's what you should be concentrating on right now." As he shut the door, he said, "I'll call you." But he left without saying "I love you."

Liz had never realized how loud the click of a door closing could be. She sat for a few moments in stunned silence, gripping the edge of her desk to force herself to stay seated. She knew better than to go after him. Jeff loved her, but he could not be manipulated or controlled. It was the most attractive and the most maddening part of the man. When his mind was made up, he planted his feet and stood his ground. Liz seldom saw that part of Jeff, but moments ago it had been the only part showing. And whatever taking "a step back" might mean, Liz knew one thing—she would not be able to bully him into having lunch, or dinner, or any other meeting with her until he had worked out whatever it was he needed to work out.

"I need time to think. You need to patch things up with your mom." He'd given her an assignment she couldn't accomplish. Not without setting aside everything noted in the planner on her desk. If he'd only given her a chance, she could have shown him. One glance at today's agenda would have told Jeff it was impossible. She couldn't leave Omaha, let alone the country . . . not without some major adjustments. And did he really expect her to miss the gala—the most important event in the foundation's year?

"You need to patch things up with your mom." That, Liz thought, would take an entire team of psychologists. She reached for her planner and scanned the next few days with an overwhelming sense of powerlessness. Never mind that she sat behind an impressive cherrywood desk. Never mind that hers was the name engraved on the brass plate perched at the edge of the desk identifying her as *President, Davis Enterprises*. Never mind that hers was the likeness in the oil painting hanging out in the lobby next to her father's.

I wonder if Daddy ever felt this way? Tears threatened. She had gone to school and earned the good grades, slaved away at her father's side, gotten engaged to the right boy—and at this moment, seated at the cherrywood desk for which she had worked so hard, all she could think about was the man who had looked so remote a few moments ago as he stood just inside her office door dressed in the gray silk suit they'd shopped for together. How, Liz wondered, could Jeff do it? How could he order her to do the impossible. . . . when what really mattered to her right now was that he was taking a step back . . . and breaking her heart.

Snatching a tissue from the silver holder on her desk, Liz swiveled her leather chair around and faced the window, washing away the most expensive makeup in town with her tears.

The term "working lunch" took on new meaning as a few minutes later, Liz opened her planner and delved into her business life. She phoned and dictated and prioritized at whirlwind speed. For about fifteen minutes. Glancing down at her watch, she couldn't believe how the day was dragging. She slid open her desk drawer, pulled out a remote, and pushed a button. On the far wall, sliding panels opened to reveal a plasma television screen. For the next few minutes, she flipped channels. How was it, she thought, that nearly every station was talking about the time?

"It's time for the weather," Paula Zahn said.

He needs time, Liz thought.

"What time is it?" Cookie Monster asked.

He needs time.

The Land that Time Forgot was showing on one of the movie channels.

He needs time.

Clicking off the television, Liz grabbed another tissue, then muttered aloud, "Thank God he took it now instead of after the wedding."

The thought of the wedding brought a fresh bout of tears. She got up and crossed the office to the door that led into her private apartment. In the washroom, she splashed cold water onto her face and patted it dry, then reached for another tissue and went back into her office, back to her desk.

The phone loomed large. She should call the house. In spite of the letter to Irene, Mary Davis was the last person in the world to go globe-trotting alone. She'd probably come to her senses by now. She was likely headed back home, embarrassed by all the dramatics.

"You need to patch things up with your mom."

No need to call, Liz thought. She'd drive out to the house. She was going to be worthless in the office anyway. And it had been weeks since she'd had a real day off. She would set the computer to deliver an "out of the office" automail. She'd have her assistant cancel the rest of the day's meetings. They could be rescheduled.

A pop-up ad on her e-mail screen promised the *Best Fares Available to Europe*. She clicked it off and scanned her new mail. Her heart lurched as she saw that *MimiMcK@aol.com* had sent her something—with no subject.

> *I left Irene a note. She probably showed you. Don't worry about me. If you care for me at all, please hire George Kincaid. Will check back to see if you reply but won't be on-line for a while. Need to take a step back and evaluate some things. You probably can't understand. Please try. European keyboard driving me crazy. Too many typos to say more. I am still your Mimi, and I love you, Lizzie-bear.*

Liz read the e-mail over and over again. *Need to take a step back.* There seemed to be an epidemic of people in her life taking steps back. How long, she wondered, had it been since she called her mother *Mimi*? Why had she stopped?

Settling back into her chair, she thought back to her thirteenth birthday party and a guest named Henry Coddington III: Henry, with slicked back hair and thick glasses that a young Lizzie Davis thought made him look scholarly.

Mary had worked hard on Liz's party, which was held in the garden and featured hot-air balloon rides for all the guests. Closing her eyes, Liz remembered how she had maneuvered to be certain she went up in the hot air balloon with Henry.

"Give *Mimi* a kiss, Lizzie-bear," Mary had demanded, just as Liz climbed aboard the balloon.

Henry snickered and whispered in her ear, "Go on, Lizzie-bear. Mimi wants a kissy-wissy from her baby."

Liz felt her face grow hot with a furious blush. "Mother," she said a little too loudly, "please. I'm not your baby anymore. And I wish you'd call me by the name my father gave me."

Liz was surprised that all these years later she could still see the expression that came over her mother's face. She'd interpreted it back then as anger. Now she knew it wasn't anger. Mary was hurt, and she hid it behind a frown that looked like anger to an oblivious, self-centered teen.

Something else came to mind. *The name my father gave me.* Had Mary taken that as a slap in the face, too? Sam Davis had named his daughter Elizabeth, spelling it with a *z* instead of an *s*. Liz didn't know if people even noticed, but now, from the adult side of her life, she wondered how much that would have hurt her mother, to have her own child named for her mother-in-law instead of herself. For the first time in her life, Liz wondered why her father had done that. Surely he must have known it would hurt Mary. Didn't he care?

Other memories came, things Liz had long since buried and tried to forget. The way her mother sometimes shrank away—almost physically—at a word or a look from Daddy. The drives home from social events when Liz had laid down in the back seat pretending to be asleep while Daddy reviewed Mimi's behavior, reminding her of better ways to respond to questions. The times she had seen Mimi swipe tears out of her eyes and murmur, "Yes, Sam. I'm sorry. I'll do better next time."

Liz turned toward the computer and reread the e-mail. *I left Irene a note. She probably showed you.* A sentence from that note came to Liz's mind. *Fear of not pleasing Sam became fear of not pleasing Liz.* It must have been that fear that made Mother think it was better for her to be alone on this trip. What did she mean by *mucking around in the past?*

Saving her mother's e-mail to a new folder, Liz shut down the computer. She sat quietly for a while, then took up her planner. Flipping ahead to scan the calendar, she speed-dialed first Millie Patton, then Derrick Miller, and finally, Harvey Fagan. Each one expressed surprise. Each one said yes, they were certain things were under control and they could handle the gala if Liz needed some downtime. Liz could sense the amazement in each voice when she closed the conversation with, "I still have my doubts about it, but I've finally come to realize Mother was right. Daddy would have wanted George Kincaid to have this project. I'll be calling George next. We'll set up a meeting for after the first of the year. In the meantime, let's make the gala special for him. I'll trust the three of you to plan an announcement with all the trimmings and fanfare to really give him a boost."

"That's not possible." Liz's voice rose a few decibels.

"I'm sorry, Miss Davis, but I've checked every airline, and there just isn't anything available until Monday."

"I'll fly standby," Liz said.

"I've checked that possibility as well. Every reliable airline already has a long list on standby. The chances of that working out are just about nil. I'd advise you to take this ticket for the 27th."

After a protracted conversation wherein Liz mentioned several alternatives and the travel agent replied she had already checked that out, Liz gave up. "Fine," she snapped, "book a ticket for the 27th."

"What about a return date?"

"I don't know. Leave it open-ended."

"One-way?" the travel agent asked. "I'd advise against that. It will raise all kinds of red flags."

"What does that mean?"

"You'll likely be searched. Repeatedly."

Liz pondered. She grabbed the calendar on her desk. "Say return on January 3."

"Morning or evening?"

"I don't care," Liz snapped. "There's a good chance I won't use it, anyway."

"There's a penalty for changing, and security—"

"Just do it, please. And have the courier bring the tickets over here as soon as you've got them printed out. I don't want to leave this to the Internet."

For the next half hour, Liz cruised from Travelocity to Orbitz to Expedia and on to a dozen other Web sites offering last-minute deals and special fares. Finding nothing—as the travel agent had predicted—she logged off just as her assistant came in with a red file folder in her hand. The woman was the picture of efficiency. She used red folders for everything pending, yet incomplete.

"I've got all the paper work that needs your attention here," she said. "But unless you had it sent to the house, you haven't received your passport yet."

NINE

Mary

IT WAS THOMAS WOLFE WHO SAID "you can't go home again." I am not exactly trying to go home, but I am on a mission involving the past, and by the time my Air France jet is bumping along the runway at Charles de Gaulle airport in Paris, I begin to think I am making the biggest mistake of my life.

There is a branch of theology called Calvinism, and while I am not a Calvinist, I do tend to be fatalistic. For most of my adult life I've found comfort in the idea that *what is supposed to happen happens.* I have, therefore, spent an inordinate part of the transatlantic flight reminding myself that things generally turn out the way they are supposed to turn out. I was *supposed* to marry Samuel Davis. I was *not* supposed to spend my life on a sailboat with an unpredictable French lover, and therefore, this little attempt of mine to go back in time is not only ridiculous, but also dangerous to what little family I have left.

A savage thunderstorm and my resulting queasy stomach fuel my doubts.

As the plane bumps along on its way to the gate, I look out the window thinking about Elizabeth. Hopefully she has read the e-mail message I sent during my layover in London by now. If not, Irene will have found the note I left and called her. I will try to locate one of those Internet cafés and check my e-mail once I've recovered a little from the jet lag.

In spite of my promise to Sam to never tell our daughter about Paris, I almost invited Elizabeth to come along. I would have managed Christmas Eve somehow. It surprises me to realize that, while I have been grieving Sam's death, part of me also seems to have been waiting for the next thing. I didn't consciously realize it until I found that little framed motto in the Old Market district. It made me contemplate the possibility that maybe my life isn't over, after all.

Sometimes I wonder if Sam deliberately planned to put himself between me and my own child. Maybe eliciting the promise to never talk about Paris was the beginning of his plan. I don't want to think he could have been that selfish and calculating, but in the two years since his death, I've begun to realize that there were many times he did or said things to encourage Liz to think less of me and more of him. Maybe he really did just want a secretary for his life instead of a wife, after all. He certainly never let me be a partner. It took a few years, but he eventually convinced me I just couldn't understand the complexities of Davis Enterprises. If I had to describe what being married to Sam Davis was like, I'd draw two boxes labeled *His* and *Hers* and then indicate a one-way door in the common wall. The door would open for "him" to pass into "her" realm. But it wouldn't swing the other way. That's how it was. For twenty-eight years.

At first, I was so overwhelmed by the Davis mansion and the life they took for granted that I gave no thought to the family business that funded the life-style. But I was a smart girl, and in a few months I had my little box well organized. I began to show an interest in some of the things on the fringes of his box. Things like business luncheons, which I suggested we have at the house once in a while. I offered to take over the company Christmas party for Sam's assistant. That was when I learned the reality of what I had begun to suspect—that the door between Sam Davis's home life and his business life swung only one way.

"Don't be ridiculous," Sam said. I can still hear that tone of voice I would grow to hate because it made me feel as if I had suggested something monumentally stupid. "Margaret has been planning that event for years. She handles it impeccably."

"Of course she does," I said. "But that's not really what a business assistant is supposed to do, is it? Margaret's a gem, and she hasn't complained, but I imagine she'd gladly hand me the party file and never look back. I'd love to invite people to the house. Make it a little more intimate. We could have a string quartet out on the veranda. . . ."

Sam's smile made me feel like a puppy being patted on the head by its master and told to run along and play in the garden. I was hurt. Of course I was just beginning to realize that true partnership and personal intimacy was something Sam Davis had little taste for. But that's another topic. My point is, it was at that moment that I understood that the idea of Davis Enterprises being a family-operated business with "hometown" friendliness was a carefully crafted public image—and completely bogus. In nearly thirty years I think perhaps a dozen of Sam's business associates actually saw the interior of the house. Even then, their exposure was limited to the formal parlor, the dining room, the library, and the veranda. Why we have eight bedrooms, I'll never know. No one was ever invited to use them.

When the plane jolts to a stop at the gate, I am jarred back to reality and nearly have a panic attack. What was I thinking, coming to Paris alone after all these years? I've been brushing up on the language a little, thanks to some CDs from the library, but I am still a far cry from thinking in French, and that is going to be a problem. *Pardon, monsieur, pourriez-vous. . . .* Blast it. I can't even remember the sentence I've practiced so much: "Please forgive my American accent, but could you help me?"

I grab my bag from beneath the seat in front of me, slip my hand into the side pocket, and withdraw the little book of travel phrases I purchased one night at the Barnes and Noble in Omaha. *Est-ce qui'il y a un café pres d'ici? Pardonnez, s'il vous plaît. Pour aller au Grand Hotel Saint-Michel? Bonjour. Au revoir.* With a gulp, I stand up and follow the other travelers, moving single file up the aisle, onto the gangway, and into the airport.

What on earth was I thinking?

The French reacted to the Eiffel Tower with demonstrations against it. I remember reading about a writer who began to dine at the restaurant on the tower because it was the only way to avoid having to look at it. Today as I walk through the airport, looking at a huge poster of the Eiffel Tower hanging on a concourse wall, I react the same way I did as a student visiting France and seeing the tower my first time. I cry. I don't bother to analyze why. I just let the tears roll as I continue toward the baggage claim area.

I came to the French language by accident. I knew I needed two years of foreign language to get into a good college. My high school offered French, Latin, and Spanish. Spanish classes were full. My uneducated, rabidly Irish parents carried on a fairly convincing campaign for Latin, it being the language of the Church and all—which guaranteed I wouldn't study Latin. That left French. Surprisingly, I was good at it. So I just kept taking it.

When I got to college I chose French as one of my majors because it was easy for me. I didn't know what I'd ever do with it. I didn't want to teach, but the more I studied French culture and history, the more I longed to visit all the places I was reading about.

My parents were amused by what was, to them, an outrageously impossible idea. The fact that I was able to afford college was a minor miracle. The thought of a McKibbin traveling to Europe was beyond their ability to process. My father couldn't understand why, if I was *going*, I didn't at least go to the land of our forefathers and learn some family history. I still haven't been to Ireland, and if I went now I'd just have this big load of guilt for not going while Mom and Dad were still alive.

When my French professor's work visa expired and he left the States, he arranged for a group of graduates to study near his hometown in France. I worked two jobs to get enough money saved to make the trip. And I still had to apply for a loan.

At any rate, we arrived at night, were bused to a dormitory at a school in Versailles, and with jet lag reigning, I fell asleep on the bus into "town" the next morning. I had dozed off when my friend, Leah, jabbed me in the ribs and said, "Look." I opened my eyes to a panorama of the City of Lights, complete with Eiffel Tower. All the late-night jobs were worth it. I was about to walk the streets of Paris, and I couldn't keep the tears back. Professor Max saw the tears and smiled at me.

"It's so. . . ."

"Français, Marie," he reminded me, waggling his finger.

"C'est . . . magnifique . . . si belle."

"Oui. C'est BEAU."

If I thought jet lag was tough when I was twenty-one, jet lag at fifty is excruciating. It takes every ounce of my willpower not to collapse on a seat at the airport and go to sleep. But there is luggage to claim and customs to process through, and thankfully, that goes very well. I am able to say a couple of words to the customs agent, and he actually seems to understand me. He even smiles.

My poring over maps of the city during the flight has resulted in a plan. I will take the B3 train into the heart of the city, transfer to the metro, and come up the stairs only a couple of blocks from the hotel. None of this evokes any memories of the past, because as a student I arrived at Orly and simply followed our professor through the maze of transportation venues.

Unfortunately, the B3 has been vandalized and shut down. A large sign directs passengers upstairs to a bus. I trek upstairs, thankful for every pound of clothing I left in Omaha. No bus comes. No other passengers arrive. I am just beginning to think I've taken a wrong turn when a young woman approaches and asks about the bus. The minute I answer her, she switches to English. British, actually.

"Is this your first visit to Paris?" she wants to know.

I shake my head. "No. But it's the first in decades. I'm sorry my French is so bad."

"But it's not," she insists. "Actually, your pronunciation is very good. I noticed your accent, though. My French is abominable, so I'm grateful you're American." She wears studious-looking rectangular glasses. Her dark brown hair is tied up in a haphazard ponytail. The weight of the overfull bag on her shoulder makes her stand lopsided. I am old enough to be her mother, and when she grunts and drops the bag to the sidewalk, I offer to haul the bag atop my wheeled suitcase.

"That's awfully nice of you," she says. She looks into the

oncoming traffic, wondering, as am I, when the promised bus will arrive. She looks at the sign. "Are you certain we're in the right spot?"

I shrug. "As certain as I can be. Of course that depends on my having actually understood the sign posted downstairs."

"Well," she sighs, "I suppose the schedules are all off now. Where are you headed? Would you want to share a taxi?"

"I have a reservation at the Grand Hotel Saint-Michel," I answer. "And sharing a taxi would be wonderful if it works for you."

"Isn't that near the Sorbonne? I think I've walked by it on my way to my favorite tearoom."

I nod.

"That's perfect." She extends her hand. "Annie Templeton. A student at the Sorbonne, much to my parents' dismay. I've a flat not too far from your hotel."

I introduce myself and try to encourage her. "My parents couldn't quite imagine or understand my coming to France, either, when I was your age. But they came around. I imagine yours will, too." I pause before adding, "I have a daughter about your age. Even she thinks I'm a bit crazy coming to Paris alone."

Annie looks at me, and I swear I can see her brown eyes warm several degrees. "She's never been here, has she."

It is a statement, not a question. I shake my head.

Annie grabs the handle of my rolling suitcase and plops her shoulder bag on it. "Well, you must get her to come. There's magic here, but until they've seen the fairies dancing on the Champs de Mars with the Eiffel Tower in the distance, some people just can't understand it." She pauses and looks at me, and her face takes on the serious expression of a woman much older than she. "But you've seen them, haven't you . . . or at least heard their voices in the church bells?"

I shrug—a little embarrassed because I am hearing Jean-Marc's voice whisper something about voices in the church bells . . . and remembering the night he put his arm around me and talked about the future while we sat side by side on a bench in a certain garden in Paris.

"Exactly as I thought," Annie Templeton's voice interrupts the memory. Abruptly, she changes the subject. "Well, let's find a taxi."

By the time we climb out of the taxi, I am convinced that Annie Templeton is an angel.

TEN

"I'm so sorry, Celine," Jean-Marc repeated in an attempt to fill the deafening silence on the line.

"Of course you are," the young woman finally answered. "You are always sorry, Papa."

"Please don't be angry, *chérie.*" He forced a bantering tone into his voice, "I'll send Mademoiselle Chevalier to *you* for the holiday if you aren't nice to your poor old papa."

"*Poor?! Old?!* Don't be ridiculous." Celine's voice grew almost shrill. "And please stop treating me like an idiot. You don't have to pretend that you are taking Dominique to visit her parents. I warned you about her. If you don't want to listen, it's none of my business. Just don't lie to me."

"I'm not lying!" Jean-Marc protested. "She's not much older than you, Celine. Please. Give me some credit for not being a complete moron. It's not so far out of the way for me to drop Mademoiselle Chevalier on my way to Paris, and I *promised* her."

"Stop it, Papa. I've no time for this. I have to invent a reason to tell my boys why their grandfather is disappointing them— again—even though he *promised* to come for Christmas."

Jean-Marc winced at her emphasis on the word. Celine was right, of course. He was keeping his promise to Dominique Chevalier. And breaking the one he had made to his own grandsons. That was bad.

"Tell them the truth."

"And what is the truth as you see it, Papa?"

"As always, it is the truth that is true. It is what I have told you. I am dropping Dominique Chevalier at her parents' villa and going on to Paris to see to something gravely important."

"It is inevitable and very interesting, don't you think, that the true truth always enables you to do exactly as you wish without thought of how it affects others?"

"Please," Jean-Marc tugged on the gold earring in his left ear. "Try to understand. This is special. Very important."

"Of course it is."

"I'll make it up to you all."

"Yes. I am certain you will try, Papa."

"I mean it."

"You always do." She paused. "You will forgive me if I do not send greetings to Mademoiselle Chevalier."

Hearing the click, Jean-Marc sighed and set the phone down. Taking the letter from his pocket, he began to read the words he had nearly memorized.

Celine

TO TELL ANYONE about Celine Dumas is impossible without telling them first about my father. It has always been that way. Being the only child of an only child skews the data in ways I probably do not even realize as yet. Although I have lived twenty-five years and have borne two sons of my own, I am still very much my father's little girl. It infuriates me that this is so. At times I sincerely wish that sea monsters existed and one would rise up and snatch a certain sailor from the deck of his ship. At other times, I fear so for his safety that I wish the *Sea Cloud* would sink in the bay so Papa would be on land for a while. Such opposing emotions are difficult to manage, but they are part of being the daughter of Jean-Marc David.

Many years ago, there was a singer in a port, and I am the result of a week-long obsession my father had with this woman whom he assures me I am nothing like. This woman, whose name I do not even know, had no interest in raising a child alone, and Papa had no interest in marrying her. Papa tells me that his heart was captured the moment he saw me, and he never considered not taking me into his life. Save for the long dark hair and my desire to have roots deeply inserted into the soil of my homeland, I am a feminine version of Papa "from stem to stern," as he likes to say in his heavily accented English. I even have his striking blue eyes, although some would say that hasn't been a good thing. The combination of Papa's blue eyes and my mother's very black hair is startling. Men seem to find it appealing. That is how I ended up the mother of twins.

My boys, Olivier and Xavier, were born six years ago. At sea. Papa says they will have salt water in their veins like him. I hope he is wrong. A passion for the sea may have gained my father nearly unbelievable adventures and provided material for his storytelling, but it has also kept him from making any firm attachments to either people or places. He is what the Americans he knows call a "free spirit."

As my father ages, I sense his spirit becoming increasingly unhappy. I really think Papa wants an anchor in the form of a home. But he says the boys and I are all the anchor he will ever need. I flatter myself to think that is true, even while I remind my father that he has kept his boyhood home all these years since my grandparents died. Save for his cutting down a few trees so he could see the bay, he's left the house untouched.

My boys adore their grandfather. His penchant for storytelling keeps them entertained. He will, no doubt, have an amazing story to explain this next absence from their lives. I sometimes suspect that Papa manufactures some of his stories. Xavier and Olivier are young and resilient now, so their grandfather's habit of changing his plans at the last minute remains charming to them. Someday the charm will wear off. I dread that day, because it will be a turning point in all our lives. The boys will have to face the same truth that I did and make a decision. The truth they will face is that, while Jean-Marc David has a great capacity for love, he has only one mistress. Her name is *Sea Cloud*, and when she calls, he goes, regardless of promises made or plans confirmed. When the boys realize this, they will either accept the great love on their grandfather's terms or they will build a wall. For many years, I did the latter.

I had just turned eighteen when I tired of what I saw as surrendering to the sea in the battle for my father's time. I was to be recognized by the mayor for my volunteer services at a local hospital. Papa was all set to attend the dinner, but when high winds and a storm came up, he excused himself and headed down to the docks to ensure that Paul had things properly secured. Never mind that Paul is a world-class sailor in his own right. Papa had to be there to see to it for himself. I made the moment into a tragedy, thinking I could force my will on my father. When it didn't work, I withdrew from him, moving out of my cabin aboard his ship—he didn't own the *Sea Cloud* yet—and into a flat the size of a closet.

It was months before I realized I was hurting myself a great deal more than I was hurting my father. I congratulate myself that when I finally comprehended this truth, I repaired the breach. He welcomed me back into his life with open arms and has never once diverted from being himself.

It bothers me to think that in the near future, I will once again be placed in the position of having Papa on his terms—or not at all. Making such a decision when my children are the ones who could be hurt is not at all the same thing as deciding for myself. But the boys are still young. At this point in their lives, they would be hurt much more by the *absence* of their grandfather than by his *disappointing* them at Christmas.

Papa says he has to be in Paris for Christmas. I want to believe him. I don't want to think of him with Dominique Chevalier. The idea gives me chills, more because of her reputation than her age. But Paris? That is more difficult to believe than Jean-Marc David and Dominique Chevalier. He is my father, but I am not blind. He's quite attractive. He has blue eyes to melt a woman's heart and a smile to capture her soul. Papa's first wife— who was not my real mother but was the only mother I knew— said that to me once. She was explaining why she loved him even as she was packing to leave.

In my memory, Papa has mentioned Paris only once. I believe an old friend of his owns a Ducati dealership there, but to my knowledge Papa has never visited the man. I can't even remember his name. Papa has, in fact, obviously avoided Paris a couple of times that I can think of. When he told me about going there on the phone just now, I could hear something in his voice. I thought it was deception, but now I'm not sure.

Either way, it seems that once again the boys and I will have to change our plans and look forward to seeing Jean-Marc David at a future day of his choosing.

While Papa is in Paris, I think I'll take the boys to Father's house in Arcachon. They love it there; they'll be able to play on the *Sea Cloud* while she's docked. Perhaps we'll even camp on board her on Christmas night. Papa won't mind. And we can surprise him when he gets back home.

ELEVEN

Mary

MY HOTEL ROOM WINDOW OPENS, not to the noisy street but to an invisible and very quiet inner courtyard in the center of the block. I didn't even try to venture out yesterday. What was perhaps a combination of nerves and jet lag and home-sickness and maybe a virus kept me in my room. I don't really know, but it doesn't matter. This morning feels different. I have done it. I am here, Jean-Marc. Are you coming?

I get up and cross the room to draw back the curtains and open the window, leaning on the windowsill and peering up at the small triangle of bright blue sky above. I close my eyes and concentrate on the sensation of warmth as the sun bathes my face. At the sound of childish laughter, I open my eyes and notice for the first time that the windows set into the wall opposite mine reveal a room lined with several long tables surrounded by chairs occupied by children. One of the girls seems to be day-dreaming, staring out the window. She sees me and smiles. I wave. She opens a book to hide her hand and waves back.

The hotel is charming, although I grimace using the word, which is surely done to death when it comes to describing the small hotels that pepper the narrow streets of central Paris. It is, however, the correct word for Au Grand Hotel Saint Michel, where the narrow entry hall leads to a small lounge on the right with a ceiling boasting gold filigree and scenic paintings à la Versailles; a small lounge on the left, where the day's edition of *Le Figaro* has been left on a couch near the window; and the check-in desk tucked into an alcove beneath the blue-carpeted winding stairs that ascend to four floors and forty-six rooms and suites. To the left of the stairway, there is an elevator about the size of a dumbwaiter. I'll be using the stairs.

This morning, a distinguished Nigerian gentleman—I know he is Nigerian because I muster my courage and ask him—sporting a white coat is polishing the brass handrail, and as I descend he greets me in French. When I answer in French, he wishes me a good day. I am thrilled because he understands me and continues to converse in French instead of switching immediately to English as Annie Templeton did at the airport bus stop.

As I step outside, I am greeted by laughter again. Up the street where students register for classes at the Sorbonne, a herd of young people are waiting to enter a nondescript door set into the stone wall of the grand old university. I smile at the thought of *old*, which means something entirely different in Paris than it does in Omaha. I remember my Professor Max reminding us that in the 1400s the French were building Notre Dame Cathedral and the Americans were . . . "Well," he said, his gray eyes smiling benignly, *"l'Amérique, ça n'existait pas au quinzième siècle."* America didn't exist in the fifteenth century. It was a lesson in cultural humility most of us needed. It was also the beginning of a shift in my view of the universe.

I turn the other way and head down the hill, turning left at the corner where I am happy to see an ATM and, just up the street, a café. The air is crisp, but not cold, and the sky is overcast, but I am determined to enjoy *le petit dejeuner* al fresco. I am relieved when I insert my bank card into the ATM and successfully retrieve euros.

Proceeding up the street, I slide into a café chair next to the sidewalk, my heart pounding as the waiter approaches. For the next few days, every new situation will undoubtedly cause a similar attack of nerves. My French is so rusty. But I want to use it. Apparently it isn't as awful as I thought, for when I request a café au lait and a croissant with butter, the waiter responds with a *"Tout de suite, madame,"* and retreats to the interior, presumably to get what I've ordered.

Across the street, an elderly woman across the street pauses to stare at an announcement tacked to the kiosk on the corner. A dowager's hump makes it impossible for her to stand upright, and she leans heavily on a cane while she reads. Her hair is hidden beneath a black scarf knotted under her chin. I think of how the world has changed since she was a child. She is probably old enough to have seen Germans and then Americans march down the Champs-Elysées. I wonder what terrors or joys filled her childish heart when her city was occupied by foreign soldiers. Thinking about that puts my own fears about Christmas Eve in perspective.

My waiter brings my coffee and halts his retreat to the café kitchen long enough to appreciate the same blonde who has caught my eye. Her purposeful stride reminds me of Elizabeth—although Elizabeth wears sensible pumps, not the designer stilettos that grace this young woman's feet. She pauses to cross the street, and I smile to myself, remembering that I once had a small waist like that, and like this *jeune fille,* I wore belted coats to show it off. I never, however, painted my lips in quite that bold a shade of pink.

The old woman drops something, and when the young lady turns to pick it up, I see the left side of her face, which is bruised just at the spot where her penciled eyebrow ends. A small cut follows the ridge of her cheekbone, too. She flashes a smile at the elderly woman, who has said something and patted her arm.

My café au lait is hot and rich, and as I lift the cup to drink it, I inhale, enjoying the aroma and closing my eyes to listen to Paris. I sit back with my eyes still closed, and for just a moment I am a young redhead waiting to be joined by the man who has stolen her heart and has asked her to wait for him at the café. They will drink their coffee and then get up and walk across the street through the iron gates set into the high fence that borders the Luxembourg Gardens. They will linger until dusk . . . then dark. . . . and their lives will be changed forever. A bus creaks to a stop. As I listen, one, then two motorcycles buzz by and horns blare. There is a screech, and I open my eyes, my heart pounding on behalf of the motorcycle riders, but the close call is only that. The motorcycles are nowhere in sight, the bus door closes, and my waiter brings me a warm croissant.

"*Merci.*" I slather the croissant first with enough butter to pack five of the pounds I've worked so hard to lose right back on my thighs. I had forgotten that you don't really see many overweight people in Paris. I have forgotten so many things. And yet, sitting here with my sidewalk view drinking café au lait, I am beginning to believe that perhaps the past can be recaptured.

No one here has an inkling of who I am, and no one cares. I am simply one of a number of people taking their morning coffee and getting on with their day. And even if there is a copy of *Le Figaro* at my table, I'm not fooling a single person. They all know I'm American. I shout it with my clothing and whisper it in subtler ways I can't explain because I don't know what they are—but they are quite evident to the French. When I was a young woman I did my best not to let the differences be intentional or obnoxious. I know I can't fit in. The thought amuses me. I've come halfway around the world to escape the life where I didn't fit in, and here I am, in another place where I don't fit in. As the French say, *c'est la misère, ça*.

It *is* a misery, too. But in my humble opinion if one is going to be miserable, one might as well be in Paris.

I HAVE BEEN in Paris for three days now. The first day, I slept. The second, I wandered past the Sorbonne and toward the Pantheon, then back down the hill and, finally, into the Cluny Museum. I had coffee three times at three different cafés. But I don't think the impact of what I have done struck me until I made the few-block trek down the Boulevard St. Michel and there, on my right, was Notre Dame Cathedral. It was an unusually warm evening, and some young men had set up a half dozen bright orange traffic cones in the street that runs parallel to the cathedral entrance. They were in-line skating, performing an intricate dance around the cones while a few pedestrians watched from the sidewalk. They bantered with the onlookers. One even flirted a little with me, and for a moment I was young again.

I went inside the cathedral, and something happened. I wonder now how many thousands—could it be millions—of souls have been uplifted as their owners stood at the back, breathless at the magnificence of soaring stone columns, sweeping arch-ways, and stained glass. The colors of the glass weren't transcendent in the evening light, but I'll go back to see that on a sunny day. This night, I slumped into a hard wooden chair and allowed myself to feel the wonder. I have read explanations of how the cathedral was built. Knowing about blocks and tackle and stonemasons did nothing to diminish my amazement.

But there was something else there for me that night. Muffled voices and shuffling feet couldn't hide it—a presence I could almost feel, it was so real. For the first time in many years I consciously registered the thought that I was literally in the presence of God. I suppose I should have felt that way before. Sam and I went to church nearly every Sunday. We even joked about being among the "frozen chosen." I've always believed there is a God. But I've never had much to do with him. I know a lot of people contemplate God when they face death. If Sam Davis did, he didn't share that with me. For myself, at first I was too busy taking care of him, and later I was too numb. But sitting alone in Notre Dame Cathedral, my eyes filled with tears as I was overcome by a longing I can't quite describe. I don't think it had anything to do with my estrangement from Elizabeth or my loneliness. I *am* nervous about Christmas Eve, and I wonder if Jean-Marc will show up, but I'm convinced the experience at Notre Dame wasn't about that. It was something else. Palpable, heavy, new.

Just in front of me, there was a small altar roped off to all but the faithful. While I was sitting nearby, a woman opened the little gate and went in. She was weeping as she lit a candle, then knelt and folded her hands to pray. It was a brief prayer. She didn't take long, but when she left, she was no longer crying and her face was peaceful. I was so tempted to follow her outside the church and ask her what happened at the altar that I stood up and moved toward the exit. But before I could find my way through the crowd, I talked myself out of being so impulsive.

The organ began to play. I sat back down, closed my eyes, and enveloped by holy sound, let my own tears come. I thought about Elizabeth and how she used to call me Mimi. I relived the first time I met Samuel Davis, so handsome and full of life. I wept for my dead husband and the love we could have shared. I wept for my daughter and the friendship I wish we had. Looking down at my hands, I wept at the prospect of growing old alone.

After I left the church I walked along the river toward the Louvre. It was nearly dark, but the lights of the Samaritaine were on and I went in, up the wonderful art deco staircase, to the book department. I bought a black leather notebook and narrow-lined paper. I had come to Paris to find something. Perhaps, I thought, if I would journal my thoughts and impressions, I would be able to clarify my search. If it didn't help, I could always throw the book into the Seine and run home to Omaha. *Home.* Contemplating the word, I accepted reality. Omaha, Nebraska, was no more home to me than Paris, France.

I clutched the handles of my shopping bag and wandered back up toward the Sorbonne, this time on the opposite side of the street. It began to drizzle, a fine rain, not too cold, not really all that annoying. From a street vendor I purchased a black umbrella and scarf, planning to revisit the Samaritaine for a coat and better walking shoes the next day. I could hide the fact that the blood in my veins is not French beneath a made-in-France-and-newly-purchased exterior.

Back in my hotel room, I changed clothes, wishing for an oversized men's shirt instead of the nightgown I had packed. Opening the small bottle of Perrier from my refrigerator, I settled on the couch with my notebook open in my lap. Finally, I wrote what I had learned about myself that day.

It doesn't matter whether I am in Omaha or Paris. I am not at home in my life.

TWELVE

"THIS IS RIDICULOUS," LIZ SAID. "There must be *something* you can do!" She clenched her copy of the passport application in her hand.

"Did you request expedited service?" the postal employee asked.

"You took the application and know very well I didn't," Liz snapped. "But that was when I didn't *need* the thing until my honeymoon in the spring."

"The only thing I can suggest," the man said, "is that you call on your congressional representative. Maybe he can do something. We can't. We're just a clearingh—"

Liz didn't hear the end of his sentence. She'd already spun around and headed for the elevator. Once on the street, she snatched a parking ticket from beneath her wiper blades and swore softly. Her heart lurched as she caught a glimpse of a gray silk suit entering the building across the street. She took a step in that direction, then stopped herself. *There is more than one gray silk suit in Omaha. And even if it was Jeff, you have to give him space. He'll miss you soon enough and call.*

Fighting back tears of frustration, Liz jerked the car door open and settled inside. She revved the engine, pulled into traffic, and headed for the office, where upon arrival she gave Peggy instructions. "Call Congressman Terry's office, and put me on the line when you have someone who can do something about this mess."

She fired up her laptop and searched in vain for an e-mail from *Mimi*. It had been over a week. Irene hadn't heard from her, either. And Jeffrey James Scott seemed entirely capable of living without her.

Jeff

TO SAY THIS has been the longest week of my life is putting it mildly. Today I actually took a detour through the perfume department at Von Maur and asked the clerk to show me a sample of Obsession—Liz's favorite scent. I'm one love-sick puppy.

The Von Maur detour happened after I saw Liz downtown. I saw her car first, parked—as usual—in the No Parking zone right in front of the building. Liz considers her time well worth the cost of the parking fines. And then there she was, coming out of the post office dressed in her electric pink suit. That's the suit she wears when she needs to feel especially self-confident. She calls it her "power suit."

It took every ounce of my willpower to keep myself from hollering her name, running across the street, and asking her to lunch. That would have ended badly, though. By badly, I mean I likely would have swept her into my arms and taken her back, no questions asked. I call that a bad ending because it is not in

Elizabeth Davis's best interest for the people who love her to let her get away with the kind of thing she almost did to George Kincaid . . . and the kind of thing she did to her own mother. I've come to realize that love has nothing to do with "never having to say you're sorry." Love is an action that does what's best for the other person.

The logical side of Jeffrey James Scott has finally risen above the raging undercurrent of passion long enough to take a good look at Elizabeth Samantha Davis, and I'm not sure I like what I see. There are things about the woman that make me so mad I think I just might regret marrying her.

It has always been a source of pride for Liz to be seen as her father's daughter. There's nothing wrong with that, of course. But I'm really hoping that somewhere inside her there's some of her mother, too. I suppose Liz sees it as a weakness, but that night while Liz was ripping into her, Mary didn't bite back. It amazed me. She had such self-control. I don't even know the details of the stuff Liz was yelling about, but Mary let her go on and on. And then *she* apologized for Liz feeling so badly. I've got to say Mary Davis was never more attractive or more loving than at that moment. I know some of it comes from maturity, but I really long to see that kind of grace in Lizzie. I think it's in there, but she won't let it out because she wants so badly to be just like her father.

Mary

December 15, 2003
    Mamalina—the best pizza I've ever eaten, and a charming, albeit toothless, waiter.

La Lutèce - Great steak-frites. Excellent people watching.

Montmartre - I have a new passion for toiles. I even made the storekeeper laugh as I pointed out bolt after bolt. "Un métre, deux métres, un métre. . . ." He happily cut the required lengths and even gave me a remnant because I was such a good customer. Montmartre is supposed to be about the church at the top of the hill. For me, it's about toile.

Le Rouvray - I stumbled on a quilt shop across from Notre Dame today. There were vintage American quilts in the window. I bought a length of gold Provençal fabric and ended up using it for a picnic cloth at the foot of the Eiffel Tower. I'm reading Jean Giono and understanding him a little better than when he was required reading in college. Stayed on the Champ de Mars reading until sunset. When the Tower lights came on, I wished for someone to share it with. Oddly, I thought of Lizzie's Jeffrey. I'll have to send them here someday.

I have stayed away from Little Athens and the garden. What awaits me in those places, I can only wonder. After the 24th, perhaps I will go alone. Please, God . . . not alone.

I have gone back to Notre Dame several times. I have begun to talk to God from my chair, which is in the fifth row on the left.

"Voilà, madame." The waiter I have come to know as Charles brings another espresso.

Looking up from my journal, I smile. *"Merci bien, Charles. Vous êtes très gentil."*

Charles bobs his head and winks at me. I have returned to this little café across from the gated entrance to the Luxembourg Gardens every morning since my arrival. By the fifth morning, the waiter anticipated my order. It is not a friendship, of course, but it is nice to be treated as a "regular."

I am pleased that even after so many years, the language seems to be returning. More than once I have been complimented for my accent, which the Parisians seem to think is not so bad. Everyone I have conversed with has been kind and helpful. Nine days remain. I have not been back to the Internet café. Perhaps it's cowardly of me, but I don't want to be hurt anymore. I don't feel up to it emotionally, especially if the 24th turns out badly. What, I wonder, will constitute a bad outcome? Will it be bad if he comes . . . or worse if he doesn't? I can't decide.

I believe I have walked at least five miles each of the days I have been here. Tomorrow I go to the Louvre. I picked up the free guide yesterday when I bought my ticket, but I have decided to wander instead of taking the typical tourist path from the Winged Victory to the Venus de Milo to the Mona Lisa. How many jewels are missed, I wonder, by tourists plotting their way mindlessly past the endless other masterpieces contained in this grand old building— which is a masterpiece in itself. When I was here all those years ago, the Pyramid didn't exist. I've seen photographs and thought it seemed completely out of place. I wonder if my opinion will change once I've been there?

A CLASSIC Citroen zoomed off the A10 from the south, onto the Périphérique and into the heart of the city. It was midnight, but Jean-Marc had set his course for a certain hotel in the fifth arrondissement, and he had planned to arrive in the middle of the night. Although there once had been a time when he would have assaulted the traffic in Paris with the relish of a race driver, those days were long past. But this way, if things didn't go well on Christmas Eve, he would be able to escape on his own terms. Never again did he want to be trapped at a soirée with no transportation but his own feet. Driving along the Seine, he remembered. . . .

"Ladies and gentlemen," an American voice said over the microphone, "I have an announcement to make."

The music stopped. Everyone looked at the distinguished American businessman holding the microphone. "Ladies and gentlemen, I wish to share with you the wonderful news of my engagement." There were smiles . . . heads nodding . . . signs of approval all around.

Jean-Marc had heard the announcement from where he was standing at the back of the room, having arrived late and being reluctant to make a scene while he looked for her. She shouldn't be hard to find though. Any minute now, her red hair—

It couldn't be true. She was getting up. Going to the stage. Standing beside the American. Looking up at him, smiling, accepting the applause.

He felt sick. Angry. He would tear the microphone out of that fool's hand—but then the girl looked up at the American and kissed him. True, it was only on the cheek. But she was *agreeing* with him. She was *smiling*.

Even now, decades later, he could remember his first thought. *So this is what it feels like to have your heart break, as the Americans say.*

Later, he would second-guess himself and wonder how it was he hadn't known. Later, he would write letters and tear them up. He would call and hang up at the sound of her voice. He would grow angry and bitter. But that night, he moved to catch her attention. Their eyes met. He saw regret. He thought he saw love. But he also saw fear. She was afraid to say "yes" to him, so she had said "yes" to the American, instead. She would go back to America, and there was nothing left for him to do but stumble out into the night and walk away.

A blaring horn brought Jean-Marc David back to the present day. He slammed on his brakes and screeched to a halt, scarcely an inch from the rear bumper of the car in front of him. Sweat stood out across his forehead. The light changed. Up ahead, he caught a glimpse of a sign. He jerked into the turning lane and slowed immediately, rolling quietly past a shop called Le Rouvray and then down a narrow side street. It was there, as his directions had indicated—the entrance to a private underground parking garage. With a sigh of relief, he parked the Citroen.

Nine days, he thought. *What are you going to do for nine days? You despise Paris, but here you are. You're like an impatient schoolboy. Old fool.*

THIRTEEN

Mary

December 16, 2003

　　I was in Le Printemps yesterday morning after my breakfast at the cafe, and it appears the French have caught a bit of the American obsession with the merchandising of Christmas. I remember Professor Max waxing quite philosophical about the differences in the holiday rituals between his adopted and native countries. He would be surprised if he could see the displays at Le Printemps. But then, maybe people don't actually buy all this stuff. I haven't been inside any Parisian homes, so I don't know.

　　Sam always treated holidays as an inconvenience—an interruption of his otherwise predictable life. I tried to make holidays special, but Sam's cooperation was given only under duress. By the time she was a teenager, Lizzie managed to spend most of her holidays somewhere else. She was usually stuck at home for Christmas Day, but once she went off to college, she didn't even come home for Christmas.

　　The worst disagreement Sam and I ever had was over Christmas. I wanted to take Lizzie, who was, at the time, three years old, to have her photograph taken with Santa Claus.

　　"Don't be ridiculous," Sam said. "The crowds are abominable. You'll wait in line forever, and after all that, the fat old bearded

man in red will scare her silly. Why go through all that just for a stupid custom?"

Somehow I convinced myself it would be all right as long as Sam didn't have to go and fight the crowds himself. So I took Lizzie. She looked adorable, and it didn't frighten her a bit. She stared up at Santa with a sort of amazed glow about her. She tugged his beard, and when it pulled away from his chin a little, she laughed. When Sam saw the photograph, he came striding into our bedroom where I was sitting at the desk addressing Christmas cards, and demanded an explanation.

"Exactly why," he said, "did you decide to ignore what I said and go ahead with this nonsense?"

"She . . . we . . . we had a good time," I said, but my heart was pounding, and I didn't sound very convincing.

He tore up the photograph and tossed the pieces into my wastebasket. "I won't have my daughter believing in fairy tales and then finding out years later that we lied to her."

Now that I think back to that moment, it seems laughable. The man who didn't want his daughter lied to expected his wife to live a lie.

Anyway, after that I dreaded Christmas. Ironically, Davis Enterprises always had one of the best Christmas parties in Omaha. The employees' children were invited, and Santa visited and showered them with gifts. Sam spent thousands of dollars on Christmas for his employees. But Lizzie wasn't invited to participate, and the atmosphere at home was bleak compared to that of her friends. We went to church on Christmas Eve. I think that as a child Lizzie probably thought of the Baby Jesus as a kind of fairy tale. Since coming to Paris and seeing the gorgeous crèche scenes set up in all the churches, I've found myself wondering what Lizzie thinks of Jesus now.

I've spent some of these days before Christmas visiting churches. I began with St. Eustache, which is lighted up at night and visible *from the top of the Samaritaine, where there's an observatory offering a delightful view of Paris by night. After St. Eustache, I went to Saint-Germain-des-Près, and then to St. Sulpice. Last Sunday morning I meant to go to a Russian Orthodox cathedral out in the Champs-Elysées, but I took a wrong turn when I got off the metro and ended up in a small Protestant service.*

The pastor there seemed to take the Bible more seriously than anyone I've ever met before. His prayers were nothing like the ones I've encountered in my past. In our church in Omaha we did congregational prayer, which means we read beautiful and very meaningful words written by someone else. I always enjoyed the experience, but I never thought much about the prayers themselves beyond appreciation for them as literature. But this congregation didn't do things en masse. The pastor spent about forty-five minutes explaining the import of the virgin birth, which gave me a lot to think about. When he prayed, it was like he was talking to someone standing at the back of the room. Someone he knew well.

The church itself was plain, and I must admit I didn't feel the presence of God like I do in the cathedrals. Of course, all the stained glass in the cathedrals was meant to instruct the illiterate about the great truths of the faith. In the little Protestant church they all bring their own Bibles, so there's no need for the "living color" version of the Bible stories. Still, I like the cathedral better for the sheer emotional impact. Looking up at the soaring arches and the vast space makes me feel certain there is a God . . . and certain He is much greater than I.

I remember reminding Jean-Marc in my letter of his denial of God's existence. Oddly enough, Jean-Marc was the one person in my past who challenged me to think about spirituality. He had a very thorough and mature belief system worked out. It didn't allow for a personal God, but it made sense to him. How I have arrived at a half a century of life without sorting these things out makes me feel incomplete—like there's an entire part of my humanity that's never been explored.

BEING ALONE here has turned out to be a positive thing. It is threatening to rain today, and I am on the 24 bus headed for the Louvre. I am happy to be alone as I contemplate the day. I have my journal and the map of the museum. I read just last night that if a person were to spend just 30 seconds before each work of art on display in the Louvre, they would spend 5 years inside that one museum. It will be good to enjoy the day without worrying about someone else's needs or desires. This is a new experience for me, and it only took my first few days in Paris to realize that I am coming to terms with just being me. It seems that I can be alone without being lonely, and I think that is quite an accomplishment.

Getting off the bus I approach the Pyramid. It is midweek and the line is not long, but people are still standing out in the rain. I open my umbrella and join them. Once beneath the glass of the Pyramid, we make our way slowly down a winding stairway and into the lobby of the great museum that was once a palace. I decide this new approach is inferior to the one I remember from long ago. Back then, we saw the Winged Victory almost immediately. I remember lifting my head as I walked up the vast staircase, never taking my eyes off the wings, wishing she had arms, wondering what line the original sculptor had given those arms, wondering what his life was like, wishing I could go back in time and watch him create this masterpiece.

It takes a while to find her today, in the new and improved Louvre. She is still magnificent. As is Venus de Milo. Today, I smile as I realize that the famous beauty is *fat* in this generation of nearly anorexic beauty standards. I look down at the floor and think what a lovely patchwork quilt pattern is contained in the marble. I look up at the ceiling and am awed by the artwork rarely studied because the thousands who come this way are glancing at Venus, checking off a list, and moving on. I wonder what the guards would do if I were to lie flat on my back so I could contemplate the ceiling for a while. I decide not to find out.

By midmorning I realize that much of the Bible is displayed on the canvasses and in the stone carvings I am viewing. Faith inspires great art, for Christian and Jews, Romans and Greeks alike. I am once again unsettled at the realization that I have no real faith of my own. In yet another facet of life, I am an observer, not a participant.

By late afternoon, I am still looking at art, but I am no longer seeing. I walk the halls, glancing briefly at the contents of a display case, noticing a piece of furniture or a painting, but no longer entering into the experience. Passing a large expanse of windows, I see that the sun has come out and is bathing the courtyard below in golden light. They are remodeling this particular courtyard. Its sweeping stairs are closed off, but as I look down I imagine an eighteenth-century carriage pulling up to those stairs. I wonder about the elegantly clad woman who descends. In my imagination her gown is sky-blue satin, trimmed in lace. Jewels adorn her neck and fingers . . . and once again, I wish I could cross the time barrier and observe another time and place. But if I could, I'd be the servant girl emptying a chamber pot. And it wouldn't be all that glamorous.

It's time to go. My stomach is rumbling, protesting the forgotten lunch hour. Back to the foyer, up the elevator to the entrance, and out into the now sunny courtyard. Just ahead is the archway Napoleon built. I realize I've neglected to go to the apartments occupied by Napoleon III. Tomorrow. I'll come back tomorrow. But now, it's to the bus stop, onto the 24, and back to the hotel.

Alighting from the bus, I am across the street from the open courtyard known as La Place de la Sorbonne. There are tea shops and cafés and bookstores flanking the well-shaded spot. It sports two fountains and a monument in memory of Auguste Comte. On this unseasonably warm late afternoon, a string ensemble is playing. I assume they are students, but the music is . . . astonishing. The obvious leader of this group is a tall young man with skin the color of café au lait and shoulder-length dreadlocks. He cradles his violin gently. The sound is sweet. A few plaintive notes draw bystanders into his world, and he begins. The artistry and energy being displayed before me are like nothing I've ever seen before. I wonder why this young man and his friends aren't playing with a symphony orchestra. Perhaps they are, and this is just something they do for fun and the occasional coin I see being tossed into an open cello case leaning against a tree.

I study the faces of the musicians. They close their eyes, listening to their own music, absorbed in the community created by the composer's dream put on paper. They glance at one another from time to time, sending fleeting, unspoken messages between them on unseen telegraph lines. This cannot be an impromptu grouping of students. The young man playing the violin steps out of the circle and begins a solo. His bow transforms notes into breathing things, and I am caught up in the moment, upset with the passersby who don't stop, wondering how anyone could resist being wrapped inside this music.

My eyes go from face to face, seeing the same involvement with the music on each face . . . and then I see Annie Templeton. Her hair is pulled back into a severe knot at the nape of her neck. She plays her cello with her eyes closed, her head tilted in a way that accents the line of her jaw. She wears chandelier earrings that hang almost to her shoulders and sway in rhythm to the music as she draws her bow across the strings of her instrument. She hasn't seen me, or if she has, she doesn't recognize me. I am content to perch on the edge of a planter and watch her elegant arms and gifted fingers bring beauty out of what was once a silent piece of wood.

I decide that in my next life, I want to play the cello.

FOURTEEN

"THIS WAY!" ANNIE SHOUTS TO me as she grabs her cello case, snaps it shut, and skitters across the plaza until she's under a faded green awning extending over the outdoor dining area of a tearoom. She recognized me during one of the pauses in the music, nodding and smiling with a warmth that made me newly aware of how alone I am in this huge city. It is good to be recognized in a crowd. Thunderclouds had been threatening for a while, but the musicians continued to play until great drops of rain began to plop at their feet. Instantly the tenuous unity of the music became an "every man for himself" dash for shelter as the heavens opened.

I follow Annie to the tearoom. We duck inside where she props her cello case in a corner, greets a girl behind the counter by name, and orders us both a cup of tea.

"Here," I say, "let me—" And I wrestle my change purse out of the bag that's become nearly a part of my anatomy since I arrived in Paris.

"But I invited you," Annie says. She requests two slices of lemon cake, picks up the tray, and heads for the table next to her cello case. Once seated, she reaches behind her neck, removes hairpins, and shakes her hair out. This motion attracts the attention of a young man who has just come into the tearoom. I look past Annie to watch him watch her, and I recognize him as the young man who seemed to be the leader of the group.

"Adolpho!" Annie calls to him. "Here we are. . . ."

Annie Templeton is in love. It is evident in the way she says his name, the delight with which she leans forward to accept a kiss on each cheek, the way she loops her arm through his, and the pride with which she introduces Adolpho to me.

I cannot tell immediately if Adolpho is in love. He is distracted, upset that his concert was interrupted. He is speaking in such rapid French I have trouble following, but I catch something about a boy named Enzo—Adolpho is upset with him— and a reference to the name Ducati, which I initially think is an odd name for a person but eventually realize is Adolpho's scooter, which apparently Enzo has borrowed. Or perhaps stolen. I can't tell which.

The fact that Adolpho *is* in love becomes apparent as I watch Annie soothe his worries over the location of his Ducati, jump up and get him a cup of tea, and convince him to sit with us. With the first gulp of tea, I see Adolpho's mood transform as he stares across the table at Annie. He gives a shrug, emits a sound that can only be interpreted as resignation, and says to me, "I apologize for the outburst. I saved a long time to buy wheels. I tend to overreact when something threatens my Ducati." He smiles warmly and reaches across the table to take Annie's hand. "You should see me when something threatens Annie." He laughs and reaches up to cup the back of her head in his open palm before jerking playfully on one dark curl. Then, leaning back, he takes a sip of tea, savoring it as if it were liquid gold.

I experience a part of Paris I never dreamed I would. As the rain outside continues, we are joined by more members of the group of musicians. They chatter and laugh and, amazingly, include me in their conversation. There is a Jamaican, two Africans, an Asian, and, surprisingly, an American among them. They have been together for a while, it seems, for they have nicknames for one another and they joke about their nationality and their class standing like family members at a reunion. I can't follow it all, but I am surprised at how well I do keep up.

We've been in the tearoom for nearly an hour when the rain lets up. The door opens to admit another customer who brings with him the fragrance of freshly washed concrete and cigar smoke.

"Enzo!" Adolpho calls out.

On seeing Adolpho, Enzo stops at the door. A furrow appears between his thick black eyebrows. He purses his lips and thrusts his hands in the pockets of his pants. I notice that one leg of his pants is filthy. Ripped at the knee.

Adolpho sees it about the same time I do and lets out a string of words I am glad I don't know.

Enzo steps backward. It is instantly silent in the tearoom.

"Oh, no," Annie mutters, and bows her head.

Adolpho pushes Enzo in the chest and drives him through the doorway and outside where, although the cloudburst is past, the sidewalk still shines with moisture. The tearoom patrons follow.

"I'd better get out there," Annie says. She looks apologetic.

"I'll keep an eye on your cello," I offer.

"Oh, it's all right where it is. It practically lives here," Annie says. "You can come—although I don't know if you'll want to."

I follow her outside. The musicians are gathered at the curb.

I can see Adolpho's dreadlocks above their heads and from their movement I know the boy is angry. He is gesturing madly. Annie pushes through the crowd and I follow, coming to the edge of the curb just in time to see Adolpho crouch down next to what was once a beautiful motorcycle. He runs his hand along the side—I will later learn it is called a *fairing*—caressing the cracked and scraped red plastic.

When Adolpho stands back up, his face is a mask of rage. Annie steps to his side. She lays her hand on his arm. "Thank God, Enzo wasn't hurt," she says to the angry young man towering over her. "He could have been killed," she says. "And *then* what would we do for a bass player?!"

Someone in the group chuckles.

Another musician calls out, "Probably *better*. Did you hear that B-flat in the third movement yesterday?"

Enzo adopts an indignant expression. "What?" he says, "You don't care that I nearly died? You should have seen this old man. . . . One minute I was right beside him, the next . . . *bif*! He turns with no warning!" Enzo is gathering steam. He tells the almost-accident with a flourish, and by the time he is finished, Adolpho, while not smiling, does seem less likely to finish the job of killing Enzo the bass-playing Ducati-lover.

"My uncle will fix it," Enzo offers. "You'll see. You'll never be able to tell it happened." Finally, he apologizes. "I'm sorry, Adolpho. Really I am."

The dreadlocked giant with Annie on his arm takes in a deep breath. Annie stands on tiptoe and whispers in his ear. He looks at me. "Annie says I should offer to take you for a ride, Mrs. Davis."

"Me?" I look at the red motorcycle. "There's no way."

"Of course there is," Annie says. She goes to the bike and

removes a red plastic cover from the tailpiece. A very small black cushion is provided to enable a passenger to perch behind the driver. She flips down a silver bar on each side. "For your feet," she says.

"I'm not crazy like Enzo," Adolpho claims. "We'll take it slow. You'll be safe." He explains, "It was very slick in the rain, but the streets are drying out."

"I . . . uh . . . I don't think so."

"Why not?" Adolpho insists. The rest of the students take up the cause. He's a good driver, they insist.

"How many of your American friends ride around Paris on a Ducati?" one says. "Come on. They've all seen Mona Lisa, but I bet they haven't done this!"

"I'll hold your bag," Annie offers. "And you can wear my helmet." She smiles at her giant. "He really is a very good driver."

The traffic does seem to have mellowed a bit. And the streets are quickly drying out. I look down the Boulevard Saint-Michel. I think of Elizabeth. I remember Jeffrey raising his glass to me. *"You go, girl."*

"No Périphérique," I say.

Adolpho looks at me with surprise.

"I read," I say, grinning. "And I've heard stories about that road. You practically deserve a medal for surviving it."

"It's not so bad this time of day," Adolpho says. He winks. "But all right. No Périphérique."

Annie hands me her helmet. She helps me put it on. It only takes two tries before I successfully scale the side of the motor-cycle and perch behind Adolpho.

"You have ridden before?" he asks.

"Never," I say.

"First rule," he says, and reaches for my hands. He pulls me forward until my arms are wrapped around him and I can lock my hands together. "Hang on."

"Second rule," he says. "Stay still. Move with me. Never against. Stay close."

"I understand," I say, keenly aware of my chest pressing into his back.

"Third rule," Annie interrupts. I look at her, and she smiles. "Have fun!"

As we pull away from the curb, the musicians cheer. I lose the sound of their voices in the purr of the Ducati's motor. I hope I live long enough to see the look on Elizabeth's face when I tell her I rode a Ducati around the Arc de Triomphe.

Aldolpho takes me around the Latin Quarter—which is the center of the city—slowly, deliberately. After the first couple of corners I feel like I have the "hang on" thing down pretty well. As the sky darkens and the City of Lights lives up to its moniker, we are zooming beneath the bridges that span the Seine. Adolpho has given me a wordless code to use to communicate with him. One squeeze means slow down, two squeezes means I'm okay. Tapping his shoulder means stop *now*. If he reaches back and taps my knee, he is asking for a report. I never tap his shoulder. He taps my knee a few times, but I always squeeze twice. And then, we are on the Périphérique, weaving in and out of traffic. And I have never felt more alive.

"You, madame," Adolpho says, bowing low and kissing my hand, "are a very good sport."

I laugh and shake my head.

"Did he scare you?" Annie asks, frowning. She has been sitting under the awning just outside the tearoom and apparently decided to use the waiting time well, as she has retrieved her cello and begun to play. I notice several euros scattered in the empty case at her side.

"I can't believe I'm saying this, but I loved it."

"And," Adolpho interjects, pretending to rubber stamp the back of my hand, "you are now Périphérique certified."

"You didn't!" Annie scolds.

"I did," Adolpho nods. He points at me. "But only because madame wanted to." He smiles. "You should come with us to the showroom tomorrow. I think maybe you need your own Ducati."

I shake my head. "I wouldn't know how to ride it."

"I could teach you," the boy says.

Annie leans forward. "He likes you. He's never offered to teach *me*."

"It would be pointless," Adolpho says. "You can't fit a cello on a Ducati."

Annie shrugs. "Point well taken." She collects the money from her cello case and puts the instrument to bed. "I have to get home," she says, and turns to me, "but if you'll trust us with your hotel name, we'll come for you tomorrow, and you can go with us to see about the bike. Unless you have other plans?"

I hesitate, only because I don't see how three of us can go anywhere on one Ducati.

Adolpho answers my unspoken question. "Enzo has his own bike. And he's paying for this." He points to the scrapes on his motorcycle. "So you could ride behind him. Although," he says, scratching his day-old beard, "I don't suppose you'll trust him."

"I could meet you there," I say impulsively. "I'll just take a taxi or the bus. Where is it?"

Adolpho provides directions.

"We'll buy you lunch," Annie says.

"Oh, no," I protest. "I'll buy the lunch. It's the least I can do for your being willing to put up with an old lady."

Adolpho shakes his head. He points to his temple. "Old is in here, madame. And any woman who climbs onto a Ducati behind a man with these"—he tugs on his dreadlocks—"is not old. She is . . . How do you Americans say it? She is *cold*."

Adolpho takes up Annie's cello case, and the two of them head up the hill toward the Sorbonne. I watch them go.

I am woman. I am cold.

FIFTEEN

WHY HASN'T HE CALLED? *How can he love me enough to want to marry me and yet just step back and not even call?* Liz swiped a tear off her cheek and put her hand on the cell phone on her bedside table. The room was dark, as was the sky outside. She had filled the two days since seeing Jeff downtown with activity, and yet she was no closer to getting her passport than she had been two days ago . . . and no less lonely.

He sees me as self-sufficient. Strong. Maybe he doesn't know how much I miss him. She picked up the cell phone and hit the first number on her autodial.

"Hello. It's Jeff's machine. You know what to do."

If I knew what to do I wouldn't be talking to your machine. Sighing, Liz put the phone down. She wasn't going to leave an inane message. She lay back, staring at the ceiling. She wasn't going to sleep, either. Climbing out of bed, she went into her home office and plopped in front of her computer. The weather channel said it was going to be unseasonably warm on Christmas Day this year. No snow. Sunny. Liz checked the weather in Paris. Fog. Drizzle. *Serves her right.*

A hotel near the Sorbonne. She wondered how hard that would be to find. She had called the travel agent the Davises always used earlier that day. They had not heard from Mary and knew nothing about her trip to Paris. Calling Irene about the subject garnered the same information delivered as cool as ice.

"Did Mother tell you where she was staying in Paris?"

"No. I told you that already."

"Would you be willing to look in her room again to see if you could find anything?"

"Already have. Hoped you'd wake up and try to contact her. There's nothing."

"Have you heard from her?"

"No."

"Well, as soon as my passport comes I'm going over."

"Good."

"Will you let me know if she contacts you? Will you try to get the hotel name?"

"Of course."

"Are you . . . are you and Cecil all right?"

"We're just fine. Don't you worry your little head about us."

"Irene, I . . ." Liz paused. She pressed her lips together. She was not going to be bullied into crawling to the servants for sympathy.

Irene was quiet.

"I'll let you know if I hear anything."

"Fine."

Click.

So much for getting help from Irene.

She sat in the dark with only the blue glow of her computer screen lighting the room. If she drove out to the house and looked around herself, she could talk to Irene and maybe smoothe things over. Irene and Cecil were good people. They'd been around for a long time. It would be a shame for there to be bad blood between them. She would drive out there. Tomorrow.

Clicking back onto the Internet, she found that the Sorbonne was located in the Latin Quarter, the fifth arrondissement. Her search for hotels in that part of Paris revealed dozens. How, she thought, would she ever find the one her mother had chosen? She tried eliminating any places rated two stars or less. A few more keystrokes left her more frustrated than ever.

Switching off her computer, Liz climbed back into bed. She lay in the dark, wishing the phone would ring. Wishing it would be Jeff's voice. Wishing she understood what was happening to her mother. Wishing her passport would come.

FOR THE FIRST time since Samuel F. Davis died, Elizabeth Davis didn't do what was expected of her. Rising early the next morning, she called her assistant and said she wouldn't be in. She dressed three times before finally deciding she would go casual. She pulled her ash-blonde hair back into a ponytail and applied minimal makeup before heading for home.

Irene and Cecil were both in the kitchen when Liz arrived. When, she wondered, had they become an *elderly* couple? It couldn't have happened overnight, but Liz hadn't noticed. Cecil and Irene were just always there—the cook, the gardener, the housekeeper. Other than complaining to her mother about their slow service or weeds in the yard, Liz realized, with a pang of guilt, that it had been a long time since she had noticed or cared about what was going on in the Baxters' lives. What was it Irene had snapped the other night? Something about Liz needing to pay attention to someone other than herself for a change?

Cecil was sitting at the same table eating the same breakfast he'd had for years.

"Two eggs, over easy," Liz said aloud. She smiled. "Do you ever try anything else?"

Cecil shook his head. "No need. I'm just an old farm boy at heart, and I'd be wishing for the eggs. What brings you home?"

God bless Cecil, Liz thought. He was doing his best to warm the temperature in the kitchen. Heaven knew it could use it. Irene hadn't said three words to her.

"Mr. Jeffrey coming out to meet you?" Cecil asked.

"No," Liz said. "I . . . I'm . . . on my own."

Cecil looked at her then, his pale blue eyes kind. "You and Mr. Jeffrey having some troubles, Missy?"

"He . . . uh . . ." Liz gulped.

"Come on over here and tell Cecil all about it," the old man said, waving her toward the bench opposite his in the nook. "I know you're a high-and-mighty, powerful business woman, but I can see in those circles under your eyes that maybe you've got a burden. I'm not very smart, but I've got a strong shoulder."

Just as Liz opened her mouth to protest that there was nothing wrong that she couldn't handle, Irene opened the oven. The aroma of cinnamon and yeast and butter took Liz back in time, and for a brief moment it was as if all the years folded back on themselves. Lizzie Davis was alone for breakfast—which happened most of the time because Daddy left early for work every day and Mother wasn't a morning person. And so it was that Cecil and Irene were the two with whom she shared breakfast and any fears she had about the upcoming day or the doubts she had about yesterday.

Elizabeth Davis was not a woman given to sentimentality, but as the aroma of Irene's cinnamon rolls wafted through the kitchen, the lack of sleep, the lack of Jeff, the absence of her mother, and the death of her father were suddenly overwhelming. Tears sprang to her eyes. Her shoulders slumped. She put one hand to her forehead, leaned her elbow on the table, and began to cry.

"Jeff's . . ." She couldn't bring herself to say the word *gone*. And besides that, he wasn't really *gone*. Was he? "Jeff said he needed some time. He hasn't called. Or . . . anything."

The cooking-clanks ceased. The oven door closed, and Irene slid onto the bench beside Cecil. She still didn't say anything, but her presence comforted. And she handed Liz a tissue. Liz thanked her, then looked from Irene to Cecil and said abruptly, "I didn't mean to be so . . . awful to her. I can't figure out why I did that. Why I said those things." She brought her hand away from her face and sat, rolling and unrolling the Kleenex. "I couldn't believe it myself. I didn't know all that was inside me. . . . But once I got started, and Mother didn't defend herself, I just . . ." She closed her eyes and shook her head. "I have to find her. I have to apologize."

"Why?" Irene said abruptly. "Because Jeffrey told you to?"

Liz looked down. "Because it's the right thing to do. Because I'm worried about her."

"Your mother will be just fine," Irene said. "She's not an idiot. Like some around here think."

"I never said she was an idiot." Liz paused, forcing conciliation into her voice. "But she's never traveled abroad, and I—"

"Just goes to show how much you know," Irene said. "I told you, she'll be fine."

Liz frowned. She looked at Cecil, who was studying the eggs

on his plate. He took a bite and looked out the window while he chewed.

"Apologizing won't mean a thing if you still feel the same way about her. If you still won't look at her and see who she is. And I mean who she really is, not the person she lets you see."

Cecil put his hand on his wife's arm. It was a gentle warning, but it caught Liz's attention.

"I know, honey," Irene said, and patted the back of his hand. "But Mister Davis is gone, and I just don't see any need to be keeping promises and secrets anymore. Not when it's doing this."

Cecil considered, nodded, and spoke up. "Time for this old man to get to the garden. Storm's a brewin', and I don't like thunder and lightning."

Irene slid over and let Cecil out. He pecked her on the cheek, then put a gnarled hand on Liz's shoulder. "You're in tough times, Lizzie-girl. Don't let them beat you. Fight for your love. That's the only thing that lasts." He patted her head and was gone.

An awkward silence reigned in the kitchen for a while after Cecil left. While Irene got up and served them both a cinnamon roll, Liz poured coffee. Finally, she broke the silence Irene wouldn't. "What did you mean when you said apologizing won't do any good if I still feel the same way about Mother?"

Irene finished chewing the piece of roll in her mouth. She looked down and fiddled with her wedding band. Liz had never known her to be so thoughtful, and it made her nervous. She shifted in her seat but determined to wait for Irene to answer, no matter how long it took.

"First, you tell me something," Irene said, and looked into Liz's eyes.

Liz nodded.

"Tell me exactly what the trouble is between you and Mr. Jeffrey."

"The way I treated Mother," Liz said without thinking.

Irene nodded. "I always did like that boy. Good for him."

"He didn't really tell me that. Exactly. Just said he needed to take a step back. Said I needed to patch things up with my mom and he needed to think some things over. But I know what he really meant." Liz looked down at the table, one finger twirling the end of her ponytail as she talked. "He's never been able to understand Mother and me. He misses his own mom so much—and he just doesn't understand that everyone can't have a perfect relationship like he had."

"Do *you* understand it?" Irene asked.

Liz shook her head.

"Well, Lizzie-girl, neither do I. Seems to me your mother has always done her best to be and do exactly whatever it was your father and you wanted her to be and do. Gave up her own interests and just molded herself into the image of Mrs. Samuel F. Davis. And I can tell you, that wasn't easy."

Hearing Irene talk this way about her mother made Liz think she must be talking about someone else.

"You don't have a clue what I'm talking about, do you?" Irene asked.

Liz shook her head.

Irene got up. "You have yourself another cinnamon roll. I'll be back directly."

"Your mama didn't just land on this planet the day Samuel Davis met her, you know," Irene said as she came back into the kitchen carrying a brown envelope and handed it to Liz. "Your father threw these away. I dug them out of the trash. Thought maybe your mama would want them back someday."

Liz opened the packet. There were only a few photographs, but there were several newspaper articles, yellowed with age.

"Mother played the violin?" she said after reading the first one.

Irene nodded. "Guess she played it really well, too. Says there she was first chair. Your father didn't want her traveling to perform."

"She lived in France?"

"That's where your parents met."

"Daddy hated to travel."

"Don't I know it. He never let *her* go back, either."

Morning turned into afternoon as Mary Elisabeth McKibbin Davis was transformed in Liz's eyes. In the end, Liz had more questions than answers. "How could he . . . How could Daddy . . . *do* this? How could he just wipe out her past?"

"He couldn't unless she let him," Irene said. "So don't be blaming him for everything. They shared it."

"Were they *ever* happy?" Liz blurted out. "Was that all just a ruse? For me?"

"Oh, now," Irene said, and she patted the back of Liz's hand. "Life isn't as simple as that. They were partners. They had you. And yes, they were happy. After a fashion." She added, her voice resonant with sincerity, "Your father was a domineering man, Lizzie. But he wasn't cruel. And he thought the sun rose and set in you."

"So . . . all those years when Mother . . . took a backseat. It was because that's what Daddy wanted."

Irene nodded. "I expect that was it exactly."

"And I just thought she was dull and uninteresting." Liz shook her head. "I believed that story about the Rolls Royce."

She shuffled through the pile of paper and pulled out a small news item. "How did she end up studying in France?"

"Scholarships, honey. She got all A's in college, you know."

"What was her major?"

"She had two. Business and French," Irene said, and pulled another piece of paper from the pile. The college diploma was stained brown and had one corner missing. Mary's name was barely legible.

"No wonder she wanted to go back to Europe," Liz murmured.

Irene nodded. "I think she's been wanting to find her old self for a while now. She's wanted to show you. She just didn't know how."

"I never took the time to listen," Liz struggled to continue. "I never *saw*. And when she tried to show me . . . when she tried to take a more active part in the foundation . . . I made fun of her." Sighing, Liz bowed her head. "I don't know my own mother." She looked up. "I've got to find her. I've got to *go* to her."

"No passport yet?"

"ARRGHH! No! I've called everyone I know, done everything I can."

"Welcome to the real world, Elizabeth," Irene said. "The one where you *can't* have everything you want when you want it." She smiled. "She'll be there through Christmas. She'll still be there when you get there. In the meantime, I suggest you call Mr. Jeffrey Scott and eat a serious helping of humble pie."

"He won't talk to me," Liz said. "At least he didn't answer my call from last night."

"Did you leave a message?"

"No. But he has caller ID." Liz looked up at Irene. "What should I do?"

The older woman got up and went to the phone. Picking up the headset she walked back to where Liz was sitting and handed it to her. "There's not a man alive who can resist an invitation to have one of Irene Baxter's cinnamon rolls."

"He'll think—"

"That you're so anxious to see him you'll even use bribery?" Irene said. "Where's the harm in that?"

Liz dialed the phone.

SIXTEEN

Mary

I AM HELPING PREPARE DINNER in Annie's tiny studio apartment when the past beckons in a new way. Annie has put me to work peeling and seeding tomatoes—why the French seed tomatoes I have no idea, but they do, and so do I—while she runs to the corner boulangerie for a loaf of bread. I finish before she returns. There is a violin case resting atop the grand piano crammed into one corner of the parlor/dining room/ living room. Unable to resist a peek, I open the case. Drawn by the patina of the wood I reach out to touch it.

It is the first time I have held a violin in my hands in close to thirty years. Grasping the frog, I draw the bow across the strings so tentatively they complain. Grimacing, I stretch my neck from side to side, settle my chin back into the chin rest, place my fingers on the strings, and this time, elicit a discernible and not unpleasant note. A lifetime, it seems, can't erase certain phrases of music. Closing my eyes, I feel my way through a simple melody.

"You didn't tell me you play," Annie calls from the doorway.

"I don't. Haven't. Not for years and years." I return the violin to its case and apologize. "I'm sorry. I know better than to do that without asking." I touch the neck of the violin. "It's a lovely instrument."

Annie shrugs. "It's all right." She grins. "In both cases."

I laugh. "Thank you. And it's more than all right as an instrument. You should have heard the one I learned on." I shudder.

"Tell me about it," Annie says, heading into the kitchen, baguette in hand.

Telling Annie about my first violin leads to a recounting of my college dreams and my life before Sam. For the next half hour, we work side by side in the kitchen while I recount the past, focusing on my youthful desires to play the violin, the realization of a dream, the debut performance.

"You're kidding me," Annie exclaims at one point. "You played with Slatkin conducting? *The* Slatkin?"

"It was only once," I say. "Don't be too impressed. I won a contest. That's all. And it was local. A fund-raiser for the St. Louis Symphony."

"But why don't you. . . ?"

"When I married my husband, he didn't want me traveling, and I would have had to do that to pursue the violin."

"So you just gave it up. Like that?"

I shake my head. "It wasn't quite as easy as that. But the music was part of . . ." I hesitate before saying it. "Sam thought the music connected me to someone else. In the end, it was better for me to put it aside. I think if I'd refused it would have caused trouble."

Annie's eyes grow large. "Mrs. Davis had a secret love," she says, tilting her head and closing her eyes. "That's the most romantic thing I've ever heard."

"I can't believe I told you," I say. I laugh nervously, shaking my head back and forth. "You, young lady, are entirely too easy to talk to."

Annie turns around and leans against the kitchen counter. "Come on, let's hear it. You know everything about Adolpho and me. What was his name?"

"Jean-Marc."

"Where is he now?"

"I don't know."

"Have you Googled him?" Annie wants to know.

"Have I . . . what?"

"Googled him. You know," Annie explains. "You go to *Google.com*. It's a search engine on the Internet. Enter his name. And . . . voilà. Information."

"You can do that?"

Annie lets her amazement at my computer illiteracy show. She nods her head, exaggerating when she answers me, "Yessss."

"My computer skills are quite limited."

"Well, you've come to the right *salon,* madame." She retreats to the next room and, with a flourish, opens the door of a scarred cabinet that houses a computer. She turns it on, and while it is warming up, she pulls out the piano bench, positions it in front of the computer, and pulls me down beside her. In less than a minute, the Google screen awaits. "So," Annie says, "type in his name."

"Just like that?" I can't imagine a digital yellow pages.

Annie nods. "Just like that. You do know how to type, don't you?"

"Hey," I protest, "I'll have you know I bought my plane ticket online. I just didn't know about this Google thing." As I talk I type in *J-e-a-n-M-a-r-c D-a-v-i-d.*

"Three first names," Annie comments.

"That's what I always used to say." I hit Enter and wait. Seconds later I have a page full of options. The second one mentions the *Sea Cloud*. I hold my breath and click, and the *Sea Cloud* appears, her sails unfurled, her hull sending a rolling curtain of foam tumbling down the side of a great wave. It reminds me of the magazine cover, although it is not the same photograph.

"There," Annie points. "It has a link about the captain."

I click. I take a deep breath. I tip my head so I can see the screen better. My hand comes up to my throat. Older. Gray hair. He is onboard the ship, staring into the distance with those incredible blue eyes. I am speechless.

"Wow," Annie says.

I am brought back to the moment with a start. "Wow what?" I ask.

"You're blushing," Annie says. She leans close, nudging my shoulder gently. "You loved him."

I cannot pull myself away from the image on the computer screen.

"Maybe," Annie says, her voice lowering a few decibels. "Maybe you still do."

I force myself to look away. "Don't be absurd," I protest. "It was almost thirty years ago." I stand up. "Let's finish dinner. You must be starving."

"But don't you want to read about it? Learn more?"

I shake my head, leaning over and clicking to close the Web site down. "No. Not now. Not this way."

"But, why not?"

Taking in a deep breath, I say the first thing that comes to mind. "Because I'm afraid."

"Of what?"

I sigh. "It's a long story."

Annie stands up, touches my forearm, and motions me to sit on the couch. She retrieves two tall glasses and pours wine. Then she curls up opposite me, grabs a huge pillow, and clutching it to her says, "Dinner will wait. My appetite's on hold, anyway."

It is amazing how something that has been held inside for so long can suddenly be so insistent on climbing out. Half afraid that by telling these things about Jean-Marc I will somehow prevent him from reappearing in my life, I begin to talk. "My parents were poor, but they loved me very much. I studied hard, got good grades, managed a scholarship, and graduated with a double major in business and French. But even before college, I'd also studied French in high school. And I loved it. It was easy for me, and the culture and history drew me like a moth to a flame. I dreamed of studying here!

"During the last semester of my senior year of college, my favorite French professor let it be known that his work visa was expiring. He'd be going home to Arcachon after the term, and if anyone wanted to study in his hometown he would arrange some independent graduate-level courses through the University at Bordeaux. My parents didn't understand it, but they saw it was very important to me and they supported my decision. So I came . . ."

I hesitate, then smile at Annie as I admit it. "I came and fell in love. Not with a man—that came later. I fell for the country first. I didn't want to go home. That autumn, my professor invited the son of a close friend of his to dinner. His name was Jean-Marc David. He was my age, and he had a small two-masted sailboat. He invited me to come sailing. I did. One day he took me out beyond the bay. We anchored for the night. I heard the sea leave and heard it return, the waves slapping against the side of the boat as the tide came in. We walked on beaches with no other human footprint. We watched the sun set . . . and watched it rise. And there was no one watching from that place except the two of us. Who wouldn't fall in love?"

Annie doesn't laugh. Instead, she says, "But it was more than just a fleeting romance. I saw your face just now—when his face appeared on the computer screen."

"Yes," I agree. "I think it was. After the first day there was something . . . uncanny about it. Almost as if one soul had been wandering the earth and suddenly realized it wasn't whole without the other." With the saying of the words aloud, I am drawn back into the past and filled with an emotion I thought long since dead. Annie is quiet. She waits. I close my eyes. "Then, another professor at the university, who happened to be the town mayor, asked me if I had ever done any modeling. I hadn't. But he begged me, and I finally said yes. I was eventually assigned to show a Rolls Royce Silver Cloud in the annual Concours d'Elégance in Arcachon. The owner of the vehicle had an American friend. Samuel Frederick Davis."

"Your husband," Annie says.

I nod.

"But . . . why? When you were already in love with Jean-Marc?"

I shrug. "I've asked myself the same question for over half my life. The only answer to that question isn't a very good one. I was afraid."

"But you came to France to study. That doesn't seem like something a fearful person would do."

"Professor Max took care of every detail of that trip. He and his wife were there as a safety net if I had any difficulties. They both spoke fluent English. It was like having a second set of parents." I pause. "Jean-Marc was a complete unknown. He was young and impetuous. Dreaming impossible things." I remember, shaking my head as I do. "He was going to work his way up to buying his own yacht and sail around the world. Encouraging him to live his dream was one thing. Abandoning my comfort zone to join him in the adventure was quite another. Sam Davis was everything Jean-Marc wasn't. Wealthy. Powerful. Settled."

"Safe," Annie offers.

"Yes," I nod. "Safe. Or so it seemed at the time."

"And so you went with the safe alternative."

I nod, newly aware of the computer looming over my right shoulder. "And," I murmur, "Jean-Marc earned his yacht." My hand trembles as I reach out for the glass and take a sip of wine. I am trying to choke back tears as I unburden. "I betrayed one of the kindest, gentlest, dearest young men in the world." I tell Annie how Jean-Marc learned of my decision to marry Sam. I describe the party and the announcement, but words fail when I try to describe the look on Jean-Marc's face.

"I tried to find him. To talk. But I never did."

"You should let Google help you contact him," Annie suggests.

"I don't need Google for that," I say and finally manage a smile as I tell Annie about my letter and Christmas Eve.

IT SEEMED to Liz that the phone rang a hundred times. In reality, Jeff answered on the third ring. "I'm sorry I didn't return your call from last night," he said. "I hit the ground running this morning and haven't come up for air until now. In fact, I was just settling in to call you, and the phone rang. And I'm not just saying that."

"Can you. . . ? Can you maybe come over? I'm at home. Home home."

"What's going on?"

"I've . . . I've been here talking to Irene. And . . . please, Jeff. I need to see you."

"Is something wrong? Something with Mary?"

Scolding herself for her inability to keep her voice from cracking, Liz answered. "I haven't heard from her. I don't know. Please, Jeff. Will you come?" She glanced over at Irene. "Irene made cinnamon rolls."

Jeff hesitated, but agreed.

"Thank you," Liz said. She hoped she wasn't reading too much into the tone of his voice. He had hesitated about coming over, but he still sounded happy to have heard from her.

She was sitting at her mother's desk chair looking out over the garden when Jeff arrived. The moon was bright enough to cast a ghostly light on the landscape that almost looked like snow. When the door behind her opened, Liz called out. "I'm over here. At Mom's desk."

When Jeff leaned over to kiss her on the cheek she closed her eyes and inhaled the familiar scent of his cologne. The thought that she might not have that scent in her future brought tears to her eyes. She cleared her throat. Motioning to the framed motto on the desk she said, "I made fun of her when she bought this." She paused. "But I want to believe it." She whispered the words, embarrassed by the warble in her voice. "It is never too late to be what you might have been." She paused before looking up at him. "Will—will you give me another chance? Please?"

Jeff looked into her eyes without smiling. But he didn't let go of her hand as he asked, "What is it you want to be, Bitsy?"

Liz sucked in a sob. "Kinder. More patient. More under-standing. Maybe . . . maybe a good daughter for a change." She let the tears come. "Do you think it's possible that she'd forgive me for the way I've treated her?"

"I think," Jeff said, taking both her hands in his, "that Mary Davis would swim the ocean just to hear you say that with her own ears. And yes, of course she will forgive you."

Liz kissed the backs of his hands. "And you, Jeff. Will you forgive me?"

"You don't owe me any apologies, Bitsy."

"I snapped at you the last time you called me that. I'm sorry."

"You thought I was belittling you," Jeff said. "I wasn't, you know. I was just trying to get you to—"

"Take myself a little less seriously?"

"Exactly." He let go of her hands and began to stroke her hair. Sighing, she leaned her head against the back of the chair. His hands came together at her forehead and with his fingertips he outlined her face, her eyebrows, her chin, with featherlight strokes. Closing her eyes, Liz whispered, "I love you."

"I know." He leaned over then and kissed the tip of her nose. His lips found hers, and he came around the front of the chair, lifted her into his arms, and kissed her again.

She snuggled against him. "I have to find Mimi."

"Mimi?" Jeff stepped back to look in her eyes.

"My name for Mom when I was a little girl."

"I'll help you find your Mimi," he whispered.

"And . . . will you come with me?" She rushed ahead before he could answer, "Not because I want to hide behind you. Because I'm afraid to do this alone. I just need your . . . support.

To get this right. To fix it." Her chin trembled and she bit her lower lip. "If it can be fixed."

"Elizabeth Davis can do just about anything she sets her mind to," Jeff said, holding her close. "You don't need me for this."

"But I want you," Liz said. She looked up at Jeff, her heart thumping when she saw the glimmer in his eyes.

"Good," Jeff said, covering her mouth with his. "That's really good to hear," he mumbled as they kissed.

Mary

THE DAY IS lonely. Annie has gone home for the holiday, taking Adolpho with her. She is anxious about how her parents will react to her dreadlocked boyfriend with cappuccino skin. They have both apologized for the fact that we never did go to the Ducati dealership—I wasn't feeling too well the day they took Adolpho's bike for repairs, and then it was time for them to leave for England.

"As soon as we get back," Adolpho promised, flashing that gorgeous smile of his.

"It's a deal," I replied. At Annie's insistence, I promised to come for dinner as soon as they return from their holiday.

I miss them more than I expected to. I have been wandering the Musée d'Orsay, as much entranced by the transformation of the building—formerly a train station—into an art museum as I am by the paintings. I wander aimlessly, surprised that I have nothing to add to my journal about the things I am seeing. It would seem that for the moment I am sated with art.

I walk down the Boule Miche and get on the 24 bus, thinking I will walk up the Champs-Elysées and dine at a new café.

Traffic on the streets seems to be at an all-time low. I make my way around the Arc de Triomphe and up the Avenue de la Grande Armée, imagining the street filled with Allied soldiers being cheered as a liberating army. Intending to head back to a café I had spotted on the other side of the Place de la Concorde, I cross the street where an unusual number of motorcycles are parked along the curb. Glancing along the street I understand why. Here is a row of motorcycle dealerships. There is Moto-Guzzi, BMW, Honda—even Harley Davidson. The vision of tattooed men with inverted aluminum bowls on their heads riding down the Champs-Elysées makes me smile.

"Mrs. Davis?"

Enzo, Adolpho's reckless friend, is lounging against a streetlamp smoking a cigarette, which he flicks into the street before coming my way. "You have come to see Ducati, eh?"

"I thought you went home for the holiday."

Enzo motions to the row of windows above the Ducati sign. "This is my uncle's business. I am working to pay for the repairs on Adolpho's bike."

I am apologetic. "I suppose it's silly. A woman my age."

"Women are like wine, Mrs. Davis. They improve with age." He isn't flirting, but he has a smile on his face. He shrugs, "I hear my uncle say that all the time."

Enzo is much more charming than I had remembered. He is tall and thin, with a carefully tended perpetually day-old beard and a warm smile that I think is genuine. Although for all I know he is laughing hysterically inside. I decide I don't care. I do want to see the motorcycles and was disappointed when it didn't work out with Annie and Adolpho. So I allow myself to be led inside, where an impressive array of bikes sits in a room with polished floors and walls covered with racing posters. I cannot believe a man can stay in control of a machine that is leaning over so radically that the rider's knee is scraping the road. Or, I should say, the racetrack.

"Can you do that?" I ask Enzo.

"No," Enzo says. At that moment a door opens and a man with gray hair comes into the showroom. "But he can. Or could. That's my Uncle Luca. And in his day, he was famous."

Luca Santo looks about my age, and after being introduced, he says, "So, the woman Enzo and Adolpho told me about finally comes to see for herself." He smiles. "You made quite an impression on my nephew." He raises his eyebrows. "Périphérique certified, I hear."

"I made a fool of myself," I say. "But I had fun." I pause. "I can't believe I'm saying it was fun."

"It's even more fun to drive yourself," Mr. Santo assures me. "Not here in Paris, of course. But touring the countryside. Provence, for example. Wonderful." He gestures as he talks, describing the delights of touring the countryside on a motorcycle. His English is fluent but the inflection is Italian. It is a charming mix, almost musical.

"You make it sound wonderful," I say. "But I don't know the first thing about riding." I am only making polite conversation. Unfortunately, Mr. Santo thinks I am expressing a desire to learn.

"In the spring, you must come to Bologna. Ducati week. They have classes for the women—"

"But surely not for beginners," I say.

"You begin here," Mr. Santo says. "You learn more there." He walks to one of the motorcycles and puts his hand on the seat. "This is the one for you." The motorcycle is smaller than most of the others. He invites me to sit on the bike. I look down at my skirt and up at him. We laugh.

"Next time," he says.

I nod. "Next time." I thank Enzo for the tour, Mr. Santo for his time, and exit the shop, knowing full well I'll never be back, yet storing up the memory. A good story for when I am back in Omaha. As I walk up the street I chuckle, imagining the look on my daughter's face if I were to arrive at a board meeting on a Ducati.

SEVENTEEN

THE YEARS SLIPPED AWAY the moment Jean-Marc stepped across the threshold of Luca Santo's Ducati dealership. He paused just inside the doorway, and was once again a young racer appraising "the stock." Among the collection of yellow and red *machinas* crammed into the small showroom, one appealed to him more than any other. Let the young men have the Supersport with its electric red fairing. He could understand the appeal of the bright yellow ST4. But for him, there was only one bike. He threw his leg over the Monster, and the instant he reached for the throttle, the past swallowed him.

He was at Imola, kneeling on the pavement to check a cable when two of a competitor's engineers approached. As they watched Jean-Marc inspect his machine, one commented on a way he thought Ducati could cut production costs. "Ducati doesn't cut costs on parts. We use the best. We make the best" had been Jean-Marc's answer.

Remembering the conversation all these years later, Jean-Marc smiled. *If Luca Santo doesn't show up soon, I'm going to be in serious danger of acquiring a new motorcycle.*

"*Mama mia,* the end of the world approaches—Jean-Marc David has come back to Paris!"

Without getting off the bike, Jean-Marc twisted around to greet his old friend. "How much for this one?" he asked.

"You think that one is nice," Luca said, motioning toward the door that led to the shop in back. "Come see what I'm just getting out of its crate. The 999R. It's going there," he said, motioning to the place of honor in the front window.

With motorcycles to discuss, Jean-Marc relaxed. The men talked as they worked, tearing the crate away from the 999R, admiring its lines, reminiscing about "the old days." Finally, the conversation turned to real life.

"And how is Magda?" Luca asked.

Jean-Marc shook his head. "I thought Magda would be the perfect woman to raise Celine. We tried as long as possible—for Celine's sake." He shrugged. "But Magda never could get past her fear of the sea. Every moment on board she was waiting for the next port, hoping I would decide to stay ashore. She wanted a house and a husband who went to work every morning and returned for dinner every night."

Luca patted him on the back. "I'm sorry."

Jean-Marc nodded. "It wasn't her fault." He smiled, "Happily, Celine was not of the same mind. She grew up at sea and thrived on it, although now she is more settled."

Quickly, he filled in the rest of the years, which had included a second marriage and a quick divorce. "That one wasn't nearly as reasonable as Magda. She tried to get a portion of the *Sea Cloud.*"

"That's always the way," Luca commiserated. "One love jealous of the other." He changed the subject. "Tell me more about Celine. The little girl is all grown up now. I bet she's a beauty."

"She has two boys," Jean-Marc said. "Twins. Xavier and Olivier—who, I think, actually like their grandfather." He shook his head. "I can't believe I'm talking about *grandsons*. How did that happen? *Two* wives . . . and *grand*children. *Mon Dieu!*"

"The years go by too quickly," Luca agreed.

"And Sophia? How is she?"

Luca crossed himself. "With God," he said. "Three years now."

"I'm sorry. I didn't know." Jean-Marc looked down at the motorcycle not knowing what else to say. *Why didn't you know?* He felt new guilt. He'd never been good at letters. But he could have made an effort. If for anyone, he should have made the effort for Luca.

"She went quickly and with little pain," Luca explained. "God was good. He gave us nearly twenty-five years together." An awkward silence hung between the two men. Finally, Luca clapped Jean-Marc on the back. "Come. Back to the new *machinas*. A few changes since you and I were on the team, eh?"

An hour later, Jean-Marc left the shop. He'd enjoyed reminiscing about the old days when, as young men, he and Luca risked their bodies test-driving the fastest motorcycles on earth. And he'd promised to return the next evening for dinner in Luca's apartment above the dealership. That, he thought, was the least he could do after showing so little interest in his friend's life for all these years. The good thing, Jean-Marc thought as he walked up the street toward the Arc de Triomphe, was that having dinner with Luca would occupy one night—leaving one less night to wait through alone. The bad thing, he realized as he ducked into a café, was he hadn't been able to tell if Luca's religious fervor had cooled down in the years since they first met. If there was one thing he did not want to deal with at the moment, it was religion. Hopefully, Luca would remember. If he didn't remember . . . Jean-Marc sighed. Settling into a chair with his back to the rest of the diners in the café, Jean-Marc ordered dinner. While he ate, he remembered. . . .

In 1974 a twenty-one-year-old Jean-Marc David lashed his boat to the dock at the Marina di Pisa. He'd been alone at sea for nearly a month. He was hungry, wet, and tired. His food stocks on board were low, his pockets nearly empty, and he was not really certain what Italian port he was in. He hadn't been sure of much of anything for weeks. The days had melded one into the next as he sailed his little boat from one port to another, around Spain, up the coast to Monte Carlo, and down the boot of Italy. He would round the toe soon and then—well, then he would have to look for work because he would be completely out of money.

The last few weeks at sea had been spent in a fever of emotions vacillating between anger and depression, laced with a generous sense of betrayal. He had relived every moment of what he had been certain was the love of a lifetime. Apparently, only he had been certain. The girl had proven to be exactly what his mother predicted.

"It is not a small thing, my son, to expect a girl to leave her country and her family, to enter a new culture, to give up everything she knows for uncertainty."

He should have listened to his mother, who was speaking not out of dislike for Mary McKibbin but from experience, having left her own homeland to marry the man who would become Jean-Marc's father. "I'm not saying I regret my own decision," his mother said. "I am saying, given what I know, this girl—she won't do it."

His mother had been right. The girl had opted out. Married

a rich compatriot and disappeared without so much as another word to him.

Young and impulsive, dramatic and creative, Jean-Marc had thought his life was ruined. And, as was his habit, he ran to the mother of all living things—the sea—to find comfort.

After leaving the Marina di Pisa, the next port turned out to be Livorno, but Jean-Marc would not learn that until he woke, hung over and sick from a combination of malnutrition and depression, in a tiny room at the back of a motorcycle shop owned by a man named Donatello Santo. Santo had a son, Luca, and in a few days Jean-Marc, who was not afraid to die and almost wished for it, was riding motorcycles through the hills of Tuscany at breakneck speed. The elder Santo hired him to work in the shop, and soon Jean-Marc David and Luca Santo were entering local races. Before long they were making names for themselves.

Jean-Marc's boat stayed docked at Livorno for a long time. Young and fearless, David and Santo became well-known in the racing world. Clad in custom racing leathers and posed beside the sleek new Desmo, they became the poster boys for Ducati. Endorsements came in, and with them came money and the means to have whatever they wanted. Women flocked around them wherever they went. Luca laughed and flirted. Jean-Marc indulged.

And then one day, Luca Santo misjudged a turn. His bike slid out from beneath him and ended up off the track on its side, its wheels spinning, its engine racing. Luca ended up beside the wall that had stopped his slide with an impact that broke more bones than a man should be able to break and still live. In the crowd that day was a renowned American bone surgeon. A racing fan in the United States, the surgeon offered his services to piece the injured racer back together. Jean-Marc was grateful for the surgeon's skill in repairing Luca's body, but he would live to regret the man's influence in another area.

Luca told him later how, when he tried to thank the man for saving his leg, the surgeon gave credit to God. Neither Luca nor Jean-Marc had ever heard anything like it. God, the surgeon said, had been his partner in the operating room that day. "When you have the creator of legs helping you put one back together," the surgeon joked, "the pieces fit better." Jean-Marc found the statement amusing. Luca was intrigued. The surgeon stayed long enough to make sure Luca's leg would be saved. Long enough for protracted conversations about life.

The day Dr. Lenert left for home was also the day he told Luca Santo that his racing career for Ducati was over. Jean-Marc was in the hospital room when his friend got the news. Amazingly, Luca didn't seem to care. "I have a leg," he said, grasping the surgeon's hand. "I am grateful." His eyes filled with tears as he bid his doctor good-bye. "And thanks to you, I have much more."

But Jean-Marc David didn't want to hear about God. Luca couldn't answer the most basic questions. *If God loves me so much*, Jean-Marc would say, *then why . . .* and he had a lot of *whys* for which Luca had no answers. Their discussions continued while Luca recuperated.

"That's not much of a religion you've got," Jean-Marc finally said, one evening when they were sitting outside the back door of Donatello Santo's shop drinking coffee and arguing. "All questions and no answers."

"I have the answer to the most important one," Luca replied.

"And what," Jean-Marc said, slurping coffee, "is the most important question?"

"What happens when we die?" Luca's gray-blue eyes were intense. "I heard the whispers in the emergency room. I saw the worried faces. The only question I really wanted answered was *What if I die?* The others . . . well," he laughed softly, "the other questions are about things that will pass." He looked at his friend. "We're going to be dead forever."

Luca went on, then, not seeming to care whether Jean-Marc wanted to hear it or not. He talked about God and holiness, about perfection and sin. All concepts Jean-Marc had grown up knowing, because like all his friends, he went to mass faithfully and memorized the catechism. As the days went by and Luca didn't shut up, it became even more apparent that he had had some sort of shift in his universe and was intent upon having Jean-Marc experience the same kind of thing. The more Luca talked, the less Jean-Marc listened. And finally, one clear spring morning not long after Luca threw away his cane and took a long walk, praising God for the healing, the sea called and Jean-Marc answered.

He was bitter about Mary McKibbin's betrayal and Luca Santo's religious phase for a long time after quitting racing. He went back to sailing and began taking tourists out for short trips to support himself. He fathered a daughter with a singer he met during a week spent in port and took on the task of raising her when her mother lost interest. After a stressful attempt to raise Celine on his own, he married quickly—more to provide a mother for his daughter than because of any great love for the woman.

Magda Romani was a customer's daughter who had romantic notions about life at sea and no interest in the reality, which included wild storms, endless maintenance, and little time ashore. When she was unable to convince Jean-Marc to take up a more land-centered way of life, the marriage ended. With the help of his nest egg kept from his motorcycle racing days, Jean-Marc bought a bigger boat and began to take small groups of wealthy tourists on cruises around the Mediterranean. In a few years, he had saved enough to upgrade again. He continued to enjoy the company of women, and eventually, in spite of Celine's protests and dislike of the woman, he got another wife. Their relationship was rocky, and there were other issues involved, but when Celine arrived home one night with the news that she was pregnant and had no intention of marrying, the second wife left. "I'm not going to raise that tramp's illegitimate child," she screeched.

During the first years of Jean-Marc's life at sea, he and Luca had stayed in touch. But Santo's glowing letters about his marriage and his God grew increasingly irritating. Finally, Jean-Marc stopped answering, and he barely noticed when Santo stopped writing.

Sitting now in the café reminiscing all these years later, Jean-Marc was newly irritated by his friend's religious fervor. Apparently Luca had accepted Sophia's death as God's will. What was it he had said? *"She is with God."* He seemed certain. He had even found a way to be grateful. *"She went quickly and with little pain. God was good. He gave us nearly twenty-five years together."*

That was the maddening thing about religious people, Jean-Marc thought: They accepted terrible things and then actually claimed to be *grateful* to the very God who—if he existed—could have prevented the tragedy in the first place. As long as he lived, he would not accept that. It was irrational. Servile. Where, he wondered, was Luca Santo's self-respect? To cower like that and just take whatever God dealt. . . . he would never do it. Part of him began to dread the next evening's dinner with Luca. Enough of the past was invading his present for the moment. He didn't need the subject of God added to the mix. He'd successfully avoided the subject for a long time. *When you've had a choice in the matter,* he reminded himself. *But the subject of God has come up. It's even been brought onboard a time or two.*

Over dessert, he remembered one of his more direct shipboard encounters with God. *When was it. . . ?* he thought. Maybe a year after receiving what would be his last letter from Santo? Yes. About then. He remembered the woman well. Less because of her interest in God and more because she reminded him of Mary McKibbin. However, the resemblance ended with appearances, as this woman constantly laced her conversation with references to deity. It wasn't obnoxious. Just odd. She bowed her head before every meal. One evening, when he thought all his passengers were long since asleep, Jean-Marc went up on deck to have a cigarette and nearly tripped over her. She'd been lying flat on her back looking up at the sky.

"Oof! Oh, I'm so sorry." She jumped up, obviously embarrassed, whether by the fact he had caught her or the fact she was clad in what appeared to be a nightgown, he could not tell.

"It is I who should apologize," Jean-Marc said. "I nearly kicked you in the head. Are you all right?"

"I'm fine," she said, tucking a curl behind her ear in a way he found charming. Reminiscent of Mary. Yes, very charming. She looked up at the sky. "I live in Chicago. I've never seen stars like this. Ever." Her hand swept across the heavens. "I was actually just sort of saying 'nice work, God'." She leaned against the railing. "I was hoping—praying, actually—you were wrong when you said it might storm."

"I'm glad I was wrong," Jean-Marc said. He motioned to the pilothouse. "You're welcome to climb up there. You'll be less likely to get stepped on."

"I don't want to be somewhere I shouldn't," she said. Again, so like Mary. That fear of overstepping. Was it an American trait, perhaps? Or a female one?

Thinking of his two wives, he now dismissed the second possibility. Neither of them had ever sacrificed their personal comfort over some "rule."

"You'll be fine up there," he had reassured her.

Over the next couple of days, fate had seemed to put the woman named Betty in his path often. At first he was suspicious, thinking perhaps she was just another single woman after a husband. He didn't like to think of himself as conceited, but the mirror told him he wasn't unattractive.

Even now, all these years later, he had to beware of the Dominique Chevaliers of the world. The years had begun to salt his dark hair with white streaks, but Dominique said that made him look "distinguished." The sea had weathered his skin, but when he looked in the mirror, he saw blue eyes shining out of a face that, while not handsome, was at least interesting. He'd even grown into his nose—somewhere in his middle 30s.

When he'd noticed Betty actually trying to avoid him once or twice, he realized she wasn't after a husband. Apparently all she wanted from Jean-Marc David was a nice cruise. He continued to find her at various places on the ship reading. As it turned out, she was reading a Bible. When he asked her about it, she joked, "I'm trying to discover the meaning of life." That was all. No sermon. Just an embarrassed little laugh. But he noticed she kept bowing her head before meals, and more than one night he saw her lying atop the pilothouse surveying the sky or leaning against the masthead singing quietly to herself.

Other religious people crossed his path after Betty. Some on land, but most were part of one sailing group or another. Not a huge number, but enough that Jean-Marc once joked to himself that if there was a God, he was tracking Jean-Marc David's progress via emissaries placed in tour groups.

The rain that had begun to fall while he ate dinner was letting up. With a clatter of dishes and scraping of chairs, many of the café's patrons rose to go, Jean-Marc among them. Outside, the scent of clean pavement and the glitter of the streetlights on the damp sidewalks tempted him to walk the distance back to his hotel on the Left Bank. It was a long way, but he had no timetable, and, he thought, if he wearied himself, perhaps he would sleep better. He crossed the Seine on the Pont de l'Archeveche, pausing to look toward Notre Dame. He had mellowed over the years, he realized. Piety didn't anger him so much now. Still, he worried that Luca Santo would think Jean-Marc David had come back into his life to be converted. He decided to postpone their dinner together. Maybe lunch after Christmas Eve. Maybe not.

EIGHTEEN

Jeff

I'M A WEAKLING. I INTENDED to stay far away from Miss Elizabeth Davis until after the first of the year. I got through not calling her that day I saw her downtown, and I figured I could probably avoid seeing her for the next couple of weeks. She'd go to Paris after Mary, and . . . well, after that, we'd see.

But then she called. Her voice on the phone was so different. Pleading, soft. She wasn't trying to manipulate. It sounded like she really needed me.

When she showed me that stack of newspaper clippings and other information about Mary, I was just as fascinated as she was. But I also felt vindicated. I had always suspected there was more to Mary Davis than met the eye. Probably because I liked her so much, and you always believe the best about people you like. But, the woman has a degree in French and a second major in business, for heaven's sake. It kind of takes Liz's reluctance to give her a real voice on the foundation board to a new level of absurdity.

The thing with Lizzie is, she's never been able to delegate anything. Her father was essentially the same way. Sam was, believe it or not, still giving orders about six hours before he died. You'd think a man would be making his peace with God, but Sam Davis was trying to make more money. It's the truth, and for the first time I think I fully realize how tragic that is. Liz wasn't at Sam's side in his last hours. He told her he wanted her in the office "with her boots on," so to speak. She finally disobeyed that command and headed home when Mary called her. By the time she got there, though, Sam was nearly gone. As far as I know, he didn't have any last words for either of them.

I don't know how this will all play out, but I think what is going on is that Liz thinks that if she builds a relationship with Mary, she is somehow betraying Sam. And that girl is so securely lashed to her image of Samuel Frederick Davis, she can't seem to entertain the idea that maybe he wasn't the man she thought.

Personally, I don't see why that has to be such a crisis. No one is perfect. Sam had great qualities—qualities I admire. There were also some things about him I didn't like. Lizzie needs to realize she can love the good and forgive the bad, and Sam can rest in peace while she gets to know her mother better.

I hope things are beginning to change. Thank heavens, Irene Baxter stowed away all that information about the pre-Sam Mary. Liz doesn't know what to think of it right now, but she'll figure it out in time. As soon as her passport comes, she—we—are on our way to Paris. I relented and told her I'd help her. We're making a list of hotels near the Sorbonne, and I'm going to start calling them tomorrow.

At the moment Liz is frightened. She's teetering on the edge of some new discoveries that may change her view of the past. She's never been good at admitting she's wrong. That's the Samuel Davis in her. But there's a softer side, too. I know it's there because I fell in love with it.

Liz

I'M FRIGHTENED. Right now I feel like nothing in my universe has ever been as it seemed. All these things about Mother I never knew. . . . I can't understand why Daddy would have made her put that all away. One of the things I love about Jeff is he isn't threatened by someone like me. I mean, I'm a strong, independent woman, and I have a measure of success— although I'm the first to admit I've had a lot handed to me on a silver platter. But I've done some things on my own, too. The company stock has risen in value since Daddy died. I'd like to think that's because I've done a good job. The foundation has raised the funds for the new oncology wing. And some smaller things have been accomplished, as well.

At any rate, Jeff isn't threatened by all that. He's his own man. He reminds me of Daddy that way. Except now I'm beginning to think Daddy wasn't the person I knew. I can't understand why he would have demanded Mother stop playing the violin. What difference could that have possibly made in a marriage? How could music have been a negative? And why didn't he give her a position in his own company? She certainly had the credentials to deserve it. I was born the first year they were married, so maybe she wanted to be home with me. I want to know if that's it . . . or if she had to give up a career. Because of Daddy.

There's so much I want to ask her, but first I have to find her. Jeff assures me we will, but looking at that list of hotels, I wonder. And my passport still hasn't come. I've sent several e-mails to Mother's mailbox. No response. She said everything is all right, but I would give anything to get another message from her.

I've taken a good long look at myself in the last few days. I don't like a lot of what I see. It's no wonder Jeff wanted to take a step back. I'm so glad Irene handed me that brown envelope. It certainly opened my eyes. The shame of it all is that it took the envelope to open them. Mother has never done anything but try to be a good mom. Most of the time, I brushed that aside as minimal effort and wondered why she didn't do something worthwhile with her life. I remember Hillary Clinton once saying something to the effect that she became a lawyer because she wanted to do something more important with her life than bake cookies. A lot of women got really angry at that. I didn't see why.

When I asked Mother about it, she just smiled and said, "There is nothing in this world more challenging than molding an eternal soul, Elizabeth. And nothing more important than investing in a marriage and a child." She reached across and patted my hand. "Your Daddy is high maintenance, sweetheart. I knew it when I told him I'd marry him. I have no right to complain." She winked, "And besides that, I make the best chocolate chip cookies this side of the Missouri."

Looking back, I remember thinking she was just trying to make herself feel good for not having accomplished very much with her life beyond a clean house. Now I see what she gave up for Daddy and me, and I am so ashamed of myself. I don't think I've ever even thanked her.

I'm so glad Jeff said he would come with me. I'm scared to death about the whole thing. I mean, where do you start to build a close relationship after twenty-eight years of wrong presuppositions and judgments? Talk about a shift in the universe. It's odd that I have no trouble at all running a board meeting, no trouble handling hostile competitors, but the thought of talking to my mother—the *real* one, not the one created in Sam Davis's image—terrifies me.

Mary

December 23, 2003

 The moment of truth is almost upon me. As December the 24th approaches, I notice I am a little more jittery than usual. I miss Annie Templeton, too. I've never grown so close to someone in such a short time. Of course that, too, is a factor of Sam. I wasn't all that close to Sam after being married to him for twenty-seven years. "That's a factor of Sam" is becoming sort of an all-inclusive term for me these days.

 It's a factor of Sam that I haven't played the violin since 1974.

 It's a factor of Sam that I didn't have any close friends.

 It's a factor of Sam that I never used my college degrees.

 But I was writing about Annie Templeton. In a couple weeks' time, Annie has begun to be the daughter I never had. The one who listens to me play the violin, who wants me to try new things, who doesn't see me through glasses fashioned by Sam. . . . and that, I suppose, is why it's best that Annie Templeton went home to England for the holiday. Being around Annie makes Liz's opinion of me hurt even more. What is developing with Annie is what I've always wanted with Liz.

 This has to stop. All the regrets about all the things Liz doesn't know about just have to stop. I don't know if Jean-Marc David is going to show up tomorrow night or not, but I've begun to realize that I can't tie my future to a man ever again. I still hope Jean-Marc comes. But I don't want to be saying "It's a factor of Jean-Marc" twenty-five years from now. At least not as an excuse for why certain good things didn't happen.

Good things. Sam brought a lot of good things into my life. I have to get past the resenting of the things he took away and start remembering the things he gave me. And, of course, at the top of that list would be Elizabeth. If life were as it seems. But, then, the truth is . . . Liz is not a factor of Sam.

Irene

NOW I KNOW my singing sounds more like a rattle in my throat than a song, but it's the best I can do, and I have reason to sing. First, it's Christmas Eve morning, and I'm making Cecil eggs for the umpteenth time, and it's a blessing to have a healthy, loving husband—even if he won't try new food for breakfast.

But it gets better. Elizabeth is coming around. Showing her those papers of her mother's was the right thing to do. Now she seems to have an almost insatiable hunger to know more. She's made me talk about her mother for hours at a time—which, come to think of it, hasn't done my singing voice any good. I'm downright hoarse from all the talking. As nearly as I can tell, Lizzie and me have pretty much relived the whole of her life right here in this kitchen during the past few days. The girl has had more questions than a giraffe has spots. She hasn't liked all the answers she's got, but I've done my best to give them straight and let Lizzie sort them out.

Another reason I'm singing is because of Mr. Jeffrey Scott. He's going to Paris with Lizzie. It seems like his and Lizzie's romance is growing by leaps and bounds. Even when he's on the phone in the other room calling hotels in Paris, it's like there's a ribbon stretching between the two of them. He's gone a while, then comes into the kitchen and pats her shoulder or kisses her cheek. Or they put on their coats and go for a walk. Or he makes himself some hot chocolate—Jeffrey doesn't like coffee—and slides next to her, and they snuggle for a while. And that reminds me of the way Cecil and I used to carry on when we were courting. Cecil isn't my first love, but he's not second-best, either, and when we were younger we did our share of cuddling. We still do, even if there is a man named "Arthur Itis" who comes between us from time to time.

Another reason I'm singing is Mrs. Davis e-mailed again. She had read Lizzie's mail—and I guess there was a lot of it—and she told Lizzie things are going to be all right and that she'll be home soon. It wasn't much, but it sure set the tone for the holidays here in Omaha, which are going to be quiet but happy. I'm going to bake four Cornish hens on Christmas Day, and Lizzie and Jeffrey and Cecil and I are going to have us a good time. And then, on the 27th, Jeffrey and Lizzie will fly on over to Paris and surprise Mrs. Davis.

That's the other reason I'm singing. Lizzie's passport came.

So Merry Christmas to all, and to all a good night.

NINETEEN

Mary

THE HOTEL IS QUIET AS I descend the stairs. Everyone seems to have found their place for the holiday, and when I go out onto the street, it too is deserted. Even the rows of cars that usually line both sides of the street are absent. I head down to the plaza where Annie and Adolpho and friends often play their open-air concerts, wondering how their holiday is going. She is an only child, and her parents have certain expectations—none of which, Annie says, she has lived up to. They want her to be a concert cellist. She wants to play both violin and cello—both more for her own amusement than as a calling. They want her to stay on their side of "the pond." She wants to experience the world. They want her to marry and have already chosen The One. She wants to marry, but his name is Adolpho.

I pause for a moment, wishing the fountains were playing their solitary water music. Down the street, a couple walk by, huddling close to one another. It's cool enough that I can see my own breath. I hope it doesn't rain. I've taken a silly amount of time with my impossible hair. It probably looks the same now as it did an hour ago when I got out of the shower. Curly hair is like that. The curl has relaxed as it's turned gray. I'm grateful for that. But most of the time I still despair over the styling. Annie says I should just let it go natural. But Annie thinks dreadlocks are attractive.

Wandering down the Boulevard Saint-Michel, I dawdle, noticing things I've ignored these past weeks. I'm trying to be casual, but as I get closer to the Seine, I walk faster and faster. I reach the river out of breath and feeling ridiculous. I shouldn't rush. If he remembers Christmas Eve twenty-nine years ago, he'll know not to come until after dark. I turn left, instead of right. Eventually, I cross the Pont Neuf—I never think of it without smiling. It's the "new bridge"—the one built in 1607. The lampposts are works of art, each one cast bronze, the base a series of clawed feet, the ornate work featuring stylized creatures who watch passersby from their perches near the lights above. I pause halfway across the bridge, thinking of all the people who pass this way every day, all the dreams and wishes and promises that have come true here or have been washed away as the water flowed below. Ahead of me is Notre Dame, her outline somewhat indistinct in the waning light before the floodlights come on.

Behind me and below, tires screech and voices shout. It would seem that even Christmas Eve doesn't improve the mood of some Parisian drivers. I look at my watch. There is still too much time. Finally, I head up the opposite side of the river. None of the bouquinistes are open this evening. Their boxes— portable "shops" hung along the concrete railing lining both sides of the Seine—are closed and locked. I wonder where the little lady who usually perches on a wrought-iron stool at the entrance is spending Christmas Eve. Dressed in one evening gown or another, complete with hat and gloves, she always smiles sweetly at those who pass by, arranging the many layers of costume jewelry around her neck, adjusting her sunglasses, hopping down with energy that belies her white hair to wrap a bouquet for a customer. Even though her shop is closed this evening, she has forgotten to take the iron stool inside. It stands beside the entryway, a throne awaiting the queen's return. I wonder what the flower lady wears for a dress-up occasion. I envision her in a rhinestone-studded tulle gown and tiara, surrounded by loving great-grandchildren who think that Great-Granny, albeit a bit dotty, is the gem of the family tree. Even eccentric little old ladies spend Christmas with their families. With a pang of loneliness, I wish for home where Irene is likely baking cinnamon rolls for her traditional Christmas Eve chili-and-rolls dinner. I hope she is making some for Elizabeth and Jeffrey. Some customs should never change.

The bells of Notre Dame ring. I walk back onto the bridge. Fog is moving in, shrouding the tops of the bell towers, reflecting the light of the city spotlights so that everything is enveloped by an amber glow. Closing my eyes, I am taken back to 1974 and another time when the bells of Notre Dame rang at the precise moment when I first said the words *I love you.* . . .

My professor had arranged a long weekend in Paris at the beginning of my studies, but it was obvious early on that a long weekend wasn't going to be enough for me. The city called to me all the weeks of my schooling in Arcachon, and as soon as I turned in the final research paper, I begged Professor Max for permission to go back to Paris.

As it turned out, Mr. Davis, the man whose friend's Rolls Royce had been in the Concours d'Elégance, said he was driving back to the city in preparation for his return to the United States and he would be happy to give me a ride.

Jean-Marc had offered to come to Paris with me—although

I knew he hated big cities. But there was a regatta the weekend I wanted to go. Jean-Marc and I had a fierce argument. He had a chance to win this year, he said, and he didn't see why I couldn't understand that. He also didn't understand why I wouldn't want to be there for him. But I had a chance not only to hear Menuhin play the Bartok Sonata but to meet him personally—courtesy of Mr. Davis—and I didn't see how Jean-Marc could be so selfish as to deny me the dream of a lifetime.

Jean-Marc stayed in Arcachon, and I rode with Mr. Davis to Paris. He even arranged for me to stay with friends of his in the part of Paris called the Marais. The Marais was interesting in its own way, but I preferred haunting the bookstores and the tearooms of the Latin Quarter. I wandered the halls of the Louvre for hours.

One day I looked up and there was Mr. Davis, asking me to call him Sam, inviting me to lunch, and generally being very charming and helpful. I met Menuhin as promised. I was on Sam Davis's arm that evening, feeling like a princess in a fairy tale, wondering when I would wake up.

Sam kept an eye on me that week. He didn't intrude, and he wasn't conspicuous, but more than once when I came out of a museum or store, there he was, waiting, inviting me to lunch or dinner. He treated me to a meal at La Tour d'Argent, laughing at my naiveté and insisting my ignorance of upscale restaurants was charming. He complimented my French—his was mediocre at best—and basically made me feel a lot like Cinderella.

But I missed Jean-Marc. Christmas Eve night I had intended to go to mass at Notre Dame to hear a well-known organist play. There was something about the city that night—it was rainy and foggy—that contributed to an uneasy feeling I had had for days. I had determined, in fact, to leave the next morning and go back to Arcachon. There wasn't much conscious thought or planning in the decision, but I was beginning to feel uncomfortable accepting all the attention Sam Davis was showering on me. It seemed somehow disloyal to Jean-Marc.

So there I was on Christmas Eve, feeling homesick for a place that wasn't really home, realizing I was in love with Jean-Marc David and wondering if he missed me at all. I sat down on a bench in the garden behind Notre Dame, not intending to cry, but suddenly wrapped up in sentiment. I closed my eyes and leaned back and listened to the bells . . . and he was there. Jean-Marc. He had taken a train and walked around the city all day trying to find me. He'd just about given up, but then remembered I had mentioned going to mass at Notre Dame. He was on his way inside when . . . there I was in the garden.

He gave me a kiss—the kind of kiss a woman never forgets. Sweet, urgent, demanding, waiting. . . . there was an entire new world wrapped up in that kiss. We whispered our love. We walked. We kissed. We never went inside the cathedral for mass.

He isn't coming. I should have known. I have waited here on this bench until I am cold and stiff. The first rush of the faithful into the church has already come out. The organ has played, the choir has sung, the bells have rung. I've walked around the garden more than once, reminding myself to appreciate the glimpses of color in the tall narrow windows. I've walked to the river and watched the water and reminisced . . . and . . . it's enough. I guess I've learned what I wanted to know. No answer is, after all, still an answer. And the things we don't do sometimes say more than the things we do.

Taking a deep breath, I look back through the fog at the church. I see the flying buttresses soaring up to the top of walls that they've held in place through several centuries, including two world wars. All around me are buildings that have outlasted many human lives and will, likely, outlast countless more. There's a lesson in it all . . . and that lesson, I think, is that I've been a fool to think my little worries are of concern to the God who inspired cathedrals.

Pathetic. I'm pathetic. What in the world am I doing . . . coming halfway around the world looking for . . . what, exactly, am I looking for?

I know what I'm *hoping* for. Love. The kind of love Sam Davis couldn't give me. The kind of love Jean-Marc promised—and I was too frightened to accept.

Say good-bye, Mary McKibbin Davis. Once and for all, say good-bye. What's done is done. You can't go home again. And whatever you are looking for, it isn't here in Paris.

I picture Jean-Marc David, wherever he is, laughing at the idea of his old flame waiting in this garden for a silly reunion he won't attend. And why would he?

You can't go home again.

You can't go home again.

You can't.

The bells begin to ring again. My tears are threatening. I get up and head for the path along the river. I'll cross the bridge to the south and take a trek through Little Athens, just for old times' sake.

"*Marie? Marie, c'est toi? C'est vraiment toi?*"

I'm just imagining it. It's the bells . . . and the—

"*C'est moi, Marie. Jean-Marc. Comment vas-tu, chérie? Mais tu es belle . . . si belle. . . . encore . . . si belle. . . .*"

Those Nordic blue eyes still smile. I open my mouth to speak, but I can't find words. He's called me *chérie* . . . dear. He thinks I'm still beautiful. I should say something, but I can't. He kisses both my cheeks. He laughs. I smile, but I still can't speak. I suppose the tears running down my cheeks say enough, for he opens his arms. And I step in.

The bells, bells, bells . . . the bells.

TWENTY

JEAN-MARC CALLS ME AT noon on Christmas Day. "I'm sorry, *chérie*. We were up so late, and I know I should be letting you sleep today, but is there a chance you'd join me for lunch? My hotel concierge knows of a little place in St. Germain that will be open."

We go, lingering over the meal, talking almost nonstop until the grandfatherly waiter sets dessert before us. Looking down at the puff pastry filled with whipped cream and garnished with a raspberry and a sprig of something green, I shake my head. "I can't. It looks divine, but I can't. I'm just too full."

"Just taste it," Jean-Marc urges. "My grandmother used to make this on special occasions." He dips his spoon in the sauce and holds it out to me. I can feel the color rising in my cheeks. Embarrassment over blushing only makes it worse. My cheeks must be glowing as I allow myself to be fed. At the first burst of flavor in my mouth I nod my head in agreement. *"Délicieux."*

"I told you." He smiles. "We'll wait awhile. You'll find room."

The years have not diminished the persuasive power of those

blue eyes. "All right," I say, and lean back with my hands in my lap. "It's your turn to talk. Do you still play Chopin?"

"Too many days at sea," he replies, shaking his head from side to side. "But I'm thinking perhaps I should take it up again. My quarters in the *Sea Cloud* are large enough. I could have a small piano. Or perhaps one of those keyboards I hear about." He smiles again. "I tried to play your favorite the other day."

"Really?" My heart is pounding. I can feel myself trembling. Trying to act as calm as possible, I take a bite of the dessert.

Jean-Marc nods. "Yes. The day I got your letter. I tucked it into my pocket and went into the conservatory at the house, sat down and—" he laughs softly—"made a mess of it."

I swallow the dessert, not even noticing how it tastes. "I was afraid the house would have been demolished to make way for some development of apartments for vacationing Parisians by now."

"It's the same as when you were there last, except I had the pines in the back taken down so I could see the bay and . . . *her*."

I smile. "My friend, Annie, practically had to resuscitate me when I saw the *Sea Cloud* on your Web site. I couldn't believe you actually did it. She belongs to you."

The blue eyes warm with pride. "For seven years now," he says.

"That's wonderful."

Jean-Marc tilts his head, considering. I notice a scar running along the curve of his jaw. I am noticing his physique entirely too much. I take another bite of dessert.

"Yes. And no. My daughter would say the ship owns me . . . not the other way around." He sighs and shrugs. "In many ways I suppose she is right. A lady like the *Sea Cloud* requires a lot of care." He looks at me. "Celine thinks I should retire. I think she finds comfort in the mental picture of her father as a doddering old man tending the roses in her garden in Tuscany."

I chuckle. "I don't think you're ready to dodder quite yet. Tell me more."

Jean-Marc tells me about buying the *Sea Cloud*. He describes his grandsons. He recounts hiring his assistant, Paul Garnier.

"Your Paul Garnier sounds like my Cecil Baxter back home," I say. "Loyal, knowledgeable, and detail oriented."

"Exactly," Jean-Marc agrees. "I don't really know what I'd do without him. He's taken care of things in Arcachon so well, sometimes I think I could disappear and not be missed for weeks."

"But that enables you to do exactly that, right? You can disappear at sea, and nothing is the worse for it." I don't remember eating it, but I've finished dessert.

Jean-Marc orders espresso, and we linger until, by the time I am back in my hotel room, I realize it is six A.M. the morning *after* Christmas in Omaha. I dial Liz's number, mentally preparing an apology. No one answers. Leaving a "Merry Christmas—I am fine" sort of message, I dial home. Again, there is no answer.

The next time the phone rings, I glance at the clock, surprised to see it is nearly noon. I fail in my attempt to hide my fatigue and to sound cheerful as I bring the headset to my ear.

"You're exhausted, *chérie*," Jean-Marc says. "I can hear it in your voice." He pauses. "How about this? I have an old friend living in Paris. We were supposed to have dinner last week, but it didn't work out. His business is closed the week of Christmas, so it's a good time for us to have lunch together. I'll go see him now. You and I can go to dinner later—after you've had some rest. Have you heard from your daughter?" When I say no, Jean-

Marc replies, "Even more reason for you to stay by the phone. I'll come by later today."

Reluctantly, I agree. After trying to call home again with no result, I fall back into bed, sleeping soundly for another hour. I spend the rest of the afternoon soaking in a hot bath, reading, and writing in my journal.

Jean-Marc arrives early that evening, and together we walk down the hill, around the corner, and toward the Luxembourg Gardens, where we make our way down a long stretch of wide walkway first, then onto less-trafficked pathways, finally coming to rest on a bench facing a dormant fountain almost overgrown by vines.

"I'd like you to meet my daughter," Jean-Marc says abruptly.

"That would be lovely."

"I almost named her for you."

Nervous laughter erupts as I react. "And what would her mother have had to say about that?!"

"Celine's mother was . . . uninvolved. I don't want to be unkind, and I've taken great care that my daughter not think of herself as an 'accident,' but . . ."

"I see." The subject of daughters makes me uncomfortable.

"You've never seen Tuscany, have you?" Jean-Marc asks.

When I say no, he begins to describe Celine's villa near Florence. And he urges me to come with him to meet her. "You can meet them all—Celine, Xavier, Olivier." His enthusiasm for the idea grows, and he concludes the invitation with, "And then we'll make our way back to Arcachon and the *Sea Cloud*." Something on my face must be telegraphing uncertainty, because suddenly he stops. "I'm sorry," he says. When he speaks again, his voice is calmer. "I've overwhelmed you." He chuckles and pats the back of my hand. "You see, I haven't changed so much since

I was an impetuous boy, have I?"

He takes my hand in his, and while I don't pull away, I do dodge the invitation. "Annie Templeton expects to call on me at the hotel when she gets back from her holiday this week. She was taking her young man home to England. . . ." I have told him about Annie briefly when I mentioned seeing his Web site. I tell him about Adolpho and Enzo, and then with my own version of impetuous behavior, I say, "You'll like them."

Jean-Marc seems to like the idea of meeting my friends. "I'd like anyone you speak of so highly," he says, then leans over and nudges my shoulder. "I do wonder, though, how it is I know so much about a British girl named Annie Templeton and so little about Elizabeth Davis. Do you realize you've said almost nothing about your daughter?"

My heart begins to thump again. I look away. "Elizabeth is intelligent, organized, beautiful. When Sam left her in charge of the company, he had full confidence she could handle it. And she's proven him right."

"So why do you not talk about her more?"

I shrug. "Liz loves me because I'm her mother, but she doesn't really respect me as a woman. She is of the generation that doesn't see being a wife and mother as a worthy full-time career."

The silence between us looms large. It is not exactly awkward, but it is not comfortable. Jean-Marc breaks it with another question. "Were you happy?"

Our eyes meet. "I was . . . content. After a while. I learned to be content." I can't say any more, and I look away, self-conscious and nervous about the direction the conversation has taken.

Jean-Marc returns to the initial subject. "And your daughter," he says. "Tell me more about her."

I speak of Jeff first, praising him as the perfect match for my strong-willed daughter before boasting a little about Elizabeth's business accomplishments. "So you can see," I conclude, "how she might fail to appreciate a full-time homemaker."

Jean-Marc is animated as he scolds, "Why do you see failure in what you have just told me about your life? Elizabeth should respect what you've done. There is no finer thing in life than to make another human being happy. From what I understand you to say, Samuel Davis was not an easy man to please. You stayed with him. And surely Elizabeth appreciates what you gave up to be the little full-time homemaker?" He waits for the answer. I don't know how to respond without seeming disloyal to Sam. He realizes the meaning of my silence. "*Mon Dieu!* You never told her about your music? About your own plans?"

I shake my head. "Sam didn't want her to know."

"And you agreed to that?"

"I . . . I had a good reason," is all I can manage to say.

He is angry now. Not at me, but at the circumstance. He gestures more forcefully as he speaks, getting up to pace back and forth while he lectures. "What possible reason could be good enough to make a woman give up the essence of who she is to look after a man who is so insecure as to demand the absurd!" When he pauses to take a breath, he looks down at me, and as quickly as it came, the anger is gone. He sits back down. "I'm sorry," he apologizes. "It's just that it really does not make any sense to me." He leans forward, resting his elbows on his knees, focusing on the ground. His voice is gentle when he asks, "Why did you write to me, *chérie?*"

"I'm not sure I know." I am fighting back tears, wishing I had never written the letter that has resulted in so much soul-searching and so many questions I cannot answer.

"I don't believe that." He gets up. "You do know. You just won't tell me." Leaning down, he reaches for my hands and pulls me to my feet. "It is all right," he reassures me. "It is a lovely evening in Paris. We will take a walk. I promise not to react so forcefully again. Tell me only what pleases you. Be yourself."

"Myself," I mutter, aware of the bitterness in my voice but unable to disguise it. I take a deep breath, and the words tumble out. "Which self shall I be? The Mary who loved the feel of sea spray on her face? The Mary who betrayed her first love? The Mary who bowed to the selfishness of an older man? The Mary who—"

"Shhhh. Stop." Jean-Marc touches my cheek. "There is no need to be so frantic. You had the opportunity to choose between adventure and security. You chose the latter." He pauses, then says slowly, "I loved you, Mary McKibbin, but I would likely have made you miserable. All the things you have just mentioned about yourself—the strengths *and* the weaknesses—are all facets of the whole woman." He traces my jawline with his finger. "And I find the way the parts have come together exquisite."

"I don't feel whole," I blurt it out, and when his blue eyes are kind, I keep going. "I feel like I've left splinters of myself everywhere I've been. I left the sea when I agreed to let Sam drive me to Paris. And you. I left you. I left my music." My voice is trembling. I'm embarrassed by it, but I don't stop talking. "I left so much behind trying to be what Sam wanted, I don't know if I even remember who I am anymore. Or if I ever will. And what's worse, I don't know if I even deserve—" I finally give up and hide my face in my hands.

"So this is what the letter is really about," Jean-Marc says, and all the while he is prying my hands away from my face and pulling me into his arms. He smells of cigarette smoke and cologne. His beard tickles the side of my face as he strokes the back of my head and talks. "Not so much about seeing an old friend . . . as about righting an old wrong. You take too much on yourself, *chérie*. You say you betrayed me. I have come to think of it in a different way. You pushed me to do something I feared." When I try to protest, he holds me tighter. "Yes, yes. I know. I had the dream. But I don't know if I ever would have really sailed away. That night, when I knew you were lost to me, I went out on my own without thinking. And that started me down a road that led to the *Sea Cloud*. I might never have done that if you had stayed with me."

He steps away, and then, reaching behind me, he brings his hands over my head, pretending to hold something heavy that he has just taken from my shoulders. "In any event," he says, "let's just take this weight off your lovely shoulders and . . ." He pantomimes throwing it into the vine-covered fountain. "There." He wipes his hands of imaginary dust before leaning down and kissing my cheek. "Gone." He traces the tear on my cheek. "What's this?"

I sniff and wipe the tear away. "Relief, I guess." I cannot look at him. Instead, I study the fountain.

"Did you really think I would have carried a grudge against a shy little American girl for nearly thirty years?" He steps before me and blocks my view of the fountain, forcing me to look up at him.

I laugh nervously and shake my head, swiping at another tear. "That would make me much more important in your life than I really was, wouldn't it?"

Sitting back down, Jean-Marc pulls me down beside him. He takes my hand. "A man never forgets his first love, Marie." He pronounces it the way he used to long ago. *Marie.* With the French *r.* "Always," he continues, "he keeps a special place for her in his heart. I loved you very much. And once I came to terms with losing you—which took a while, I will admit—I also did my best to keep bitterness from creeping in." He puts his open palm across his heart. "I have kept the memory of you safe. And while at times it hurt me . . . at times it gave me wings."

I inhale deeply, feeling some of the tension leave my body. "I'm just so sorry for hurting you that way."

"Enough." He speaks the word even as he stands up and pulls me up off the bench beside him. "Enough apologies, enough sadness." Leading me along, he makes his way out of the garden and across the street to a flower shop. He snatches up two huge bouquets and then leads us toward the Seine. We emerge onto the Quai de Conti, where Jean-Marc takes me down the stairs and along the river to an empty bench beneath a tree.

"These," he says, holding out the bouquets, "are the hurts of the past." He pulls a blossom off its stem and tosses it into the water. "There is the night Sam Davis announced you were his. This"—he takes another blossom and does the same—"is the train ride back to Arcachon alone . . . setting sail without you. . . ."

He continues pulling blossoms from the bouquet and tossing them into the river, recounting disappointments until the first of the two bouquets is nothing more than bare stems. Laying the other bouquet down, he puts his arms around me. "You see, Marie. They float away. All the hurts. And still, you are in my arms." He kisses the back of my neck and I feel goose bumps rise on my arms.

"Now," he holds up the other bouquet and pulls a blossom off and hands it to me. "Your turn."

Taking the flower in my hand, I step to the water's edge and whisper, "The look in your eyes that night . . . thinking about the empty slip where your boat should have been . . . the letter I never wrote. . . ." I follow Jean-Marc's example, sending my regrets down the Seine until only one flower is left. Inhaling its scent, I joke that I have run out of sorrows. I sit down beside Jean-Marc, watching the blossoms float out of sight, keenly aware of the one that remains.

THE NEXT EVENING, Jean-Marc and I head down the Boulevard Saint-Michel, past the shops selling everything from used textbooks to umbrellas, from Doc Martens shoes to Levis, past the iron-fenced ruins of Roman baths, and into the several-block area known as Little Athens where narrow streets are drenched with the varied aromas of cuisine from around the world.

As we round a corner Jean-Marc leans over and whispers, "Do you remember how we could hardly pass a doorway without someone smiling at you and trying to lure us inside? And how jealous I was?"

I shake my head and laugh, "We won't have to be concerned about that tonight."

"Monsieur, vous avez une belle femme." The speaker calls out from where he is leaning against the doorframe of his tiny Arabic restaurant.

I can feel myself blushing at the man's flagrant flirtation. The fact that he's assumed I am Jean-Marc's wife adds to my embarrassment.

"Ce n'est pas ma femme, monsieur, mais vous avez raison," Jean-Marc banters as he takes my hand and tucks it beneath his arm, *"elle est belle."* Ever the gentleman, Jean-Marc corrects the man's assumption about our being married but agrees with the comment about my beauty.

"Pas votre femme?" the Arab replies, clucking his tongue. *"C'est dommage."*

"You see, Marie," Jean-Marc says, patting my hand, "European men have better eyes. We see with our heart . . . which reveals the woman inside."

When we pass another restaurant, and yet another man winks at me, I protest. "I know it's their job to flirt—" I can't resist a chuckle—"but I had forgotten how good they are at it."

A short distance up the street I stop to admire an artistically woven collection of sticks and natural stems serving as an awning across both the doorway and the display window of a restaurant called Les Argonauts. Hung with varicolored glass bulbs and ornaments, the creation serves both to draw attention to the restaurant and to celebrate the holidays. The proprietor, a short, swarthy man with glorious dark eyes, waves toward the display window, where a mouth-watering array of meats and seafood rests atop shaved ice. I marvel at the artistic display, pointing to a swirl of bright red shrimp and lobster tails garnished with lemon and lime slices and a fresh herb I don't recognize.

The restaurateur thanks me for the compliment, adding in English, "But it is in the cooking that the art is fully realized." He motions toward the doorway and points inside where rows of tables extend from wall to wall, with only a narrow passageway down the center left open to give guests and waiters access to the tables. The aroma of grilling meat wafts toward the door. "We grill fresh lamb for you. We have music." He leans toward me with a conspiratorial whisper and a wink. "Dancing!"

"Je ne danse pas," I say quickly and shake my head.

"No dancing?" the man protests. "But, madame, not to dance is not to live." He addresses Jean-Marc. "You come inside. Eat with us. You no like, you no pay. And—" he raises both eyebrows and nods at us both before leaning closer again as if to share a secret—"I give you free glass of good wine. You toast to friendship, eh?"

Jean-Marc inhales deeply. "It does smell wonderful, *chérie.*"

We follow the Greek inside. He shows us to a table toward the back, close to a tiny stage where two men perched on high stools quietly strum the Greek version of a guitar. I can't remember the name of the instrument, and it bothers me. Once seated, I look up at the timbered ceiling hung with every size, shape, and color of paper lanterns imaginable. The restaurant is awash in charm—and oblivious to fire codes.

The Greek summons a waiter. "For *m'sieur et madame,* special service tonight, eh?"

The waiter nods. Watching their unspoken communication, I wonder how many thousands of times this guy has lured customers into his establishment with the same routine of compliment-the-lady, promise-free-food, treat-them-like-old-friends.

With some encouragement from Jean-Marc, the waiter lets it be known that he is a relative newcomer to Paris, a student with family in Chicago, and he plans to join them someday and open his own Greek restaurant in America. He shares his plans with a wink in my direction. "What better way to spend a life than to give pleasure to beautiful women, eh?" Then he turns to Jean-Marc, "You must convince her m'sieur—it appears the American lady does not believe what all Greeks know." He grins at me. "Wine and women—they both improve with age."

As the waiter struts away to place our order with the cook, I swirl the wine in my glass and take a sip. I am feeling awkward and out of place.

Jean-Marc reaches across the table and lifts my chin, his eyes searching mine as he asks, "What has happened to you, *mon amie*? In times past, you would have given that young man a happy reply, and the two of you would likely have ended the evening by dancing in the aisle behind me. All in fun."

"I got old," I reply. "And I can see through their . . . flattery." I shake my head. "It's just a game. Of lies."

"It is a game, of course," Jean-Marc agrees, "but there was a time when you enjoyed life enough to play."

Before I can answer, the waiter, Alain, arrives with the food—oversized platters bearing skewers of grilled meat along with baked potatoes and salad. The musicians begin to sing, and conversation without shouting becomes impossible. With my first bite of a gigantic prawn, I realize that, while the Greek restaurateur might have played a familiar game to lure us inside, his promises about his food were true. Between each sampling of succulent lamb and tender steak on the skewers, a fresh wedge of tomato or green pepper provides the perfect way of cleansing the palate for the next delight. I am barely halfway through my meal when the musicians end their rousing folk song and resume quietly providing background music for the diners. Jean-Marc returns to his storytelling, and I am content to savor my dinner and listen.

We are enjoying our after-dinner coffee when Jean-Marc sets his cup down and says, "Enough about the past. What does Mary Davis have in mind for her future now that she is an independent woman of means?"

The motto back on my desk in Omaha flashes through my

mind. I shrug, then tell him about the memorial foundation and its work.

"This foundation, then—it is your new passion?"

I shake my head. "Not really. It's good work. Important. But, Elizabeth is very efficient. She doesn't really need my help with any of it." Leaning back in my chair, I take a sip of water before saying, "Liz doesn't really see me as an asset to the foundation. She thinks of me as little more than the decorative element in Samuel Davis's life."

"Were you?"

"Was I what?"

"Only the decorative element."

"In some ways, yes," I say, hurrying to add, "in some ways, no."

"And were you happy?"

Those Nordic blue eyes are pulling me in again. How could this be happening—after all these years. What was that poem he'd whispered one night on the beach. . . ? *"I have no power over my eyes."* I realize that if I am not careful, I am going to have no power over my words. I look away. "As I said the other day, I learned to be content." I force a smile. "Sam's world was fairly well defined. He liked order. Predictability. Dinner precisely at seven and all that. I did it well."

"I imagine you did," Jean-Marc says, nodding slowly.

Behind him, our waiter is coaxing an American woman, with an *I Love NY* T-shirt stretched across her ample bosom, from her chair. Directing her to stand beside him, he demonstrates a simple dance step. They move sideways up the narrow central aisle toward our table. The woman's boisterous American friends begin to hoot and clap their approval, and Alain and the young woman link arms and make their way back down the aisle.

Suddenly Jean-Marc stands up and holds out his hand to me.

I shake my head *no* and look around, hoping no one has noticed.

He pleads, "For old times' sake, *mon amie*."

When Alain calls out encouragement, the rest of the diners join in, urging me on. My cheeks are blazing as I stand up and follow Jean-Marc to the front of the restaurant. I am grateful when another couple joins us.

As Jean-Marc raises his palms above his head, I reach up and lace my fingers through his, leaning close enough for him to hear me say, "I will kill you for this later. And dump your body into the Seine."

Jean-Marc's blue eyes sparkle as he throws his head back and laughs. "To die for dancing with a beautiful woman—it is an honorable death, *n'est-ce pas?*"

The restaurant resounds with music and clapping as we make our way up the aisle to the slow, swaying rhythm provided by strumming guitars. Gradually, the musicians quicken the pace. More patrons join in, linking arms, stepping back and forth, back and forth.

Alain reaches above him and slaps a row of bells hanging among the paper lanterns, then rips the scarf serving as a belt from around his waist and tosses it to Jean-Marc, who snatches it from the air and flings it around my waist. He holds each end, never violating the circle of open space between us. For the first time since our reunion in the garden behind Notre Dame, I do not look away from Jean-Marc's Nordic blue eyes. In the midst of the music and the bells, the aroma of grilled steak and cigarette smoke, the light of lanterns above and candles on the tables, the years disappear. I lift my hands above my head and clap in time with the music. Somewhere between the last two verses of the raucous song, the weight of years and expectations, of guilt and dead dreams falls away, and I am once again a girl in love with a boy, lost in the music, where neither wrinkles nor gray hair nor age matter. With the last notes of the song, Jean-Marc tosses the scarf aside and lifts me into his arms. He whirls around, laughing, and kissing my cheek as he carries me the few steps to our table. When he puts me down he kisses me again—but not on the cheek. I kiss back.

The musicians begin another song—soft guitar and gentle voices, and we plop into our chairs, breathless and laughing, sharing secretive smiles. Jean-Marc lifts his water glass, and we toast one another before he switches to wine, emptying his glass before snatching up a slice of the baguette between us. He tears off the crust and pops it into his mouth.

"It would seem," he says, "that you *do* dance, after all."

We walk back to my hotel arm in arm. Just outside the hotel entrance, Jean-Marc links his other arm through mine and, while he hums the tune, we repeat the Greek folk dance, moving down the sidewalk to the corner, back to the doorway, inside and toward the winding stairs where two new hotel guests stand waiting for the elevator, unaware of the discrepancy in size between the square footage required for their luggage and the interior of the tiny elevator.

The woman turns and looks at me. She glances at Jean-Marc and then back at me in disbelief.

"Mother?"

TWENTY-ONE

Jeff

TO SAY IT WAS AWKWARD is the understatement of the century. Whoever this French guy is—and believe me, I intend to find out—he was as smooth as glass.

"You must be the lovely Elizabeth." He spoke right up. In English. "I've been hearing wonderful things about you from your mother," he said. The smile he gave Mary was . . . well, proprietary. But at that particular moment I was more worried about Liz, who I could sense was just about ready to combust. So I stepped in.

"I'm Jeffrey Scott, Liz's fiancé," I said, and stuck out my hand.

"Jean-Marc David," the guy said, taking my hand. His grip was strong. He looked straight at me. *Nothing to hide,* he seemed to be saying. Which, of course, I had assumed. Not because of him, but because I know Mary. I expected more of an explanation, however. I thought Mary would speak up. But she didn't. After Mr. David shook my hand, he turned to Mary, kissed her—on the cheek, at least—and bowed out. I would have given a lot of money to know what he whispered in Mary's ear before he nodded to Liz and me.

The elevator came. Mary spoke up. "You're never going to get all of your luggage in there," she said. She grabbed the handle of one of Liz's bags. "I'll bring this one up with me. What floor are you on?"

"Fifth," Liz said. "Jeff has 503. I have 510."

"510," Mary repeated. She waved the two of us onto the elevator. The last thing I saw as the elevator door slid shut was Mary turning to look toward the hotel entrance. Like she was looking for Jean-Marc David.

Mary

"I WAS WORRIED about you, Mother." Liz moves deliberately, taking the suitcase from me, rolling it across the carpet into the bedroom. "I guess I didn't need to be," she says over her shoulder.

"I told you not to worry," I reply. "And I've tried to call more than once. There was never an answer. Now I see why. You were on your way here."

"Yes, well, I didn't realize how thoroughly you'd recovered from . . . whatever it was that resulted in that collection of sleeping pills." She grabs her purse up off the bed, rummaging for what I assume is the key to the small lock dangling off the front of her suitcase. "Silly me. I thought Paris was some sort of attempt to distract yourself from grief." Finding the key, she fumbles with the lock.

Thank God for Jeffrey, because I have been momentarily struck dumb. He puts his hand over hers, opens the lock, lays the key on the bedside table, and then slides his hand up Liz's back and to the nape of her neck. He pulls her to himself, and she leans against him, her back to me, her head on his shoulder. I am surprised and pleased when she doesn't push him away in some immature display of personal strength.

I stand mute, staring at Jeff.

"Well, Mary," Jeff finally speaks up. "It's probably not my place, but . . ."

Liz reaches around him, holding tight, as if waiting for him to speak. Again, I am pleased to see it. Even if the two are to join forces against me, the alliance will, in the end, be good for their future together.

He clears his throat and continues. "I guess we'd both like to hear about Mr. David." Taking Liz's hand, he leads her into the little parlor where they sit on the couch. I follow, standing by the window, opening the drapes while I collect my thoughts.

"And I'd like to know why he slunk away like that!" Liz adds.

I turn around. The rage in her blue eyes is so reminiscent of Sam that I lean away, physically trying to avoid it. Down below, in the tiny courtyard that serves as a break area for the hotel kitchen staff, I can see a couple, the girl with her back to the stone wall, the boy leaning toward her, stroking her cheek.

"He didn't slink away. He realized you were upset and was trying to be thoughtful."

Liz glares at me for a minute. She is obviously waiting for me to explain Jean-Marc, but I can't find the words.

She erupts. "How could you, Mother? How could you keep it all from me? What possible reason was there?"

"What are you talking about?" My stomach is churning, and I steel myself for the answer.

"What am I talking about?!" Liz leans forward. "Irene told

me . . . us—" she glances at Jeff—"everything."

"Everything?" I feel sweat trickling down my neck, between my shoulder blades. My heart is pounding.

"Yes. Everything. She saved newspaper clippings. Photographs. Things you threw out."

I want desperately to remember what Irene could have found, but Sam was the one who discarded my past. I thought my marriage was over the day he found the envelope in my closet. If it hadn't been for our daughter, perhaps it would have been. I close my eyes as Liz talks, trying to erase the memory of Sam's anger . . . and the bruises I hid even from Irene.

"The woman who pretended to have no interest in business has *two* degrees! The woman who pretended to be nearly tone-deaf was practically a violin concertmaster! The parents who pretended they didn't want to travel met in France!" Liz swallows before continuing, "You kept all that from me. And you . . . you ran off!"

I can't tell if her tears are evidence of anger or hurt. Either way, I relax a little as Jeff takes her hand. Liz clingss to him even as she continues her tirade.

"And when I drop everything to fly over here . . . to tell you I'm sorry . . . to try to make up, you waltz in on the arm of some French . . . escort you've latched on to from who knows where!"

"Jean-Marc David is not just some escort I—how did you put it?—latched on to. He's an old friend."

Liz's left eyebrow lifts as she ponders the information. Then she scowls. "How old?"

I meet her gaze and don't look away. "I knew him before I met your father."

Liz closes her eyes. Her nostrils flare. "Who *are* you?" she mutters wearily and slumps back against Jeff. She won't look at me.

When the alarm on his wristwatch goes off, we all three jump, but the silence continues.

Finally I say, "I'm sorry about the way this has happened. But I'm not sorry you've met Jean-Marc. I'll tell you about it. But not right now. You are both exhausted, and you need your jet-lag day to get rested."

"And you need time to talk to *him*," Liz mutters.

I nod. "We had dinner together tonight. We were stopping here so I could get a warmer jacket when we all collided down-stairs. You need to sleep, and I really don't see any reason to cancel my plans to take a walk with Jean-Marc." I stand up. "I'm in 314. I won't be out late, and if you need anything the con-cierge speaks fluent English. If you get hungry, the tearoom next door makes delicious sandwiches, but if you're smart you will eat light, if at all."

I point to what looks like a nightstand beneath the television set. "I recommend the Orangina in the refrigerator." At the door, I pause and look back at them, feeling sad about the emo-tions swirling just beneath the surface, but also proud of myself for taking control of the situation. "I love you both. I'm in the habit of having my morning coffee at the little café just off the plaza in front of the Sorbonne. Go out the door and to the bot-tom of the hill, turn right, walk about a block. You'll see foun-tains and a bronze statue off to your right. I'll be at the tearoom halfway up the plaza in the morning. If you aren't ready to talk, and you don't want to come, I'll understand."

I smile at Jeff. "And with you here, I won't worry about Liz."

I look at Liz, whose cold stare has mellowed a little. "Jean-Marc doesn't have to be a *bad* surprise, you know." I think I sound quite convincing. *If only I can convince myself.*

THE MOMENT her mother closed the hotel room door, Liz jumped up off the couch and went into the other room. Hauling her suitcase up onto the bed, she opened it—and let out an exclamation of horror and a very unladylike word.

"What is it?" Jeff followed her into the room.

"This isn't mine," Liz slumped onto the bed, holding a man's dress shirt in her hand. "I can't believe it."

"Don't touch anything else," Jeff took the shirt out of her hand. "Mary said the concierge speaks English. I'll take care of this."

"What am I going to do? What if the other person—"

"*You,*" Jeff said, zipping the luggage closed and setting it beside him, "are going to forget about this mix-up for now and get into that bed. The other person has probably discovered the mistake, and whoever he is, I doubt he'll have any use for two pairs of size-eight black slacks and whatever else it was you decided to bring."

"My makeup was in that bag," Liz muttered as she pulled back the comforter and slid into bed.

"I don't think Paris cares whether you wear makeup or not, sweetheart," Jeff said as he drew the drapes closed. "Get some sleep. Mary was right. We both need some rest." He headed for the door.

Answers, Liz thought. *We need answers.* She was asleep before she could say it aloud.

THE ELEVATOR door slid open, and the first thing Jeff saw was Mary sitting next to Jean-Marc David on an elegant sofa in the hotel lobby.

"Something wrong?" Jean-Marc got up.

"Is Lizzie all right?" Mary's expression was typical "worried mother."

"She's probably asleep by now." Jeff pointed to the luggage at his side. "But we've picked up someone else's bag by mistake."

Instantly Mr. David reached into his pocket for his car keys. "I'll take you. We'll make it right."

"There's no need," Jeff said. "I'm certain the concierge will—"

"Of course he would," Jean-Marc interrupted. "But at least let me call." He was already flipping open a cell phone, already asking for the number for Lufthansa.

For a moment, Jeff wondered how the man could possibly know what airline to call, but then he saw the airport security sticker on the side of the bag. *Smart man.*

"Unfortunately," Jean-Marc said, clicking his cell phone shut and sliding it into his pocket after a short conversation, "you must be present with the luggage tags to make the exchange, but they seem to have the other bag—along with a gentleman who is most eager to make the exchange. Please. Allow me to drive you. My car is parked in a garage only a few minutes away."

This guy was offering to spend half his night fixing a stupid mistake made by someone who had barely been civil to him not an hour ago. And Mary was looking at him with a smile Jeff had never seen. She looked years younger. Jeff decided that from all appearances, Jean-Marc David must be a good guy. He would give Mr. David the benefit of the doubt. Besides, he was starting to feel the jet lag. He was too tired to make the effort not to like him.

Mary

I LIE IN the dark looking up at the ceiling. The thing part of me feared most—the *same* thing part of me wanted to happen more than anything—has happened. I didn't plan it, I didn't arrange it, I didn't manipulate it. In fact, I literally ran away from home to avoid it. Ever since Sam died, and the more distant Elizabeth seemed to get from me, the more often I thought about breaking my promise to Sam to never talk about Paris. I still don't know exactly what I'll do. In the end, I suppose the only thing a mother really cares about is what's best for her child. At this point, I simply do not know the answer to that question.

I pray the first original prayer I've uttered since I was a very little girl. *Dear God . . . if you have ever considered involving yourself in my life . . . now would be a good time.*

TWENTY-TWO

PRAYER WAS DIFFICULT BUSINESS. He could sing with the best of them—he was, after all, from the land that gave the world *Madame Butterfly* and *La Bohème*. He liked to read, and so Bible reading had easily become a normal part of his day—as basic as putting on his shoes or having the first cup of coffee each morning. But prayer? Prayer was another matter, especially when no progress could be seen, no answer detected. Being faithful on behalf of people he didn't see every day was even more difficult. And that, Luca Santo reasoned, was why he hadn't mentioned his old friend Jean-Marc David to God in some time. But understanding the reason didn't necessarily relieve the guilt he felt now that Jean-Marc had reappeared. If God had gone to such great lengths to bring Jean-Marc back into his life, then God must have an agenda with the man. He should never have stopped praying. Luca hoped he could further the agenda and avoid raising any kind of barrier to whatever it was that God might be doing.

It might be too late for that, he realized. Already Jean-Marc had cancelled a dinner and a lunch they had planned. Luca wracked his brain trying to think of what he might have said to make Jean-Marc reluctant to spend more time with him. All he could think of was one harmless reference to God's goodness in Sophia's passing. Surely, Luca thought, that wouldn't have scared the man off. No, he should never have stopped praying.

"I am here, Father," Luca said at breakfast. "And I don't know how to pray for my friend. It was so many years ago when I came to you on his behalf. You remember, Father, how he reacted. He flung my words about you back in my face. He said my turning to you was only a crutch—something to help me not become bitter when I couldn't race anymore. He said religion was for men who couldn't meet life on their own terms. I don't know if he still has that streak of rage in him. I don't want to chase him away again. If I am the one you have chosen to speak . . . give me the words, and I will say them.

"Already he has cancelled two times. Now I've invited him to dinner again, and he says he is coming. He says he has some-one he wants me to meet. I fear it's yet another woman." Luca added hot milk to his coffee and stirred it. He didn't have to tell God about Jean-Marc David's reputation with women. But then, Luca reminded himself, that was a long time ago. Maybe things had changed.

He looked out the tall, narrow kitchen window, happy to see a blue sky. Too many gray days left him feeling restless, like something wasn't quite right with his world. Sighing, he took a long gulp of café au lait and opened his Bible.

The phone rang.

"I'm so sorry, but something has come up—an unexpected arrival. I'm afraid Mary and I won't be able . . ."

So it *was* a woman that kept him away from lunch and din-ner. Luca wanted to know more. The name Mary . . . meant something. What was it? Surely it couldn't be—

"Mary, did you say? Not *the* Mary—surely not her?"

There was silence on the other end of the line. Before Jean-Marc said a word, Luca knew.

"Yes. My old friend. My first love. Can you believe it? She wrote about a month ago to say she was coming back to Paris for a visit. But suddenly her daughter and the daughter's fiancé have arrived." Jean-Marc paused. "Mary wasn't expecting them . . . and they certainly were not expecting me. I don't know what's going to happen, but we—"

"Bring them with you." Luca said the words even as his conscious mind protested. *What on earth are you saying, idiot?*

"What?"

"Bring them with you." He repeated the invitation. "Bring them all. If you think it will help to have an old friend as a buffer. . . . Is a buffer what is needed?"

"I don't know what's needed," Jean-Marc said. "The daughter is . . . well, not very pleased with my presence, it would seem. Her fiancé is nice enough. I took him to the airport late last night. There was a mix-up with the luggage."

"You drove him to the airport?"

"Yes. I'm crazy."

Crazy to make a good impression, Luca thought. He walked to the window, phone in hand, looking out on the city traffic. "Well, I don't want to interfere, but I'd love to meet the woman for whom Jean-Marc David would come back to Paris."

"I hate to impose."

"I'm only making pasta and a salad. It's easy to add a little extra. I'd be honored to have them. Bring some bread and wine. We'll celebrate reunions."

Jean-Marc hesitated, promising to get back to him. After

hanging up the phone, Luca went back to the window, staring at the traffic below. It was, at times, very hard to believe that God truly was big enough to keep track of all the people scurrying about in his world. *Lord, I believe . . . help my unbelief.* Luca cast the prayer heavenward and added another request on behalf of Jean-Marc David, Mary, her daughter, and the fiancé. And for himself. "Wisdom, Father. I need wisdom. And a little help with the cooking wouldn't hurt, either."

Laughing to himself, Luca made his way into the living room and opened the cupboard where he kept Sophia's favorite dishes. The cheerful colors in the Tuscan pottery would be just what the drab room needed to set the stage for a reunion. As he pulled a table away from the wall and added leaves, the idea of inviting Enzo popped into his head. The boy had been good about working off the debt owed for repairs on Adolpho's Multistrada. He would be impressed to meet Jean-Marc David. And another "buffer" around the table couldn't hurt.

SHE WAS NOT going to like the man, no matter what he said.

But then Jean-Marc David winked at her across the table and commented on her beauty. Although Liz tried to be casual about it, she could not control the blush rising to her cheeks.

She was *not* going to like the man, no matter what he did.

But then he served the main dish to Mary before himself, and when Mary turned to smile at him Liz realized that for the first time in . . . forever, her mother's *eyes* were smiling.

She was *not* going to like the man, no matter what.

But then Mr. Santo asked a question about the *Sea Cloud* and launched Jean-Marc on a series of sailing stories. It opened a window on a world Liz knew nothing about. Jeff asked questions. The young Enzo was entranced. Mr. David was charming—even humble. It was hard not to be drawn in. And maddening.

All through dinner, while she learned the Italian way to wind pasta on a fork and held her own in a debate about French versus Italian wines, Liz looked for something to dislike about Jean-Marc David.

He talked with his hands. Liz noticed her mother had started to do that, too. That was irritating.

He seemed to have a special smile for Mary. Which was, Liz reminded herself, all part of Mr. David's role as the Charming European. It was all pretense. Show. But then she began to second-guess herself.

Was it just pretense and show when Mr. Santo bowed and kissed the back of your hand earlier? Was it just pretense and show when he did the same to Mother? No, Liz reasoned. That was Mr. Santo being friendly. Was it pretense when he referred to Mary's coming into the Ducati dealership and called it destiny? No. It was just a charming reaction to a coincidence. And was it pretense when Mr. Santo proposed a toast to Mary after Enzo described her motorcycle ride? No, Liz admitted. That was Mr. Santo being a good host and trying to put his guest—her mother was beet red with embarrassment—at ease.

But when Mr. David proposed a second toast, Liz tensed up. She scolded herself. Maybe she was being unfair to be so negative. She had to admit that for an old guy he was genuinely attractive. She could do without the earring, though.

As the evening wore on, Liz watched her mother. It did seem

there were a lot of unspoken conversations taking place between Mary and Mr. David. All of it good. She was just beginning to think maybe Mr. David's presence in her mother's life could be a positive thing, when he put his arm across the back of her chair. It was all Liz could do to stay in her seat. Who did he think he was? She was *married*. All right, Liz thought, she was a widow. But still . . .

Jeff sensed her mood, and when Mary got up to help Mr. Santo clear the table, he leaned over and whispered, "Lighten up, Bitsy."

"I can't," Liz whispered back.

Enzo asked a leading question about what he called "the olden days" of motorcycle racing—before there was much competition.

Mr. Santo rose to the challenge. "Not much competition? Have you heard of Agostini? Walter Villa?" One after the other, he named famous motorcyclists from his era, and one by one he told how either he or Jean-Marc David had prevailed in this race or that. He urged Jean-Marc to tell more stories. The men entertained their audience like two well-rehearsed comedians with perfect timing. In spite of herself, Liz was taken in. With the rest of the diners, she collapsed with laughter at Jean-Marc's self-deprecating tale of a race he lost. Then, try as she would, she could not prevent the hiccups that ensued.

"I'm *hic* so *hic* sorry," she gasped. "This hasn't happened *hic* in ages. *Hic.*"

"I have the same problem," Jean-Marc said. He got up and went to the kitchen and came back with salt and a shopping bag. "Salt on the tongue, breathe from the bag."

"Does it *hic* really work?" Liz said.

"Not at all," Jean-Marc said. "But it takes your mind off the hiccups." His blue eyes sparkled.

More laughter . . . and then Jean-Marc was hiccupping, too, and he and Liz were laughing and hiccupping together . . . until . . .

Dear God in heaven. Flashbacks from the evening converged before her. Things Mr. David did. Certain gestures. The tilt of his head. She had thought at one point that surely she had seen a photo of the man. He seemed so familiar. She couldn't figure it out. Even now, she didn't want to think—

Liz covered her mouth with her hands and wished the floor would open and swallow her.

Mr. David looked at her with an odd smile.

Liz looked at her mother, who was getting up to pour more coffee.

Jeff didn't seem to realize anything was wrong. How could he be so blind? Maybe she was wrong. Still, her chest was being held with a tight band that kept getting tighter. She took a drink of water. No change. Coffee. No change. Finally, she stood up, her hand at her throat.

"Excuse me," she said. "But I'm afraid this may be more than just hiccups. I'm really not feeling well."

Luca Santo jumped up. "What is it? How can I help?"

Jeff stood up and put his arm around her. "What is it, baby?"

Mumbling something she hoped Mr. Santo would accept as an apology, Liz leaned on Jeff. "We have to leave. Now." When her mother spoke up, Liz glared at her. "Don't let me spoil your evening." She looked past her to Mr. David, then back at Mary. Liz shrugged and arched one eyebrow in a way she had thought was a Davis trait—until this evening. She looked at Jean-Marc.

Mary's face went pale. Liz gave a little nod. "By all means, enjoy your little reunion."

She pushed away from Jeff, silenced Luca Santo's attempts to help her with a wave of her hand, and stumbled through the door, down the stairs, and out onto the street. She could hear Jeff's hurried footsteps behind her. Once downstairs, she slumped against the glass window of the Ducati showroom.

"What is it? It was going so well, and then . . ." Jeff put his hand on her shoulder. "And I know you aren't really sick, so tell me what's going on."

Liz shook her head. She swallowed and blurted out, "How could she?"

"Who?"

"My mother." Liz said it like a swear word.

"How could she what?"

"Put me in that room. With him." She forced herself to stand upright. "And let me just—" She closed her eyes and shook her head. "I don't believe it. It can't be."

"Liz, what on earth are you talking about?"

"It's like I've been caught in a time warp. Sucked into a different dimension." She leaned her head back against the plate glass window and closed her eyes. "I don't *know* that woman upstairs."

Jeff agreed. "It *isn't* exactly the Mary Davis we know, is it?"

Liz snorted. "That would be the understatement of the year."

"It's just a part of her we've never seen. But I've been watching her tonight, and . . . I mean, have you really *looked* at her? Have you *listened*? When have we ever seen her smile like that? How long has it been since you heard her really laugh? When Mr. Santo was telling that story about he and Mr. David playing that prank on one of their racing buddies, she was laughing so hard there were tears shining in her eyes."

"That would explain it," Liz said.

"Explain what?"

"You've been watching Mother." She looked at Jeff, her eyes brimming with tears. "I was watching *him*."

"Him who? Luca? Jean-Marc?"

"Since when is he 'Jean-Marc' to you?" Liz said.

Jeff shrugged. "He asked me to call him that. You were there." Taking her by the shoulders, he looked into her eyes and shook her gently. "What is going on, Elizabeth?"

"Is everything all right?" Luca Santo had opened a window on the second story and was calling down to the street.

Jeff looked up. "She's better. We'll be right back up."

Santo nodded and withdrew, closing the window.

"You can go back in if you want to," Liz said. "I'm going back to the hotel. And back home. As soon as I can get on a flight."

"Stop talking nonsense."

"Fine," Liz lifted her chin and stared at him through gathering tears. "How about you go back up there and watch Jean-Marc David for a little while. How about you look at the color of his eyes." Liz pointed to her own eyes. "That weird shade everybody always had to comment on when I was growing up. While you're at it, watch his mannerisms. See if they remind you of anyone."

"What are you saying?"

Even as he asked the question, Liz could tell he was beginning to understand. He gave her a stricken look. "That can't be."

"Can't it?" Liz pulled away from him.

"But you were born—"

"In September. Prematurely, they always said. And my

parents were married the previous January. At least that's when they celebrated their anniversary," Liz said. "Who knows what date is on the marriage license?" Her voice trembled. "My entire life is a lie."

Jeff held her until she had calmed down a little. "I'll go up and tell them you aren't feeling well. I'll ask Luca to call a taxi for us."

"I don't want my mother rushing down here trying to make everything all right," Liz said.

"Don't worry," Jeff said. "I'll take care of it."

While he was gone, Liz relived the evening. She had resisted the idea of liking Jean-Marc David. Little by little, he had scaled the wall she erected, torn down her defenses. Closing her eyes, she put them back up. She was not going to like that man. It didn't matter what anyone said or did. Least of all, her mother.

Liz walked to the corner and looked toward the Arc de Triomphe.

A young couple blazed by on a motorcycle.

Up the street, an old man doddered along, tapping the sidewalk with his cane.

The charm that was Paris faded. Looking up at the night sky, she let the tears come.

Mary

I WOBBLE down the stairs from Luca Santo's apartment to the street. *"No. Please, Jean-Marc. Let me go alone. I'll call you tomorrow." "Thank you for your hospitality, Mr. Santo." "Liz? Oh, I'm sure she'll be fine. You know how it is with travel. Everything is different. The body sometimes rebels. Thank you for understanding."*

"Yes, of course I'll let you know if a doctor is needed. You're so kind. Thank you for your hospitality."

It is a long walk from here to the Latin Quarter. *You can't go home again.* I wish I'd never thought of the phrase. Wish Liz had not come. Wish—no, not that. I am not sorry I wrote the letter. Nor am I sorry to have Jean-Marc back in my life. Sighing, I head up the street. Perhaps on my way back to the hotel I will stop at Notre Dame and light a candle. It couldn't hurt. Might it help?

AFTER ENZO left, Jean-Marc and Luca Santo finished clearing the table and reassembling Luca's apartment. They washed dishes in relative silence. Finally, Luca said, "I'm making more coffee. Will you join me?"

The two men settled just inside the doorway to the narrow balcony at the back of the apartment. The silence between them was broken when—while gazing at the ornate ironwork framing a view of the city that included Notre Dame's two identical towers and a misty but still visible outline of the Eiffel Tower—Jean-Marc said, "I wouldn't have expected such a view."

Luca followed Jean-Marc's lead, ignoring the recent dinner party. "I never planned to live over the business. But when Sophia saw that view she refused to look at any other apartments." He stretched and sighed. "We had a good life." He waited for Jean-Marc to say something, but his friend remained quiet. Pensive.

"Your Mary is a lovely woman," Luca offered.

Jean-Marc snorted softly, shaking his head. "She isn't *mine.*

She never was." He sipped coffee, then returned his gaze to the view.

"And what an odd coincidence that she already knew Enzo and had visited my dealership."

Though it was obvious Jean-Marc was preoccupied and not interested in conversation, Luca persisted. "Tell me something. Were you offended by my praying over the meal?"

Shrugging, Jean-Marc said, "Of course not. Why would I be offended?"

"Religion is a crutch for weak men. If you ever do anything besides go to church, call me."

"Ouch," Jean-Marc pretended to dodge a bullet. "Was I that harsh?"

"You were."

Jean-Marc opened his mouth to speak, shut it, cleared his throat. "Tell me something, Luca." He inhaled deeply, finally blurting it out. "The girl. Elizabeth. I thought—I'm probably imagining it, but . . ."

"Yes?" Luca said.

"You know what I'm going to say, don't you?" His voice trembled. "I'm afraid to say it aloud."

"Whether you say it or not, you can't think of anything else. I imagine neither can she."

"There's something in her manner—the way she tilts her head when she's angry," Jean-Marc looked down at the floor, then back out the window. "And she has my eyes."

TWENTY-THREE

Mary

"YOU CAN'T DO THIS TO ME," Liz cries out. She sits like a wounded bird on the edge of the couch in her suite, clutching her chest, leaning over. When I reach out to her, she flings my hand away and jumps up. Raking her hands through her hair, she rushes to the window, lifts it open, and screams into the night.

"Elizabeth." Jeff goes to her, grasps her by the shoulders, and pulls her against him while he closes the window. "Stop it. Now."

Liz balls each hand up into a fist and pounds his chest. She cries out. "Don't *tell* me to stop. My mother's just told me my life is a lie. I'm not the daughter of Samuel Davis. My father is some vagabond sailor who—"

"No." I interrupt her. "Your father is Samuel Frederick Davis. That hasn't changed."

"Right. And I suppose these are *his* eyes." She shakes her head. "And to think people used to wonder where the color came from." She looks accusingly at me. "And you had some wild story about a great-great-grandmother and a painting that was destroyed when the roof leaked."

"That was your father's story, not mine."

"And I suppose lying to me for my entire life was his idea, too?"

"Oh, Lizzie," I beg, "Please. Stop. This . . . information . . . doesn't really change anything. Your father couldn't have children. When I told him about you, we were already engaged. He was shocked. But he was thrilled. He had a chance to be a father, after all. *He* was there when you were born. It was *his* arms that held you. It was *Sam* who gave every ounce of his love and attention to you. Nothing can ever change that. Nothing."

"Nothing except a little dinner between old friends in Paris."

I want to defend myself. I want to tell her everything. But I won't. Telling her everything would only hurt her more. She has a little girl's idyllic view of her father, and I will not interfere with it. I close my eyes, trying to find the strength to not damage Lizzie's memories of Sam in defense of myself. *God. Are you there? HELP.*

"You know what, sweetheart," I say, amazed that my voice is so calm. "I want to answer all the questions I possibly can. But not this way. Not now." I look at Jeff. He nods agreement and I continue. "I'll be in my room. Take some time. Talk this over with Jeff. When you've calmed down—when you've had some sleep—call me. I'll come right away."

"Unless you're on a date." The sarcasm in her voice hits hard.

I ignore the attack. "I won't be on a date. I'll come. I love you, Lizzie. Nothing will ever change that. I love you and—" My voice catches. I remind myself to breathe. *God. HELP.* "I'd give anything if you hadn't come to Paris. If you hadn't discovered this. But you did come. You met Jean-Marc. You've discovered a secret I kept because I wanted to obey your father. This new information doesn't change anything about your daddy and you or the love you shared or the legacy he left you. In time, it might even prove to be a good thing."

"What does he want from you?" Her voice is shrill.

"I don't know what you mean."

"What does he want? What's the point in his looking you up now? After all this time?"

It takes a moment for me to absorb the implication of her question. "As you may recall from our conversation at dinner, Jean-Marc David is the captain of a rather famous yacht called the *Sea Cloud*, Liz. He's in no need of Davis money, if that's what you mean. And besides that, he didn't look me up. *I* wrote to him."

I keep talking, afraid if I stop to think, I'll hold back. "I've been so . . . unhappy, Lizzie. Even desperate, sometimes. One night, I was alone in my room, and yes, I had a bottle of pills." I am ashamed, and I turn away. "It just seemed like my life was so . . . meaningless. You didn't need me, your father was gone. I was adrift. And I had the pills, but I was afraid. So, instead of taking the pills, I wrote a letter. To an old friend."

When I look at Liz her face is a mask. She won't look at me. "A long time ago, I hurt Jean-Marc. Terribly. It's haunted me for years. And since your dad died the guilt has reared its head even more often. The thought kept coming back that maybe, just maybe, if I went back in time, if I resolved that part of the past, maybe I'd be able to move forward. Be able to face life again. So I wrote the letter. I had no idea if he would even get it. But he did, and he came." I pause. "It was never supposed to involve you at all. It wasn't even about you."

"I'd love to have been there when you told *him*," she says.

"When I told him what?" As I ask the question, I realize

223

what she means. "I didn't tell him about you. I promised your father I'd never mention Paris to you *and* that Jean-Marc would never know about you." I feel a rising tide of emotion as I begin to suspect the reason for Jean-Marc's becoming suddenly quiet after Liz left the dinner party. Is he somewhere in Paris contemplating the existence of a second daughter? I argue with myself. Surely he didn't suspect. There's no reason for him to think it. Unless he noticed all the things Liz noticed. *God. HELP.*

Finally, Liz looks at me. "Are you telling me Mr. David doesn't know?" Her Nordic blue eyes are cold. Calculating. I meet her gaze evenly.

"I . . . I don't know. Maybe he's guessed. But I didn't say anything. How many times do I have to tell you? That's *not* why I wrote the letter. It's *not* why I came to Paris." I am desperate to reach out to her, but I hold back, knowing instinctively that she'll shrink away. And that would break my heart. I feel fragile . . . and yet, somehow I realize I am stronger. Strong enough to finally put an end to this confrontation.

Mary

December 28, 2003

> *I told Lizzie I didn't come to Paris to tell Jean-Marc about her. Is that true? Beneath the conscious thought, was there a hidden agenda I didn't admit to myself? I need to think. I'll ramble on paper for a while and perhaps I'll get all this mess into some sort of informational bundle I can manage. The phone hasn't rung. I have no messages. I don't know if that means Jean-Marc isn't as perceptive as Liz . . . or if it means he knows and has run for his life. I want to contact him, but I don't think I should. If he's guessed, he*

needs time. If he hasn't, I don't want to explain why Liz acted the way she did. Not tonight. So . . .

I came to Paris because . . .

I pause. Thinking. The answer is simple. I came to Paris because I am fifty years old and I want to believe that silly little motto I found in the Old Market back home. I want to believe that it is never too late to be what I might have been.

So the logical question is . . .

What might I have been?

1. A violinist. I didn't want to become a concertmaster. I just wanted music to be part of my life. But because he knew Jean-Marc loved to hear me play the violin, Sam didn't want it in my life at all. I suppose he was afraid I would think of Jean-Marc when I played. The tragedy in it is that when I played, I always thought of ethereal things like ocean waves, birds in flight, things from nature, sometimes angels. Sometimes even God. The music didn't connect me to Jean-Marc. But Sam didn't believe that, and he wouldn't let it go. One day he got so angry he broke my bow . . .

I pause. I will not relive that part of the past. It is gone. I return to my musings about the present.

2. An adventurer. The world is such an exciting place. I like the idea of learning about new cultures. I never want to stop. In many ways, I suppose I did end up on an adventure after all, although it wasn't the adventure I expected. Certainly Sam Davis's life was a foreign country to me. I learned a lot about a part of society I never belonged in. And I like to think I did it well. Sam was proud of me in his way. He just didn't say it aloud.

3. A sailor's wife. That's a silly one. Part of what made me go to Sam was the knowledge that at twenty-one, Jean-Marc David wasn't the type to be tied down to a wife and child. I'm saddened to learn that he's been married twice and neither marriage worked out. Do I wish for a serious relationship with him now? I don't know. Twenty-nine years ago I was carried away by the romantic circumstances. Now I have a more mature understanding of what it takes to build a marriage. But my heart still beats faster when he smiles at me. And his kiss. . . . well, I guess I still have fires that can be lit. Knowing that is both thrilling and terrifying.

4. A vagabond. It saddens me that Jean-Marc has never settled down. I don't mean that I think he should have given up the sea. But he could have planted the kind of roots that could have gone with him wherever the Sea Cloud took him. When we were young, the image of a vagabond life probably made him more attractive to me. But now he seems sad that he's so disconnected. Maybe that's just me forcing my ideas onto him. But I don't think I ever wanted to be a vagabond. And I don't think Jean-Marc wants that now. He speaks of his daughter—his OTHER daughter, Celine—with a kind of heartbreaking wistfulness.

5. A divorcee. Well, I could have been that . . . twice. I would have made Jean-Marc miserable. And I could have failed Sam. But I didn't make Jean-Marc miserable for long . . . and I didn't fail Sam, either. Thank God.

I don't know what I expected from Paris, really. It does feel like I've been given a kind of indulgence against the sin of desertion. Jean-Marc doesn't hate me. He still likes me, in fact. And I still enjoy him. But I want more than a rekindled romance. I want to get in touch with the musician and the traveler and all those parts of me I put away for Sam. I don't want to waste any more time being bitter. I did what I did, and I did the best I could. I was a good wife to Sam, and I am a good mother to Liz. I don't know what I want to be next. Who knows, maybe I'll be a better ME than I've been. I'd like it if that included being the friend—at the very least, a friend—of a French sailor. But if Liz is right, and Jean-Marc has guessed that she is his daughter, I may not have that option.

Would I come to Paris again if I'd known what was going to happen?

Yes. The music is back in my life. I have some delightful new young friends. I'm going to look into buying a violin. Who knows, I may even take Mr. Santo up on his offer to teach me to ride a Ducati.

What do I want? I want to take Liz and Jeff to Arcachon and to see where I went to school. I want us all to be friends with Jean-Marc. And I want Liz and Jeff to go home and let me have some more time for myself—a time without regrets, without worries.

I lay the pen aside, rubbing my right wrist, which has grown numb in the hour I've been conducting my "stream of consciousness" writing exercise. Maybe I'm becoming an actual journaler. Meredith at the club told me I should journal when Sam died. It may be the one sensible piece of advice Meredith has ever given. I should have listened to her. When I reread what I've just written it seems I've come to a new kind of clarity and peace. It is surprising—and perhaps telling—that I haven't mentioned going on the *Sea Cloud* at all. I say I want to take Liz to Arcachon . . . but apparently I don't see Jean-Marc's ship as a necessary part of Mary Davis's revelation of herself to her daughter. Interesting.

I look at the phone, managing a sad little laugh as I think of Snoopy and how forlorn he looked as he said *a watched supper bowl never fills*. Or something like that. A watched phone never rings, either.

I am exhausted. I kick off my shoes and lay back on the couch. My last thoughts, which are getting fuzzy, are about Luca Santo and how he prayed before the meal earlier tonight. It reminded me of the pastor in that little Protestant church. The "Hi, God, this is your buddy" kind of prayer. It intrigues me.

I'm not prepared to go on a religious pilgrimage, but I'd like to ask that pastor a few questions about the Bible he gave me the last time I visited his church. And maybe talk to Luca Santo about his faith. If he's open to that kind of discussion. If he doesn't think it's rude. If . . .

TWENTY-FOUR

Mary

A JANGLING NOISE BRINGS ME from a deep slumber, but only halfway to consciousness. I wish someone would stop— and then I realize it isn't just a noise, it's the phone. I sit up with a grunt, rubbing my neck, which has not benefited from spending the night on this little couch. It is still dark outside.

"Hello?"

"It's Jean-Marc."

"Yes."

"Would you meet me in the garden? Please. I can't sleep."

He knows.

I hesitate just a minute, thinking of Liz, two floors above me. Is she finally asleep or is she pacing the floor? Has Jeff managed to calm her down? Should I check . . . or let her be? I remember her sarcasm—saying that I would be here for her *unless* I had a date.

"I'm on my way." I hang up the phone, scratch a "just in case" note on a piece of paper, grab my coat and the room key, and head upstairs.

At first, there is no response to my knock, but after a moment, Jeff comes to the door.

"She's asleep," he says and is quick to add, "I've been snoozing on the couch . . . in case she needs—"

I nod and interrupt him. "Good. Then you can toss this out."

Jeff reads the note, which says *I have gone for a walk in Luxembourg Garden. Back soon.*

"Jean-Marc called. He didn't say anything, but I assume he's had the same revelation as Liz."

Jeff nods. After looking toward the bedroom he steps into the hall, drawing the door nearly closed behind him. "Mary, I don't know how this will all work out, but I do want you to know that none of this changes my feelings about you. Or about Mr. David, for that matter. I like him, and I respect you."

"You respect me? After the mess I've created?"

He shakes his head. "This *mess,* as you call it, isn't your fault. And I admire you for getting stronger instead of folding."

"You're very sweet, but the mess *is* my fault. Be sure your sins will find you out. Even after nearly thirty years." My eyes fill with tears.

"You didn't mean for Liz to find out. I believe you. If there's anything in your shifting world that's a constant, it's your love for and loyalty to Liz. And once she works her way through the shock she'll realize that, too." He puts his hand out and grasps me by the shoulder. "I'm still on your team, Mary. Things will work out."

I am at a loss to know how things will work out, but I don't say that. I simply thank Jeff and head toward the stairs. I hear the door to Liz's suite close behind me and thank God she didn't come to Paris alone.

I may have thought about God more in these past few weeks in Paris than in the last thirty years in Omaha. As I make my way past the café where I've had breakfast every morning since coming back and toward Jean-Marc, I remember my half-prayer to God about helping me. If this is his idea of help, I'm not sure I want God in my life. Of course, I realize in a moment of theological clarity, that if he is God, then he is in my life whether I acknowledge him or not. If he can't invade a person's life unless they invite him . . . doesn't that put the creation in charge? And what kind of God is that—to be subject to a human will? In a muddle of confusion and ignorance, I give up.

Jean-Marc has preceded me into the garden. I see him up ahead, standing beside the broad expanse of concrete that in springtime will be filled with water and speckled with model boats captained by lively children. But this morning, the pool is empty and there are no voices.

He hears my approaching footsteps and turns. As soon as I get near enough that he doesn't have to raise his voice he says, "She has my eyes."

I nod.

He takes in a great, wavering breath. "That first night at the hotel, I didn't notice." He shakes his head. "Oddly enough it wasn't even her eyes that first caught my attention. There is a certain tilt of her head when she is intent on a subject. When she asks a question. Suddenly I thought of Celine. And then I began to pay closer attention. And those hiccups—" He stops short. "Why didn't you tell me?"

I sigh. "I was young. Terrified. I didn't think you would want the responsibility. And I didn't want you to do anything out of obligation."

"You didn't trust me," he says.

I avoid the term. "I didn't even know I was pregnant until after Sam proposed. I was shocked. I used my pregnancy to give him an excuse to back out. But then he amazed me. He said he didn't care. That he would raise the baby as his own if I would agree to cut all ties with you." I shrug. "You had already taken off."

Jean-Marc slumps down onto the edge of the pool, so suddenly that I reach out and put my hand on his shoulder. He takes my hand, kisses the back of it, pulls me down beside him. "You were right not to trust me. I would have run out on you. Eventually."

"My coming back wasn't about any of this. I didn't expect Liz to come, and I certainly never intended for her to know. I just wanted to apologize. To see how you were and move on. I'm so sorry, Jean-Marc. I never intended to hurt you. I am so very sorry."

He shakes his head. "We sent our regrets down the river, remember?" He looks up at the sky. "Maybe I would have married you . . . but you are right. Eventually I would have felt trapped. Perhaps not right away, but in time." He nudges my shoulder, "You weren't cut out for a sailor's life, Mary McKibbin. You needed roots, and I have never been a man to grow them." He smiles. "Elizabeth is lovely. Talented, bright. A tribute to you."

"Whatever she is is due mostly to Sam's investment in her." I do my best to explain Elizabeth and Sam's relationship to Jean-Marc. In the telling, I try not to paint Sam in a bad light, but it is obvious I have revealed my own sense of hurt and alienation, because Jean-Marc takes my hand while I am speaking.

When I finally pause, he says, "She's missed a lot, not knowing you better. Perhaps, now that she is here, a garden in Paris can stand for more than just two young lovers who have become old friends. Perhaps the garden will witness a new beginning for mother and daughter." He pats my hand. "If these trees could talk, my friend, they'd have stories to tell. Maybe you'll give them one more story about a reunion and a new beginning."

My eyes fill with tears, and a profound sadness sweeps over me. "I wish I could believe you. But I don't have much hope that she'll get over this." I draw in a raggedy, emotional breath. Jean-Marc puts his arm around me. I lean into him.

"So I am not the only one who had a revelation at dinner," he mutters.

I shake my head and reach up to wipe the tears off my cheeks.

He hugs me close and lifts me to my feet. As we walk along, Jean-Marc says, "Luca Santo tells me that God often gives people more than one chance."

"More than one chance at what?"

"Happiness. Understanding. Forgiveness. Whatever unspoken needs a man has. A God of second chances, Luca calls his God." As the early morning sun bathes the palace walls, I am now acutely aware of everything around the two of us, including the cars passing on the street just beyond the iron fence that surrounds the grounds of the Luxembourg palace and gardens.

I apologize again. "I never meant—"

"Ssh." He puts his finger to my lips. "That last flower—the one you didn't want to send down the river. . . ."

"Yes. Regret that you'd never know Elizabeth. That she would never know you. That she would spend her life trying to be like Sam . . . and never know the things you could have taught her, the things that could perhaps balance out Sam's weaknesses."

"You don't need *me* to do that," he says. He turns then and puts one hand on each of my shoulders. "Give her yourself, *chérie*. Show her that girl you hid away for all these years. Let her hear the music . . . listen to the laughter I remember . . . feel the sea spray in her face." At mention of the sea, he smiles. "If she will let me—if she would come—we could give her the sea together." He pauses. "Would she come to the *Sea Cloud*?"

I shake my head. "I doubt it."

"You know, Mary, when your letter arrived . . . I kept it in my pocket for days. Finally I went out to the dune. I meant to tear it up and throw it into the sea." He shrugs. "You are not the only one with regrets. And not only God is willing to give second chances. If she will come . . . or whether she will or not, I'd like it very much if you would think about coming aboard the *Sea Cloud* this spring. And perhaps, a trip to Italy to meet Celine and my grandsons."

"What will Celine think of all this?"

He sighs. "I don't know. She'll have some time to absorb it before you come."

"I have to get back to the hotel."

He sighs deeply. "Of course. I'll walk you there."

"Thank you, but . . ."

He nods. "I understand." He cups my face in his hands and whispers, "For old times' sake," and kisses me. He wraps me in his arms. It is a friendly hug, not a passionate one. Before letting go, he says, "I am going to breakfast with Luca Santo. If you change your mind and decide to come for a visit, I'll be sure Luca has all the information you need to find me at any hour of the night or day."

I murmur my thanks, and then he kisses me again. "That one," he says, "was for the future's sake." He smiles and winks.

He is still the flirtatious sailor, and I still respond to his passion with increased blood pressure.

I watch Jean-Marc walk away from me, and I am not tempted to call him back. He has said he will wait. I believe, this time, he will. I turn away and head toward the hotel where I live. . . . *Where I live.* I like the idea. I tuck it away and turn my attention back to Elizabeth.

I don't have any idea what I will say today. What I will do. Whether my daughter will come to me—or run away forever. As I make my way back to the hotel alone, a phrase keeps repeating itself in my mind. *A God of second chances.*

TWENTY-FIVE

Mary

ONCE AGAIN I AM CALLED out of a heavy sleep by a noise, but this time it is not the phone. Rather, it is a knock at my door. Without even looking at the clock, I rise, pull on a pair of slacks and an oversized shirt, and stumble to the door, barefoot and bleary-eyed.

"Yes?"

"We're back! And we have news!"

I open the door and in tumble Annie Templeton, Adolpho, and Enzo.

"We woke you. I'm sorry, we'll come back." Annie is ready to charge right back out into the hallway, but I am grateful for my young friends' arrival and their distraction from the realization that Elizabeth Davis has not called her mother . . . and it is nearly noon.

"No. Wait. Just give me a minute." I retreat to the bedroom, closing the door behind me. My personal record for morning toilette used to be about ten minutes. I think I accomplish this one in three.

Just as I have rejoined my young friends in the sitting room of my suite, another knock at the door sounds. This time it is Liz and Jeff—Liz red-eyed and pale, Jeff giving me his version of an encouraging smile. At least I hope I've interpreted it correctly.

With the introduction of strangers to buffer our "recent history," Liz seems to regain her footing. She greets the three young people and smiles at Adolpho, "So you're the one who has my mother speeding around Paris on a motorcycle?" She puts her hand on my shoulder as she speaks, and I marvel anew at her ability to turn the corner from personal angst to polite society. No one would guess we are anything but a loving mother and daughter.

"You have news?" I ask Annie. She smiles up at Adolpho and looks back at me. "Can you come, all of you"—she includes Liz and Jeff in the invitation—"to the tearoom? We're celebrating and we'd love to have you there!"

"Celebrating what?"

"The surprise . . . in the tearoom." Adolpho looks down at me with a conspiratorial smile. He looks at Jeff and Liz. "It's wonderful you are here, because part of the surprise is for Mary."

I am truly confused. I hesitate, and Liz speaks up, accepting the invitation for us all—which feels more like home, but I decide that, in this case, it is a good thing. Maybe some human buffers for a few hours is a good idea. Maybe God knows what he is doing, and maybe Annie's return is an answer to my plea for help. Even as I am thinking of these things, I am mocking myself for the absurdity of the musings. God planning tea parties. Ha.

We break ranks, Liz and Jeff and I to get ready, and the others to go ahead of us and prepare whatever surprise awaits.

The tearoom is filled with the members of the chamber

music group and a few faces I don't recognize, but this is obviously a planned celebration, and I am deeply touched to have been included.

Adolpho stands up, thanks everyone for coming, accepts a few good-natured jeers, and then takes Annie's hand and says simply, "We're engaged."

The tearoom erupts with cheers and whistles, stomping of feet, and shouts for Adolpho to make a speech, which he does. He concludes by reading a poem to Annie. The room grows quiet, and when he finishes and looks at his fiancée, it is with such sweetness the entire room almost sighs audibly. I notice that Jeff has taken Liz's hand during the reading of the poem.

When Enzo makes a joke the spell is broken. A few of the group members open their instrument cases—I had not even noticed the instruments when we arrived—and music fills the air. It is not the classical wonder I am used to hearing from the group, but rather folksy or bluesy—something I can't quite identify. When Annie opens her violin case and thrusts her instrument into my hand, I shake my head and try to push it away.

"Please," she says. "Make it our engagement gift."

"I can't," I say, suddenly very much aware of Liz's disbelieving stare and what I think is a little frown of disapproval. "Maybe another time."

But the rest of the young people have gotten into the act now, and I am suddenly at the center of attention in the room. If I refuse, Annie will be hurt. If I acquiesce, I will be embarrassed. Looking at Annie's face, I decide that embarrassing myself is better than disappointing a girl at her engagement party, and so after much self-deprecating humor, I tuck the instrument beneath my chin and, closing my eyes, place my fingers on what I hope is the first chord in a simple folk tune I learned years ago.

My fingers waver, I misdirect the bow, and the violin squawks. "See?" I say, trying to hand it back to Annie.

"See what," Annie smiles. She looks at Liz. "Is she always like this when you ask her to play?"

Liz mumbles something noncommittal.

"We haven't heard her play in years," Jeff says. He gives me a knowing look. "Please, Mary. Do play something."

It's an obscure tune, but as I call it out of the past and struggle to find the heart of Annie's violin, I close my eyes again and try to forget the people in the room and my own nervousness and unpracticed ear. I remember more than I expected to. It isn't half bad, I think. It's not half good, either. *Just middling.* It's been years since I thought of that phrase. Sam's mother—the original Elizabeth—used it often when giving her opinion of cooking or entertaining. *"You can't be just middling, Mary McKibbin,"* she'd say. *"You're a Davis now."*

The kids clap for my mediocrity, and I shrug and shove Annie's instrument back at her. "I told you it wouldn't be good. It's been too long."

"It was beautiful, Mimi," Liz says.

I look at her and am shocked—both that she has called me her pet name for me . . . and that she has tears in her eyes.

"You used to sing that to me when I was very little." She frowns. "But you stopped. And even when I asked, you wouldn't ever sing it again. Why'd you stop?"

"Daddy didn't like it," I say.

Enzo speaks up. "It's an old Provençal lullaby. Very old." He looks at me. "Where did you learn it?"

"Before Daddy," Liz says. She is looking at me, but I can't read her mood.

I nod and say to Enzo, "Jean-Marc's mother used to sing it."

"Ah," Enzo grins, "the famous Maman David."

I shake my head, bring my open palms up to my face and try to hide my laughter.

"What?" Liz asks.

"You have to explain that," Annie demands.

Enzo looks at Adolpho, who shrugs. Apparently this is Adolpho giving permission, for Enzo begins. . . . "The legend Uncle Luca told us when we were growing up is that Hélène David—that would be Jean-Marc's mama—was captured by gypsies when she was young. She lived among them until she was thirteen years old, at which time she ran away with the circus."

The story has taken on a ridiculous edge, and the listeners hoot and howl their derision.

"Say what you want," Enzo insists. "It's true. My own uncle Luca Santo told me. Maman David was a renowned singer. Until she met Jean-Marc's father and fell in love. They married and settled in Arcachon, and Maman David refused to tell anything of her past until she was a very old woman—save for that song, which was sung in Provençal to her son and for the rest of her life. And now, Maman David rests beneath the soil, and the song and this story are all that remain." Enzo finishes the story with a flourish of his hand and a low bow.

We have dominated the tearoom for over an hour before first one, then another of the ensemble begins to depart. Finally, Adolpho and Annie must go, too. While she is packing her violin away, Annie leans over to say, "Now I can tell you the other surprise Adolpho was talking about. I took the liberty of making an appointment for you. At Monsieur Rousseau's."

I explain to Liz and Jeff, "Monsieur Rousseau has a small shop across from Notre Dame. I thought I might buy a violin." I turn to Annie, "I'm having second thoughts. I'll let you know."

"Go," Liz says abruptly. Jeff takes her hand. She nods. "And maybe—if you don't mind—maybe I'll come along?"

My first thought is that perhaps there is a God of second chances, after all.

"*Sì?*" His daydreaming interrupted, Luca Santo answered the door buzzer in his native language.

"*E'io, Jean-Marc.*"

"*Acceso in su, il mio amico.*" Releasing the intercom button, Luca went to put the Bible on his kitchen table, out of sight, then hesitated and decided to leave it out. *If I offend, Lord, let it be for the right reason.*

Jean-Marc's face revealed a sleepless night.

"You look terrible."

Shrugging, Jean-Marc nearly fell into the threadbare over-stuffed chair beside the balcony door.

"Can I get you coffee?"

"*Grazie.*" Jean-Marc got up and followed Luca into the kitchen. He pulled out a chair and sat down. He pointed to the Bible. "You read different things than you did in the old days."

"*Sì.*"

After assembling the cone and a filter, grinding and measuring coffee, Luca excused himself to get cups and saucers from Sophia's dishes stored in the other room.

When he came back into the kitchen, a cup and saucer in each hand, Jean-Marc had the open Bible in front of him and was pointing to Sophia's name—penned in Luca's handwriting—in the margin.

"What's this?" Jean-Marc asked.

Leaning down, Luca peered at the passage—about Christ descending from heaven—through the lower half of his bifocal glasses. He grunted. "A promise to me that I will see my Sophia again." Just as he spoke, the teakettle began to whistle, and Luca busied himself pouring hot water through the coffee filter, inhaling deeply of the aroma of fresh coffee. "Is there any better aroma in the world than fresh coffee?" He grinned at Jean-Marc. "I know, I know. You're thinking of sea spray and fish."

"Actually," Jean-Marc replied, "I thought first of the freshly turned earth around Celine's villa in the spring." He closed the Bible and pushed it toward the center of the table to make room for the cup and saucer Luca set before him. "I asked Mary to visit there in the spring. And to bring Elizabeth and Jeffrey."

"You're leaving, then." It was a statement, not a question.

"You think I shouldn't go?"

Luca shrugged. "I don't know."

"You think I'm repeating old mistakes. Running away."

"I didn't say that," Luca added cream to his coffee. "Actually, old friend, I don't know what I think. Except that I wish you might consider asking God for help. Despite what you think, he is much more than a crutch for weak-minded men. Although I admit *I* turned to him more completely when I was at my weakest." When Jean-Marc was quiet, Luca continued, "To my surprise, it seems to be how God operates. He takes the weakness of a man and transforms it into strength." He pointed at the Bible. "It even says that when I am weak, he is strong."

"What kind of a God wants weakness? Of what use would that be to him?"

Luca smiled. "I know. It seems impossible. But it is true. Men come to him with weakness and empty hands and lives. He makes them strong and fills their lives with himself."

"I have neither empty hands nor an empty life," Jean-Marc said quickly.

"I thought the same thing," Luca agreed. "Until I saw my life through God's eyes."

"And then?"

"Then I read the words of this book—'all our righteous acts are like filthy rags.'" Luca sat back, forcing himself to take a drink of his coffee, praying for just the right words. "I didn't have anything to offer to God. I had to accept that my future depended ultimately on him . . . not on me."

"You said this God gives second chances," Jean-Marc said.

"I think," Luca replied, "he gives hundredth chances, if that is what is required for him to collect a soul."

Jean-Marc peered out the tiny window above the kitchen table. For a long while, the two men drank coffee, saying nothing.

When Jean-Marc finally broke the silence between them, he told Luca about his talk with Mary. "And so, it ends the same way it did years ago. I go back to Arcachon with nothing. And hope to hear from the girl." He forced a laugh. "Which is, I suppose, what I deserve." He looked at Luca. "Am I doing the right thing?"

"Only God knows," Luca said.

"I told Mary I'd make certain you knew how to find me." Jean-Marc reached into his pocket and pulled out his wallet where he'd inserted a slip of paper among the euros. He laid it on the table before standing up. The men shook hands. Halfway to the door, Jean-Marc paused to ask a question. "Tell me something, Luca. If I decide to ponder this idea of a God of second chances . . . how do I do that? Should I go back to Mass?"

Luca hesitated. "You could. But it is a sad truth that many of our wonderful and gloriously beautiful churches are little more than mausoleums now—buildings filled with traditions that do little to bring a man face-to-face with a personal God." He paused, internally resisting what he sensed God telling him to do, then relenting and retreating to the kitchen table for his Bible. "I think," he said, "what is more likely to speak to you, my friend, is simple. See what God says about himself." He thrust the book at Jean-Marc. "Start with the Gospel of John. See what you think." Smiling, he clapped his old friend on the back and followed him to the door. "You can always drop in on a broken-down racing buddy in Paris if you decide you want to discuss what you read."

Jean-Marc accepted the Bible, then appraised Luca from head to toe. "You aren't so broken-down as I expected," he said. "Although a little sun would do you good. Maybe you'll come south, too."

"Careful," Luca said. "You'll go crazy if everyone you've invited to visit really does come."

"Maybe," Jean-Marc replied, "just maybe it's time to come out of the cave."

As Jean-Marc retreated down the stairs to the street, Luca called out, "You know, Jean-Marc, God has not just written of himself in that book. He's written of himself everywhere. You just haven't had the eyes to see. Look for him the next time you take the *Sea Cloud* out."

Jean-Marc looked back up the stairs. "Maybe I will."

Luca wished his friend traveling mercies and closed the door with a sigh of regret, already missing the book that had carried him through the darkest time in his life. Settling back into his favorite chair, he looked out over the city, wishing he had said things more clearly, hoping Jean-Marc would not toss his treasured Bible in the first garbage can he saw on the street, and wondering how Elizabeth Davis and her mother were doing. He was painfully aware that his concern and interest applied more to the mother than the daughter. *What does that mean, Father?*

TWENTY-SIX

Mary

IT IS DINNERTIME IN PARIS. Jean-Marc has left the city, but not before leaving an envelope with the concierge. It contains a note to me and a letter for Liz that he told me I can give her or not, Jean-Marc says. *Whatever you think is best*. While I appreciate his attempt to be thoughtful and careful with this new knowledge of his, I resent the responsibility it has laid at my door. And the fact that he seems to have fled the scene.

His note to me is simple. He is grateful we have found each other, he wants to know the woman I have become, and he hopes the garden in Paris is a beginning . . . not an ending. Again, I wonder: How can anything begin if the parties involved run away? I decide not to read his letter to Liz, but to give it to her via the hotel concierge and let her decide what to do.

It is the day after the celebration with Annie and Adolpho in the tearoom. I spend most of it waiting to hear from Liz. When I do not, I go for a walk. Back into the garden, back toward the cathedral, around Little Athens, and finally, into a very old and simple church called St. Severin. It has none of the stained-glass grandeur of a cathedral, but the choir is practicing in a room

247

somewhere, and their song echoes in the empty church. When I close my eyes, I am overwhelmed by a desire to know the God who inspires such music.

Who are you . . . where are you. . . ? I want to know you.

On my way back to the hotel, I decide that while I may not be able to find God today, I can try to find my daughter. As I pick up the phone to call Liz's room, I find myself mouthing an awkward prayer. *Help. Please. I don't deserve it, but if you really are there, and if you really do care about me . . . then please help.*

No one answers the phone in Liz's room.

THE DRIVE HOME to Arcachon was longer than Jean-Marc David remembered. He arrived exhausted and, instead of heading home, opted for the yacht club. As always, the moment his feet landed on the deck of his ship, the cares of the world seemed less cumbersome. Going below, he unlocked his cabin, threw himself into bed, and fell instantly into a deep sleep. Hours later, he awakened to what sounded like children's feet running on deck. His feet had barely hit the floor when there was a knock on his door accompanied by familiar voices calling for "Grand-père."

"Your grandfather is not here," Jean-Marc called out. "I fought him at dawn and cooked him in stew. And now I am the captain of the ship." He climbed out of bed, doing his best to sound like a pirate as he flung open the door and finished the impromptu poem by bending over to shout, "Boo-BOOO!"

Xavier and Olivier screamed with delight, spun about, and ran for the stairs. Jean-Marc caught them just as they reached the stairway, and scooped them up—one under each arm. Then he turned sideways, hauled them back to his cabin, and flung them onto the bed. He jumped in after them, wrestling and tickling until they begged for mercy, which Jean-Marc granted only at the sound of his daughter's voice scolding him.

"Papa! You'll make them sick!"

He peered around the pillow the boys had been using to smother him. "But they were winning," he protested, looking at each of the boys and back at Celine. "They've grown so strong, I can't believe it. Truly, if you had not come to rescue me . . . they would have won."

Cheering, Xavier and Olivier pumped their hands in the air and collapsed atop Jean-Marc, who threatened to begin the wrestling match again, but was deterred by the vision of Celine, hands on hips, an expression of mild disapproval on her face. Climbing out of the bed, Jean-Marc kissed Celine on both cheeks. "I'm so glad you came. Have you had breakfast?"

"Three hours ago."

Reaching for the hat hanging on a hook by the door, Jean-Marc clamped it on his head. "Oof," he said, rubbing his eyes. "I slept much longer than I meant to." He turned to the boys, "Give your grandfather time to get dressed. I'll take you all to . . . lunch?" He looked at Celine, questioning. Shrugging, she smiled and said *yes* before motioning for the boys to come with her. As quickly as the ruckus began, it ended, with Jean-Marc closing the door and reaching for his suitcase. He changed into khaki pants and a gray sweater, then pulled on a navy blue blazer, deciding not to shave. Being the local "veteran of the seas" had its advantages. He was *expected* to be "colorful." Just before heading up on deck he took a small bundle from the side pocket of his duffel. Unwrapping it, he placed Luca Santo's Bible atop a pile of navigational charts.

Celine

I DON'T know what's happened to him, but something has. I think it's good, but it's so abrupt I find myself holding back. The most obvious change is that he honestly seems to care about Olivier and Xavier. Not that he wasn't kind before, but I always felt it was out of duty, not out of a real sense of joy over having grandsons. He seems different now. I catch him watching them, concentrating, almost as if he is trying to memorize their movements.

He has been living on the ship these past few days, which is not so different in itself, but Paul Garnier says Papa spends most of his time in his cabin reading. He emerges twice a day, once for lunch and once after dinner when he drives up to the house, inquires about the boys, and then . . . *plays* with them. Cards. Table games. Sometimes he takes them down to Pinelli's for ice cream. The boys are beginning to expect it, and I hope this change is permanent, because they are going to be very hurt if this man they are falling in love with suddenly decides to become his old self again. By that I mean, if he sails away and doesn't contact them for a long while.

He is different with me, as well. He hasn't spoken of his time in Paris, other than to say the traffic was abominable and he doesn't know how anyone can stand to live there. He also mentioned his old motorcycling friend—named Luca something— and said they had had dinner. But dinner with one old friend wouldn't keep him in Paris for all those days. I want to ask him, but I've determined I won't. Prying before he is ready to talk can only create a deeper kind of silence in him. That's just how he is.

JEAN-MARC resisted the call of the sea for longer than ever before, but eventually, the sea had her way. Telling himself it would be just a short jaunt up the coast and back by sundown, he called on Paul Garnier to help him. Together, the men guided the *Sea Cloud* across the bay, delighting as always in the snapping sound as first one, then another sail filled with wind. Standing at the helm, Jean-Marc closed his eyes, relishing the hushed *swisshhh* as the bow sliced through the cold water. His heart swelled with pride at the sure knowledge that behind him, just inside the wall-high panes of glass that housed the yacht club, a group of admirers was gathered to watch the *Sea Cloud* glide away.

As they slipped through the mouth of the bay and moved toward the open sea, Paul nodded toward the horizon. Jean-Marc squinted at the wall of clouds. "We'll just tack to the south for half an hour or so and then run downhill," he said. "We'll be moored long before those come to anything."

Fifteen minutes later, with the sea growing more choppy, Jean-Marc decided to cut the voyage short and head for port. Half an hour later, in the face of rising wind and swelling seas, both men doused the sails and donned their life jackets. Jean-Marc started the engine and ran before the wind with only the small storm jib flying, while Paul scurried about, storing everything loose in the cockpit, closing ports, and securing hatches.

When the wind began to roar and they couldn't hear each other's voices, the men used hand signals learned over the years of sailing together. With Jean-Marc at the wheel fighting to keep the yacht from slewing abeam to the wind and waves, Paul moved between checking the radar screen below and climbing to the deck to look for other boats.

Never think you have dominance over the sea. The day you become too sure of yourself is the day she will take your life. How often, Jean-Marc wondered, had he given that speech to the youngsters up at the yacht club? As gray-green clouds swirled above him, he wondered if he was about to become proof of his own lecture. *But not Paul. Please, God. Surely not Paul.*

For what seemed like hours, the men battled the waves and wind. And then, as suddenly as it had come up, the storm abated. As if a giant hand had reached across the sky and pulled them aside, the clouds broke up and brilliant rays of light from the setting sun streamed through, creating a patchwork of light on the water around the *Sea Cloud*.

"That," Paul said, taking in a deep breath, "is the strangest thing we've ever encountered."

Jean-Marc nodded as both men pulled off their life jackets.

"Just when you think you know what you're doing, nature throws something freakish at you." Paul swiped his damp palms down the thighs of his pants. "For a minute there, I thought we—"

"Yes," Jean-Marc interrupted. "So did I." He paused before deciding to ask the question he'd been contemplating for days. "Would you have been ready?"

"Ready?"

"If that had been God in that wind, calling your soul to account, what would you have said?"

Paul shrugged, laughing nervously. "I don't want to think about it. Let's get the ship to the pier." He grabbed a line, looking up to watch a sail billow out, shining bright white against the dark storm clouds receding in the distance.

Jean-Marc spun the wheel, hoping Paul hadn't noticed how his hands trembled as he guided the *Sea Cloud* toward her home pier. For the first time in years, the sea had been unable to soothe his inner turmoil. She had, in effect, mirrored his emotions, tossing him and the *Sea Cloud* to and fro like a toy to be broken at will.

In the distance, lightning flashed as the dark bank of clouds moved away. *In a few hours, if the front stays together, it'll be pouring rain in Paris.* Where, he wondered, was Mary today? And Elizabeth. Would she seek her mother out . . . or be estranged for days or weeks to come? He had suffered that kind of separation with Celine. Mary, God help her, shouldn't have to endure that.

God. Thoughts of God were beginning to invade his philosophical matrix. He still resisted Christianity as a simplistic philosophy of life. And yet, as he pondered whether Elizabeth would ever come to terms with the revelations of the past few days, whether Mary would ever be happy, part of him coveted the peace of mind Santo evidenced in every conversation.

As he deftly guided the *Sea Cloud* safely home, Jean-Marc thought about this new twist to the saga of his life. He wanted the answer to the question he'd asked Paul. What if death had come riding in on those waves and collected his soul. . . . what then? He had always said that death was the end. He had always said that to believe anything else was just a crutch for weak men who thought too much of their own worth. Since seeing faith in Luca's life—and reading the Gospel of John—he was beginning to wonder. The man he'd encountered in Luca's Bible was nothing like the weak, sickly-looking creature portrayed in so many works of art.

As Paul jumped onto the pier and moored the *Sea Cloud*, Celine and the boys clattered down the pier. "We thought . . . We—" Celine burst into relieved tears.

Surprised by the moisture rising in his own eyes, Jean-Marc took his daughter in his arms and hugged her tight. "But of course I'm all right." He leaned back and with a dirty thumb swiped the tears from her cheeks. Tousling the hair of Xavier and Olivier, he made a joke. But beneath the laughter he sensed something new. A revelation of sorts. He realized that he loved this little family very much and no longer wanted the sea to be his mistress, his family, his life. Jean-Marc David was looking for more.

TWENTY-SEVEN

Mary

JUST AS JEAN-MARC AND I sent blossoms down the Seine, so I am learning to put away the regrets of the past and create a present that will ensure a future with fewer regrets. I am too much of a realist to hope for *no* regrets, but I am definitely in pursuit of the present.

I don't know if it is God answering my plea for help or if it's just a stroke of good luck, but either way, the next time I call her room, Liz is there. And she agrees to let me treat her and Jeff to dinner. We meet in the lobby of the hotel and walk down the Boulevard Saint-Michel in silence. When we come alongside the now-familiar iron fence around the Roman baths, Liz stops to read the sign.

"My French is awful," she says. "I hardly remember a thing. Would you translate this for me?"

I do, nodding toward the museum flanking the site. "The Cluny is a wonderful museum."

"Is it open tomorrow?" Liz asks. "We could go—together. If you want. I mean, if you don't have other plans. With Annie or someone."

Never has Elizabeth Davis sounded so unsure of herself. I hate the idea that it is I who has swept the foundation from beneath her, and yet I wonder if she realizes that what she is feeling at this moment is exactly the way I have felt for most of my life. I decide not to make the point. "I do have plans. To go to the Cluny Museum. With you." I am rejoicing that apparently she and Jeff aren't going to run away home, after all—which is what I had expected to be told over dinner.

We stroll across the street and into Little Athens. Now the shop owners are calling out to Elizabeth, making her blush. Jeff puts his arm around her protectively, and I take up the banter with the shop owners. *"Elle est belle, n'est-ce pas? C'est ma fille."* I turn to Elizabeth. "They don't mean any harm. It's just a game."

We arrive at the small crêperie where I have decided to take them instead of Les Argonauts. It's quieter, more intimate, and I am hoping the atmosphere will be conducive to talking—if Liz decides she wants to talk.

The crêpes are delicious, the atmosphere at our table guarded. I wait for Liz to speak of Jean-Marc or what has happened. She doesn't. She does, however, want to know the story of how I met Annie Templeton and Adolpho. I conclude the story by reconfirming my invitation to visit the Cluny the next day.

"But you've been there," Liz protests. "You'll be bored as can be."

"I can't imagine it," I say. We agree on a time.

After the morning in the Cluny, I take Jeff and Liz to the busiest café I know—La Lutèce on the Boulevard Saint Michel. We consume steak-frites and watch passersby. At some point in the meal, it seems we agree—without saying the words—to call a moratorium on decisions about Jean-Marc David. We decide to enjoy Paris. Later that evening we eat pizza at Mamalina. I boast of my beautiful daughter and her fiancé to the toothless old waiter, and do my best to translate for Liz and Jeff.

While I may have been sated with the exploration of art on my own, I learn that everything seems new now that I don't have to pretend I haven't seen it before. I can share all the anecdotes Professor Max told, and more. We make the rounds. The Musée d'Orsay, the Louvre, Giverny, Versailles. Even the tiny attic where composer Erik Satie wrote and lived in a room the size of a wardrobe.

One afternoon, we are joined by Annie and Adolpho. We linger at Montmartre and eat at Le Consulat. There is live music, and along with Annie and Adolpho, we sing raucously and toast much more often than we should.

And, as is so often the case with humanity, with things improved between Liz and me, I neglect reading the little Bible and am not moved to pray—until the day when, after standing in a long line in the rain, we three climb the winding staircase to the tiny Sainte Chapelle. I am looking at the window that shows the crucifixion of Christ, and exactly at the moment when I am beginning to think about why God would let such a good man die such a death, the sun illuminates the window next to the one I am examining. I turn to look, and the sunbeams broaden. The process continues until the sun has broken out from the clouds and one entire side of the chapel is on fire with light and color. The tourists around me *ooh* and *aah,* and I think I have stepped into the middle of a ruby. I am transported beyond the place and the time, and again the longing rises in me to understand the faith that resulted in such devotion as the apostles displayed— such willingness to endure persecution to the point of death. I realize that I've never felt that desperately devoted to anyone or anything—save, perhaps, Elizabeth. I stand amazed. I want to understand.

I am shy about mentioning my religious questions to Liz. I don't know why. Perhaps it is that after all the years of feeling distanced from her, I don't want to raise any more barriers. And I don't want her to think of me as weak again. There have been times when she almost mocked Irene Baxter's references to "the good Lord." If this were happening at home, I could talk to Irene.

I think again of Luca Santo and his table grace and how it seemed so personal and fresh. But I haven't heard from him since Jean-Marc left Paris, and I'm certainly not going to call him. He might misunderstand. He is, after all, a successful widower. With an athletic build, gorgeous hair, and, well, I have noticed more than I thought.

If God is God, and he really is chasing me down, and if Luca Santo has answers to some of my questions, then God can certainly send him to answer them without any help from me.

If you want to talk to me, God, I'll try to listen.

At breakfast the next morning I announce to Liz and Jeff, "My appointment at the violin shop is at ten this morning. Did you still want to come along? Annie called last night and said she's convinced Monsieur Rousseau to let me see a couple of his better instruments."

We agree to meet in the lobby at 9:30.

Back in my room, I pull the Bible out. I am ashamed of my ignorance of what is supposed to be one of the greatest books in existence. It takes quite a while to find the four passages noted in the front—the passages the pastor apparently thinks speak for themselves. I take out a piece of paper and write in my own words what I think they say. I regret that there is no English Bible in the nightstand drawer as there would be in a hotel back home.

"YOU'RE JEALOUS of Annie Templeton," Jeff said after breakfast.

"Don't be ridiculous," Liz protested. "I just thought that when we're having this family crisis, Mother would put off shopping for a violin . . , with Annie." She added, "You'd think she'd be concentrating on—"

"You?"

"On the situation."

"I think she's doing a great job. She isn't rushing you. She's trying to give you space. Would you prefer that she accost you and demand you decide how you feel and settle everything by, say, tomorrow at noon?"

"That's not what I mean."

"Well, then, should she linger in the hotel waiting for us all to decide how we feel about things? Stop living? Again?"

"What do you mean *again*?"

"Isn't that exactly what was worrying you before? That she'd stopped living? It seems to me, she's doing the best she can, trying not to let your attitude ruin her life, trying to find her way—"

"Attitude? *My* attitude?"

"Don't pick a fight, Liz. Think. It doesn't take a genius to realize you need time to assimilate some things. But while you do that, we are, after all in *Paris*. And Mary's doing exactly what we've wished she would. She's finding her way and establishing a life. Making new friends. Going out. So, I repeat . . . don't be jealous. Go help your mother shop for a violin."

Mary

"Ah," THE old man says. He waggles his finger and winks. "You have the touch, madame. As soft as velvet."

As I draw the bow across one of a dozen violins on display in the tiny shop tucked into a side street across from Notre Dame Cathedral, I am both relieved and surprised. The appreciation in Monsieur Rousseau's eyes seems genuine.

"She hasn't played seriously in nearly thirty years," Annie Templeton says.

The old man's eyebrows go up.

"She was a concertmaster," Annie says.

I can feel myself blushing, and I protest. "Once. For a local production. That's all."

Annie whispers something to the shop owner, who smiles and crosses the room to where a single violin is on display inside a locked case. "Usually one must make more formal arrangements," he says, "but for Miss Templeton's American friend, I make an exception." He points at the violin. "Would madame like to play the Amati?"

I shake my head. "Thank you, but . . ."

Liz has been looking out the window toward the street while I play first one, then another of the handmade instruments in the shop. When Monsieur Rousseau mentions the special violin and I hesitate, she turns around. "Don't concern yourself about the money, Mother."

"It isn't the money," I reply.

Liz crosses the shop to peer at the violin through the glass. "The finish doesn't look right," she says.

"That's patina," Annie explains.

"How much is it?"

When Monsieur Rousseau quotes the price, Liz gasps.

Annie says, "He has a Guarneri in the safe."

"Do you want to try it?" Liz asks me.

I shake my head. "Absolutely not. A person doesn't just ask to try an instrument like that," I explain. "There would be special security, required credentials—who knows what."

While I explain to Liz, the shopkeeper walks to the front door, locks it, and pulls down the shade. Now he moves to the counter beside the display case, pulling a thick piece of black felt from beneath the counter and unfolding it. Taking the ring of keys from his belt loop, he unlocks the case, and with all the reverence of an acolyte lighting a holy flame, he takes the Amati out, tunes it, and lays it on the black felt. He briefly explains how the violin came to be in his possession, then holds it up for me. "A chance of a lifetime, madame. To create beauty in partnership with a master."

My heart is pounding as I tuck my chin into the Amati's chin rest and prepare to draw the bow across the strings. I close my eyes thinking of all the centuries of musicians who have touched this enchanting instrument, and I am very much intimidated by each one. The sweetness of the sound as I play the Provençal lullaby once, then twice, then again, brings tears to my eyes.

Monsieur Rousseau nods. "You understand."

I lower the bow and hand the violin back to him.

"You aren't taking it?" Liz says. "But you . . . you love it."

"I do. But I don't deserve it." One last time, I caress the body of the violin. "This deserves Isaac Stern . . . not Mary Davis from Omaha." I take a deep breath and turn toward Monsieur Rousseau. "Thank you for the privilege of touching it." He returns the violin to its climate-controlled display case. "Let's go," I say. "I can't possibly make a decision today. Not after touching an Amati—and being in the same shop with a Guarneri."

The shopkeeper bows. He unlocks the door and opens the shop to passersby. And he does not try to convince me to buy his Amati.

We leave the violin shop and walk along the quai. Annie takes her leave, headed for a practice session with the string ensemble. Liz and I wander along the Seine, halfheartedly poking through the art prints and old books displayed by the *bouquinistes*. We start to cross the Pont Neuf, then pause to watch a *bateau mouche* navigate the Seine.

"Annie's nice," Liz says.

"She is a darling girl," I agree.

"Jeff says I'm jealous of her."

I frown and look at her. "Are you?"

"I think I'm jealous—a little—of the . . . easiness in your relationship. The idea that there's no tension."

"Well, considering what I've put you through in recent days, I'd say it's a minor miracle we're standing on this bridge together—and that it's quite normal for there to be some tension between us."

Liz blurts out, "Do you mind if I ask you a question?"

"Ask away."

"What made you come back? What made you want to see him again?"

"I told you. I hurt him. I guess I wanted to say I was sorry."

"You could have written a letter." Her voice is tinged with sadness.

"Yes. I could have apologized in the letter and let it go at that." I inhale deeply. "So there must be more to it than that. I think I was looking for a way to . . . find the girl I used to be."

"The violinist?"

"Not so much her as the girl who heard the music in her head . . . and danced . . . and laughed." I pause.

I can feel Liz looking at me. "Were you *ever* happy? With just Daddy and me?"

The hurt in her voice as she asks the question brings tears to my eyes. "Oh, my yes. The first time you said *Mimi*. When you took your first steps. Your first dance recital. Every time you asked me to read you a story. When you got your MBA. . . ."

"And with Daddy. . . ?"

"You don't have to let go of Daddy to learn about me," I reassure her. "He was a very good man. I learned to love him."

"But he made you bury part of yourself," she says. "How could he do that?"

"Well, at the heart of it, I think he was a lot like me—afraid that somehow he didn't measure up. I think he was threatened by Jean-Marc—who was daring and handsome—threatened by the idea of me sailing away with a modern-day pirate. And that eventually made him scared to let me keep the music and retain parts of my old life. He was afraid it would somehow inevitably draw me away from him."

"He was selfish," Liz said.

"He was *human*," I reply. "And, yes, he was selfish. But so am I."

"What?" She turns and looks at me.

"I'm not going to let you go easily, Elizabeth Davis. You may be Samuel Davis's daughter, but you're my daughter, too. And I'm going to fight for you."

"Oh, Mimi," she says, and begins to cry. "You don't have to fight for me. I'm not going anywhere." And then she is in my arms, and we are both crying.

TWENTY-EIGHT

"YOU CAN'T TELL IT EVER HAPPENED," Adolpho said, walking around his Ducati, his hands on his hips. He whistled in appreciation and nodded his head. "Good work."

Enzo shrugged. "Don't thank me. All I did was work to pay for the cost. Uncle Luca did the repairs."

"It wasn't me," Luca spoke up from his desk near the front window. "Donato did it. He's had special training at the factory in Bologna. Thank him."

Adolpho threw a leg over his motorcycle, turned the key, started it up, and revved the motor before shutting it down. "What do you think? Is she the right bike for me? I've registered to take some practice laps on the track next spring."

Luca looked up from his books and made a face. "Still you speak of racing. Haven't my aching knees and stiff shoulders taught you anything?"

"Only to be more careful than you . . . and not to get involved in a rivalry like the one you had with Jean-Marc David," Adolpho replied.

"What are you and your fiancée doing for New Year's Eve?" Luca asked abruptly.

"We can't decide."

"I have tickets to the ballet."

Adolpho held up his hand. "Don't ask us. Please."

"It's the Opéra Garnier, Adolpho," Luca said. "The most beautiful opera house in the world. You'll be—"

"NOT on New Year's Eve, Mr. Santo. *Please.*"

"All right," Luca relented with a laugh. "I won't torture you."

Enzo spoke up. "Why don't you ask Mrs. Davis?"

"I have four tickets," Luca said, turning to his nephew. "I suppose you feel the same way about it as Adolpho?"

Grinning, Enzo nodded.

Adolpho spoke up. "Mrs. Davis was a musician. A very good one. She's been looking at violins over at that little shop near the Quai de la Tournelle." At Luca's blank look, Adolpho continued, "They are handmade. The best instruments for the best musicians. And priced accordingly. Mrs. Davis would probably love the ballet. You should ask her. Her daughter and the fiancé are still here. That makes four."

"I don't know what Jean-Marc would say about it. I don't want to do anything to cause trouble."

"What? You like Mrs. Davis?" Enzo's voice was hopeful.

Luca shook his finger at his nephew. "Don't start with me. I'm too old for such nonsense." He lifted his chin and gave a shrug. "But I'm not blind. An attractive escort and good company for New Year's Eve would be nice."

"Take her," Adolpho interrupted. "You can tell your friend you were just making sure his lady wasn't alone for New Year's Eve."

"Right, Aldolpho," Enzo agreed. "I'd be happy to do that for you, too, by the way. Is Annie free New Year's Eve?" he joked.

"It's not the same thing," was the reply. "We're engaged. Mrs. Davis and Mr. David—"

"All right, you two, all right," Luca stood up from his desk and waved them into silence. "Enough discussions. I think I'm old enough to handle my own New Year's celebration. I'll ask them. What hotel was it, Adolpho?"

Mary

WHEN THE PHONE rings, I am expecting Jeff, not Luca Santo. I stammer like an idiot, and he misinterprets the problem and switches instantly from French to English.

"I have learned from my nephew's friend, Adolpho, that you are a musician," he begins.

"Adolpho is being very kind," I protest. "I like to play the violin, but I'm far from any level of expertise."

"Just the same, Adolpho thought you and your daughter might enjoy an evening of ballet. A customer provided me four tickets for New Year's Eve. Would you do me the honor? Along with your daughter and her fiancé? It's the early performance. I could meet you there . . ." He rattles off the metro directions, and suddenly I realize, although I don't believe it, that he is possibly taking us to the famed Opéra Garnier.

"Excuse me . . . Mr. Santo."

"Luca. Please."

"All right then. Luca. Am I understanding you correctly? You are inviting us to the Opéra Garnier?"

"Yes. Of course. Is it not to your liking?"

"I . . . I don't know what to say. I've always dreamed of attending a performance there, but isn't it always sold out far in advance?"

I hear him smiling. "It pleases you, then."

"More than you could possibly know."

"Is it all right . . . the three of you meeting me there? I don't own a car, you see, so—"

"It's fine. It's wonderful. I don't know how to thank you."

When I tell Liz, she doesn't understand.

"Sweetheart," I say, "It's the *opera*. Napoleon built it. . . . The inside is legendary in its beauty. It will be like . . . oh, I don't know how to even tell you. I've only seen pictures of the interior, but I've always wanted to go." I grab her hand. "We have to go shopping!"

"WOW."

Jeff is standing in the lobby of the hotel waiting for us, and when Liz and I step out of the elevator he looks us up and down.

"You don't think it's too young?" I am still doubtful about the floor-length cascade of black spandex Liz talked me into buying. I catch a glimpse of myself in the mirror across the way, and while I love the way the rhinestones cascade off my left shoulder and down the sleeve . . . and the way the chandelier earrings glimmer against my neck, I am still doubtful that a woman my age should wear anything so eye-catching.

Jeff kisses me on the cheek. "You look fab-oo-lus." He is mimicking Billy Crystal as Fernando Lamas, and I can't help but relax a little.

"And you!" He touches Liz's elbow and takes a long look from head to toe at her strapless indigo gown. "Wow."

With a glance at Jeff, the concierge goes to the door and looks outside, then comes to tell us our taxi has arrived. It is a limousine. I look at Jeff who winks and shrugs. "A little help from our friends," he says. As we pull away from the front door, the concierge gives me the thumbs-up sign.

The Opéra Garnier, I tell Liz and Jeff as our car winds its way through the streets, across the Seine and toward the Place de l'Opéra, dates from the time of Napoleon III. "It's built over an underground water source. Remember the Phantom of the Opera poling his boat along deep below the stage? And the interior—gilt and marble—and the staircase!" When we drive up, the building's columns are illuminated by floodlights, and the gilt figures between the columns shine.

"Oh, my," is all Liz can say.

"Yes," I agree, looking up and sighing. "Indeed."

Jeff speaks to the limousine driver, who tells us where he will pick us up after the performance, and as we turn to ascend the stairs, Luca steps out from behind one of the columns. He is wearing a tuxedo beneath an evening coat. The white silk scarf tucked beneath the collar of the coat has fringe that dangles on either side of the coat buttons. I am surprised at the ease with which he wears a tuxedo. He calls to me, extending his hand, and then offering his arm as he greets Liz and Jeff, he leads us inside and up the grand staircase. We pass the famous sculpture titled *La Danse*. I gape, openmouthed, at the glorious ceilings, the inlaid floors, and the jeweled and obviously wealthy company we are keeping. I wonder if it is my imagination or if Luca really is the subject of admiring female glances as we pass by.

Upstairs we go, to the right, where Luca hands an usher the

four tickets and we are taken to a door that is unlocked just for us. We step into a tiny anteroom, large enough for a chaise lounge and a coatrack. Luca helps me with my coat, and leads me through the velvet drape, where I realize we are in a private box with a wonderful view of the stage. I look up at the magnificent crystal chandelier made famous by *The Phantom of the Opera*.

The curtain rises, the orchestra begins to play, and in what seems like only moments, it is intermission. The four of us spill out of our box, into the hallway, and follow Luca to a gallery where refreshments are being served.

"It's like dining at Versailles," Liz says, and she nudges Jeff, who follows her gaze up to the ceiling and to yet another elaborately frescoed work of art.

"Someone should write a book," Jeff says. "*The Ceilings of Paris*."

Luca laughs and nods. "Someone probably has. It could be a series, you know. I humbly remind you the greatest masters of such things come from *my* homeland. Which you should visit sometime. Especially Florence." He raises his glass and finishes his drink, then looks at me. "I have a villa near there." He smiles at Liz. "You are all welcome to it anytime. I recommend October. The tourists are gone—as is the heat." He pauses, "Perhaps we could tempt Jean-Marc to the marina at Pisa . . . although he much prefers Livorno. Either one would work."

"There you go, Mary," Jeff teases. "You can recover from your broken leg at a villa in Tuscany or onboard the *Sea Cloud*. Either way, it sounds like something you should definitely plan on doing."

Luca is understandably confused by the comment, which Jeff hastens to explain in spite of my efforts to keep him quiet. "She's planning some Ducati days with Annie and Adolpho."

I raise my hand to hide my face, which I know is electric red. "Please, Jeff, this is embarrassing."

"And why would you be embarrassed?" Luca says. "My only reaction is to be a little hurt that you didn't talk to me after I promised you I would teach you."

Intermission is over, and the conversation is interrupted. I am grateful to be headed back to the private loge. As the crowd presses in on us, Luca encourages me to tuck my hand under his elbow. "So you don't get lost," he explains.

After the performance, the limousine is waiting at the appointed spot. It is only polite to offer to take Luca to his apartment, and once there, Luca also does the polite thing and invites everyone up for a drink—or coffee, if they prefer.

"From my balcony," he says, "you will have a wonderful view from which to see in the New Year. If you would honor me." He hands a bill to the limo driver who looks down at the number in the corner of the bill and salutes smartly. He will wait, he says, and wishes our party a happy new year.

The talk is of the ballet at first, but then it moves on, and in a short time Luca Santo is talking about Italy.

"Tell us about yourself," I ask. "Do you have children?"

No, Luca says with a shake of the head. He and his Sophia were not blessed. He sighs. "It was something we discussed with God often. But he always said *no*. I learned to accept. But I regret."

There is a brief silence, and then outside Luca's window a firecracker explodes.

"It's time!" Luca says, jumping up to throw back the curtains and open the door. We all crowd onto the balcony and *ooh* and *aah* at the fireworks display above the city.

I notice that when Jeff slides his arm around Liz's waist she leans into his embrace. I am suddenly very aware of Luca standing behind me, ostensibly looking up to watch the sky. When I think I notice him watching me out of the corner of his eye, I scold myself that I'm imagining things. I also serve up a healthy dose of guilt over my attraction to the man. I came to Paris to see Jean-Marc. And things are far from settled. My life is complicated enough right now without indulging in some middle-aged fantasy. I tell myself to grow up, already! At last the city grows quiet except for an occasional burst of color here and there or an occasional horn or firecracker going off in one garden or another.

"If you don't mind—if it doesn't offend you," Luca finally says, "it has been my habit to begin a new year with a simple prayer. Would you join me before you go?"

He holds out his hands, which Liz and I take, and the four of us form a circle. We bow our heads, and Luca prays. "Thank you, Father, who has brought us through the difficult days behind us. Thank you, Father, who has brought us many joys. We ask you to walk with us into this new year before us. And please, Father, just enough of sorrow to bring us to step nearer to you. For the friends who are away from us, we ask the same. Amen."

With the amen, Luca squeezes my hand. When I look at him he says, "God's will be done on land and sea, eh?"

WHEN I AWAKEN on the first morning of the New

Year, my first thought is of Jean-Marc. I have dreamt of him in the night and am tempted to call him. I roll over in bed, taking stock of the little room. My black gown from the night before lies in a pile on the floor. Next to it are the strappy black stilettos and the tiny evening bag. I think over my evening at the opera, realizing somewhat happily that even with the stilettos on, I wasn't as tall as Luca Santo. Which, I remind myself, doesn't matter a bit. Except that he offered me his villa in Tuscany. I am once again mentally recounting the reasons to beware of Luca Santo when the telephone rings, and it is his voice that greets me.

"I just got up and made coffee, and I thought how nice a beginning to the year if I didn't drink it alone." He hurries to add, "So I am wondering if my new American friends would join me? The city will be quiet this morning. It's a rare opportunity to experience in Paris."

I consider . . . for about a second and a half. "I'll call Liz and Jeff's rooms and let you know. For myself, it sounds lovely."

"There is no need to call me back," Luca says. "I will meet whoever wishes to come in the garden near the Place de la Concorde. If it's not too far? The metro and the buses might be slow today."

I walk to the window and pull the drapes back. The sun is shining. "It's a beautiful day," I say. "And a long walk sounds lovely."

"No children?" Luca says, looking behind me for the missing Jeff and Liz.

I shake my head. "They wanted to sleep in—and, I think, have a day to themselves." Suddenly wondering if Luca has misinterpreted my coming alone, I feel self-conscious.

"I walked by a little café that's open. Their hot chocolate is especially nice."

We are seated only a moment when Luca asks, "Have you heard from Jean-Marc?"

I shake my head.

"I should perhaps tell you that he stopped by my apartment on his way out of Paris." Luca stirs his chocolate, then licks the spoon before continuing. He looks at me and smiles. "Of course, I already knew about the beautiful Mary McKibbin from our youth. But now Jean-Marc tells me . . ." His dark eyes are kind as he continues. "He tells me about your Elizabeth."

Not knowing what to say, I gulp and look down at my cup.

His voice is gentle when he says, "I only tell you this so you will please not feel awkward with me, and so you will please let me know if there is a way I can help. Even if it is only to pray."

"Prayers are welcome," I say. "Answers would be more helpful." I close my eyes, fighting the weariness that threatens to overwhelm me and bring on a fresh bout of tears.

Luca misinterprets the expression on my face. "Please forgive me. I don't mean to put the finger in to stir soup that is not mine."

"I'm not upset. Not the way you think." I lean back in my chair and rake my hands through my curls. "Liz has come to some kind of peace about it. At least for now." I force a smile. "Although I don't know how a person does that after a lifetime of false assumptions."

Luca replies in a voice warm with conviction. "Give God time to work. It is never too late for that."

"You obviously know a lot more about God than I do."

He shrugs. "I have solid faith, but I'm only a student of God."

"Jean-Marc says that religion is only—"

"A crutch for weak-minded men." Luca smiles. "Yes. I've heard him say it many times. Do you agree with him?"

I shake my head. "I don't think so. But I don't really think it matters if it's weakness that makes a person call on God. We're all weak in one way or another. Some of us just pretend better than others." I pause. "I did it for nearly thirty years. I'd still be doing it with Liz if she hadn't followed me here." I tell him about the woman I saw praying. "What does it matter if she was showing her weakness? She left that church at peace. I could see it on her face." When Luca nods with what I think is understanding, I ask, "Tell me how you came to know God."

"The long or the short?"

"Either," I say. "As you like."

He doesn't spare himself as he paints the self-portrait. I understand completely when he says, "Who would have thought God would care to reach out to such a man, eh? It took courage for that doctor to look me in the eye the day he said my career was over. When I think back, I can still see the smile as he said, 'But if you let him do it, God can take this ending and make it a new beginning. That wreck could turn out to be the best thing that ever happened to you. I don't really believe in accidents, you know.' When he said that, I wanted to throw something at him. 'You think God pushed me off that curve and into that wall?' I shouted. And the American doctor just stood there smiling, asking, 'Did he get your attention?'"

Luca paused. "He left the room. He didn't come back until the next day. When he came, I asked more questions. Finally, I stopped fighting. I said 'yes' to God. And that changed everything."

"How did things change?" I so want to understand.

Luca thinks about my question for a long while before he answers. When he does, he is apologetic. "I don't know if it makes any sense to you," he says. He puts his open hand across his chest. "The changes were in here. A confidence without being so cocky. A peace that God was listening. That he cared for me. A desire to please him. And a weight—gone." He gives a flourish with each hand that concludes with his palms toward the sky. "Just gone." He grins at me. "It makes no sense. But the doctor was right. That wreck was the best thing that ever happened to me." He shrugs. "You should talk to someone else. A pastor, maybe."

"Did this . . . change . . . did it happen all at once?"

He shakes his head. "Slowly. I remain Luca Santo—with many things still needing change."

When I say nothing, he asks, "So . . . you are thinking this man is dangerously close to being mad and you are wanting to escape, yes?"

I shake my head. "No. I'm thinking this man may be from God." When he looks at me doubtfully, I ask, "So. Do *you* have time for a story?" I tell him more than I intended, and by the time I finish, Luca Santo knows much of my life story, much of the difficulty with Elizabeth, and all about my recent quest for God.

"The difficulties with Elizabeth and the questions about our friend Jean-Marc—these, I can only pray about," Luca says. "The quest for God—I can help you with that." Very simply, he walks me through Scripture that says the same things I learned from the verses written in the front of the Bible the Protestant pastor gave me weeks ago. And, just as simply, I end my quest for God, not in a cathedral . . . but in a café in Paris.

TWENTY-NINE

AS HE TUCKED THE SMALL package into his duffle bag, Jean-Marc smiled. How he had agonized over the note that would accompany Luca Santo's Bible back to its owner. Part of him wished that he could be there to watch Luca read it. There would be a day ... someday. Right now, he was keeping his promise to spend some time with Celine and the boys. And he had another letter to write. Once he was ensconced in the guest cottage at Celine's villa, there would be time. The rumble of thunder in the distance reminded him of the approaching storm. They should be on their way.

"Celine!" He shouted up the stairs.

"Five minutes, Papa," his daughter yelled back.

A flash of lightning drew his attention down the hall and toward the conservatory. He made his way down the hallway and took a seat at the old piano, thinking back to that morning back in November when he had sat in this very place with a letter from Mary Davis tucked into the pocket of his shirt. Another letter—actually, only a note—resided there now. As rain pelted the windows, obscuring the view of the bay below, Jean-Marc took the new missive from his pocket and read.

> *Dear Jean-Marc,*
>
> *Please forgive me for calling you by your first name. I mean no disrespect. In this situation, Mr. David seems too formal. You can understand, I am sure, that I am not ready to call you Papa, either.*
>
> *This is my attempt to open a door. I am both frightened and excited about what will happen as a result. Mother and I have had many hours to talk since you left Paris. I am not at all certain I understand everything that has happened, but I am not willing to give up on the hope that someday all will be well again between everyone affected by what we have discovered.*
>
> *I wish you well, and while I am not certain this means that Jeff and I will accept your invitation to come and visit you in the spring, I do want to open this avenue of communication and, as Mother has been saying lately, see what God may do with it.*
>
> *Jeff and I are going back to Omaha early in the morning. Mother has promised to mail this for me. I will leave it to her to tell you of her own news.*
>
> *My best wishes to you and your family.*
>
> *Liz Davis*
> *P.O. Box 1121*
> *Omaha, Nebraska 68313-743A*
> *or, if you prefer . . .*
> *esdavis@davisenterprises.com*

Rereading the letter, Jean-Marc reminded himself not to read too much hope into the words. He must not agonize over things out of his control. Elizabeth had provided an address and, as she said, opened a door. He intended to go to the threshold and hope to be invited in.

At the sound of Xavier and Olivier clattering down the stairs and outside, Jean-Marc folded the note into fourths, and tucked it back into his pocket. His fingers once again found the notes to a familiar melody, the lullaby his mother used to sing. *I should play it for the boys,* he thought, wondering if Celine owned a piano. If not, that would be the first thing he would contribute to the family. Perhaps he could even teach the boys himself. In years to come, he wanted them to have more to remember about their grand-père than his sailing away from them.

"We are ready, Papa!" Celine called from the landing.

Finishing the song, Jean-Marc closed the piano and headed for the back door.

"Shall I check the front door?" Celine asked. "Is everything turned off?"

"Paul will be around later in the day to check on things," Jean-Marc said. He scratched a note and hung it on the hook next to the key for his Triumph. *Use it as if it was yours.*

Seeing the note, Celine raised her eyebrows in surprise.

"He's a good man," Jean-Marc said, shrugging. "He should enjoy life a little more."

An hour out of Arcachon, with Xavier and Olivier dozing in the back seat, Celine spoke up. "I don't mean to meddle, Papa . . . but I can't deny my curiosity any longer. What happened in Paris?"

"I told you," Jean-Marc said. "I saw an old friend."

"Mr. Santo?"

"Yes." He cleared his throat. "Thank you for forgiving me, by the way. For disappointing the boys. I've done enough of that. I'm going to try to make it up to them, and to you." He reached over and squeezed her hand. "I haven't always been a very good father, have I?"

"You've been yourself, Papa."

"A diplomatic answer," Jean-Marc said. After a few moments,

he asked, "Do you still think I lied to you about Dominique Chevalier?"

Celine sighed and looked out the passenger window. "I know you didn't. She called the house while you were gone." After another few moments, she nodded toward the back seat at the boys. "Don't break their hearts, Papa. Please. It took me a long time to learn that loving you on your terms was better than not having a father at all. I'd rather the boys not have to face that decision about their grandfather."

"I won't do that," Jean-Marc said.

"You say it now," Celine replied. "But you may have forgotten just how small the cottage at my villa is. There is no view of the sea from those hills. And sooner or later she will call. You'll leave. And you'll break their hearts."

A clap of thunder sounded above them. The heavens opened, drenching the road with great sheets of rain. For a few moments, Jean-Marc said nothing, concentrating on guiding the car on the mountain road. When the downpour lessened, he said, "The days of my disappearing for weeks at a time are over. When I'm gone, I'll e-mail. And I'll call every Friday to talk to those boys." He swallowed hard. "They're going to grow up fast. I don't want to miss it. I know you probably don't believe this change will last, and I don't blame you, but in time, you will see."

"And so I repeat," Celine said, "what happened in Paris?"

"A reunion," Jean-Marc said, "followed by a beginning. At least I think it's a beginning. Time will tell."

"And you don't want to talk about it anymore," Celine said. "All right, Papa. I won't harp on it. Whatever—or whomever—it was, I am thankful. From what I can see, Paris was very good to you."

Jean-Marc nodded. "And it had nothing to do with Dominique Chevalier."

"Oh . . . I don't think I'll have to worry about her nosing around any more," Celine said.

"Really? Is my charm fading?"

"It has nothing to do with your charm," Celine said. "I made her really angry. She hung up on me."

"What did you say? I've been trying to get her to hang up on me for months," Jean-Marc chuckled.

"I told her you don't need another daughter."

Mary

THE SKY IS a brilliant shade of blue when I accompany Liz and Jeff to the airport for their return flight to Omaha.

"Thank you for understanding," I say as I hug my daughter.

"I almost wish we could stay longer, too," she answers.

"Well, it's good that at least one of the women at the head of the Samuel Frederick Davis Foundation is responsible enough to go home and attend to business."

"I called Millie Patton this morning for a final report on the gala. The auction netted enough for us to break ground in the spring." Liz smiles. "I'm thinking we might schedule that event around a trip to Tuscany."

Jeff steps in to give me a hug.

"Would you do something for us?" Liz asks me. "Would you get a bouquet of flowers and give them to Annie at her recital? Tell her we're thinking of her. And if she wants an audition with the Omaha Symphony, we'll talk to George Kincaid for her. I understand he knows the conductor quite well."

Jeff pulls out the handle on Liz's rolling bag.

"I know. Time to go." She takes the bag and gives me one last hug with her free arm. "I love you, Mimi," she whispers. I am surprised at the level of emotion in her voice and the tears in her eyes.

"I love you, too, Lizzie-girl." I order Jeffrey to take good care of my baby girl, and slip back into the taxi. I have the driver take me to the northernmost part of the city where I spend the rest of the day wandering in the never-ending maze of antique shops that form the market at Clignancourt.

Annie Templeton's violin recital is a triumph. The string ensemble members are there, but they are not the first ones on their feet to cheer her performance. Her professor does that, and he is rapidly joined by the music department faculty. As soon as she lays aside her instrument, Adolpho leaps onto the stage and gives her the bouquet I have purchased at Liz's instruction. Everyone heads to the tearoom to celebrate, and I find myself seated with Luca Santo who once again brings up the topic of motorcycle-riding lessons for me. As I look around the tearoom, a pang of nostalgia hits. I will miss these young people when I return to Omaha in a few days. It disturbs me to realize I will also miss Luca Santo. Jean-Marc has not contacted me since he left Paris. I wonder why.

"You are far away," Luca says, calling me back to the moment.

I nod and stir my tea.

"Would you do me a favor?" he asks.

"Of course."

"I have been looking for some investment properties near here. There is one I like, but the price is high, and I'm not sure about some of the design details. Would you mind taking a look and telling me what you think? A woman's opinion would help."

We once again give Annie our congratulations. Luca walks me back to my hotel, tells me he will call me about viewing the property, and says good-night with a kiss on each cheek. I hum to myself on my way to my room.

THE MORNING I am to meet Luca to give him my opinion of his investment property, the weather has taken a decided turn for the worse. The sky is bleak, and a chilling wind blows debris down the street at a dizzying speed. When Luca arrives, he is windblown and shivering. We head downstairs for coffee. Seated across from him, I try not to notice the gentleness of his gray-blue eyes and the way his gray hair contrasts with his olive skin. I fail. He still wants to teach me to ride a motorcycle, and insists that I'll love the Ducati 650. We talk for nearly an hour. I have more questions about God. And motorcycles.

When we leave the hotel, Luca does his best to shield me from the wind. We have gone several blocks when he stops where a small door has been set into a large expanse of wood closing off a lovely courtyard from the busy street outside. It is quiet and the air is still. Carefully tended evergreens and a vine climbing on the far wall create the impression of a secret and enchanted garden.

"Over here," Luca says, leading me across the courtyard to a doorway on the opposite side. "It's a private entrance," he says, and takes a key from his pocket and unlocks the door.

"Aah . . ." Admiration and delight are all I can express.

"This color," he asks, indicating the bright yellow entryway. "If I buy, should I repaint?"

"No. It's perfect." I love the contrast between the yellow walls and crisp white woodwork. The entryway stairs sweep up to a loft which, Luca says, the previous tenants used for their bedroom. Directly ahead is a conservatory with high windows and a tall double set of doors that lead out onto a balcony, where the overhang boasts a generous trimming of elaborate ironwork.

It is only then that I realize the conservatory has been—or will be—inhabited by a musician, for a grand piano sits in the far corner, tucked beneath the overhang created by the stairs. Immediately I think how it needs to be moved near the windows. And as quickly as I see the piano and think it should be moved, I see the violin case resting on the sleek black piano top.

I look at it, then at Luca, who is leaning against the window frame with arms folded and a smile on his face.

"What's this?" I ask.

He shrugs. "Look and see."

I feel a lump rising in my throat. I open the case. Before me lies the Amati.

"It took some convincing," Luca explains. "But between Annie and Elizabeth and myself, we finally were able to get Monsieur Rousseau to part with his treasure."

I don't touch the violin. Instead, I turn and look at Luca. "But . . . why?" I motion around us to the empty room, the high ceiling, the view.

Luca smiles. "I admit to a little lie. A *fib* I believe is your word. The color of the paint is . . . well, it's not a mistake. It's just as your daughter requested."

"My daughter?"

"It is true that I have been looking for property. But not

exactly as an investment. More as a help to your Elizabeth."

"Liz. . . ?"

"*Sì. Elizabet.* She has bought for you this apartment." Luca nods at the violin. "But read the note. She tells you all about it."

I am trembling as I slide the scrap of onionskin paper from where Liz tucked it beneath the strings of the Amati. I read it, and always the gentleman, Luca is beside me, ready with a tissue to mop up the tears that course down my cheeks.

You see, Mimi—it is never *too late to be what you might have been.*

Watch for ***A Hilltop in Tuscany***
The sequel to *A Garden in Paris*

Everything about Liz Davis shouts success. Davis Enterprises has just been featured in *Money* magazine. She's engaged to one of Omaha's "Top Five Young Businessmen." Her fractured relationship with her mother, Mary, has mended, and even though Mary now lives in Paris, the two of them have never been closer.

But when Liz returns to Omaha to oversee the family estate in her mother's absence, her world begins to unravel. First, she finds troubling information stored on her deceased father's computer. Then, her fiancé accepts a promotion that not only requires him to move hundreds of miles away—but also postpones their wedding.

When all her coping mechanisms fail, a once-confident Liz arrives on her mother's doorstep in Paris. But Mary is on her way to Italy where the *Sea Cloud* will soon be anchored. . . .

A Journey of Sacrifice, Forgiveness & Hope

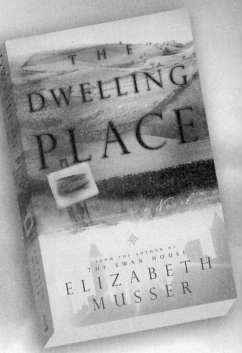

The bestselling author of *The Swan House* offers a story of sacrifice and hope that finds a daughter and mother linked by love but separated by secrets. When her mother insists on visiting a site in Scotland called the Dwelling Place, Ellie Bartholomew yearns to uncover the secret meaning the place seems to hold in hopes of finding answers to her own yearnings.

Sprinkled with humor, heartache, and history, this companion to *The Swan House* follows the journey of a young woman to make her dreams come true.

The Dwelling Place by Elizabeth Musser

BETHANYHOUSE